CRIMES COLLIDE VOL. 1
A MYSTERY SHORT STORY SERIES

KRISTINE KATHRYN RUSCH
AND DEAN WESLEY SMITH

PUBLISHING

Crimes Collide, Vol. 1
Copyright © 2022 by by Kristine Kathryn Rusch and Dean Wesley Smith
Published by WMG Publishing
Cover and layout copyright © 2022 by WMG Publishing
Cover design by Allyson Longueira/WMG Publishing
Cover art copyright © grandfailure/Depositphotos
ISBN-12: 978-1-56146-718-1
ISBN-10: 1-56146-718-9

Due to limitations of space, expanded copyright information can be found on page 355.

Contents

LIGHT OR COZY

KRISTINE KATHRYN RUSCH

It's my fault. It really is.

The book you're holding in your hands is my fault. Dean wanted to do a project for Kickstarter's January Make 100 in 2022. We'd done The Year of the Cat in 2020, which was a blast. Then we did Colliding Worlds in 2021. Colliding Worlds is a compilation of 120 stories (yeah, we added one more book as a stretch goal). Each volume has ten from me and ten from Dean.

So I said, "How about mysteries? We have a lot of mysteries." Dean said sure. He wanted to call it Colliding Crimes which is a *great* story idea, but I didn't like it as the title for an anthology series like this one. I switched the words to Crimes Collide.

We put these volumes together the way we assembled Colliding Worlds. I went first, and picked general titles. Then I found ten of my stories to fit into the title.

This one's working title, for me and Dean, was "Light or Cozy." Because, really, as my students know, I don't like cozy mysteries much. Okay, okay, I read all of Agatha Christie when I was twelve, and I have a ridiculous fondness for Kenneth Branagh's Hercule Poirot movies, but to read...? Naw, I don't like cozies. Except Dean's. Except cozies with a Christmas theme. Except...

Okay. I kinda like cozies.

And I was stunned to see how many I had written. A few more than Dean, actually. I had included the "light" for me, but it turns out the "light" needed to be there for him.

Dean likes to say that we are very different writers—and we are. Even without looking at the book design, you'd be able to tell which story was written by whom. We made it easy for you. My stories come first in this volume, and then we turn to his. His are filled with voice, and mine are more traditional, in this volume at least.

These stories might be "light" or "cozy" but they're certainly not insignificant. They're a lot of fun.

We think you'll enjoy all of them. We had fun writing them.

Ten Stories by
Kristine Kathryn Rusch

Stomping Mad

A Spade Conundrum

Kristine Kathryn Rusch

Stomping Mad

A Spade Conundrum

She called herself the Martha Stewart of Science Fiction, and she looked the part: Homecoming-queen pretty with a touch of maliciousness behind the eyes, a fakely tolerant acceptance of everyone fannish, and an ability to throw the best room party at any given Worldcon in any given year.

So when a body was found in her party suite, the case came to me. Folks in fandom call me the Sam Spade of Science Fiction, but I'm actually more like the Nero Wolfe: a man who prefers good food and good conversation, a man who is huge, both in his appetite and in his education. I don't go out much, except to science fiction conventions (a world in and of themselves) and to dinner with the rare comrade. I surround myself with books, computers, and televisions. I do not have orchids or an Archie Goodwin, but I do possess a sharp eye for detail and a critical understanding of the dark side of human nature.

I have, in the past, solved over a dozen cases, ranging from finding the source of a doomsday virus that threatened to shut down the world's largest fan database to discovering who had stolen the Best Artist Hugo two hours before the award ceremony. My reputation had grown during the last British Fantasy Convention when I—an American—worked with

Scotland Yard to recover a diamond worth £1,000,000 that a Big Name Fan had forgotten to put in the hotel's safe.

But I had never faced a more convoluted criminal mind until that Friday afternoon at the First Annual Jurassic Parkathon, a media convention held in Anaheim.

———

The convention was officially called Dinocon I because Crichton's people, or Spielberg's people, or some studio's people wouldn't give permission to use the Jurassic Park name with a non-sanctioned project. I normally don't get involved with a media con, especially one held in Anaheim, but this one had a million dollar budget and a state-of-the-art computer system, and I simply couldn't resist the challenge.

So I was in Ops with most of the folks running the con when the call came through. Ops, for those of you who've never seen one, is a hotel function room with most of the furniture removed, replaced with tables covered with computer equipment, too many chairs, and tons of print out paper. Most of the people working Ops look haggard and stressed by the time the convention starts, and many of them are ready to collapse by the time it's over. So we really didn't need to hear some security person, young by the sound of him, on the two-way radio:

"Hey, ah, we got a, um, Situation X, here."

Everyone in Ops snapped to attention. The actual term was a File X—always a pun, everything a pun—and it was only supposed to be used for an extreme emergency.

"Copy that," Doris, a muscular woman the size of Stallone, said. She headed security, and had at every major con I'd ever worked on. Security is important at sf conventions, perhaps *the* most important thing, because these cons, as most of you know, aren't your simple suit-tie-and-briefcase affairs. The big conventions have three levels: the fans, most of whom dress in costume (some medieval barbarians, some Captain Kirk, some space aliens); the pros, most of whom write, act, or somehow work in the science fiction field; the dealers, most of whom sell sf paraphernalia—books, videos, posters, and the ubiquitous Bajoran earrings. Media cons had more earrings, videos, and actors; fewer books, writers, and intellectual discussions. Behind it all is the con-com, the army of people who run the entire shebang, and put out any and all fires along the way. Security deals with most of those: from regular hotel guests who are scared by the werewolf in the elevator to the teenagers who've stayed up all night playing the card game *Magic*, and who suddenly think it fun to pull the fire alarm on the second floor.

Never, in my twenty years of fandom, have we gotten a call for this kind emergency, and never have I heard a security person sound so scared.

"It's in room 4708. Can someone come here?" The security kid's voice cracked, confirming my suspicion: he was a volunteer, and he was eighteen at most.

"What's the nature of the emergency?" Doris asked.

"I don't think you want me to describe it on an open channel," the kid said.

"All right, be right there," Doris said, and left.

We mused about the "Situation" X for a moment. "Maybe," Ruth, the con chair, said, "he saw a fur bikini for the first time."

"It's the masquerade tonight," John said behind her, and we all laughed. He probably saw a costume, got scared, and decided to call it in. We'd all had that happen before.

"Or maybe it's pea soup," said Ben, and I, being most senior on the staff, groaned. I remembered that one, which had now eased into fannish legend. Just after *The Exorcist* came out, some fans in Baltimore held a room party and served pea soup along with the usual potato chips, cheese, and beer. After midnight, when the crowd got really drunk, someone had the brilliant idea of imitating Linda Blair in the famous vomit sequence. Of course, everyone had to do it, and by the time security arrived, a sea of pea soup was running down the corridor like the Blob without the assistance of the special effects people.

"Please, ghod, anything but that," I said.

At that moment, the phone rang. Ruth answered, and handed it to me, her tired face filled with confusion and surprise. "It's Doris," she said. "For you."

I slid my chair back and grabbed the phone, feeling as confused as Ruth looked. Doris could have radioed me. That would have been procedure. Maybe something was really up in 4708.

"Yeah?" I said.

"Spade," she said—my fannish friends had called me Spade since I solved the first case almost twelve years before—"you've gotta come up here. Now."

"What's going on?" I asked.

"An absolute disaster," she said, and hung up.

"Why didn't she use the radio?" Ruth asked.

I shrugged. "I guess she didn't want anyone else wandering up to the room." I eased myself out of my special chair, the one that I insist a con-com bring to every convention if they want my services, and with a push of a button, shut down the financial files on Dinocon's main computer. Then I made my way slowly—because I never hurry—to the fourth floor of the main convention hotel.

Dinocon had 8,000 registered attendees, and it was only Friday afternoon. The convention was scheduled to go through Sunday, and another 2,000 people were expected at the door on Saturday. Most of these folks were already crowding the halls, having conversations with friends they hadn't seen for a while and trying to discover where that night's parties would be held. I squeezed my way through—negotiating packed hallways was never easy for a man of my bulk—and made it to the elevator in time to nab the last spot. No one complained, though, as I squooshed people toward the back. Part of that was my con-com badge—regular con attendees knew better than to harass a person in a con-com badge—and part of it was my reputation.

"Hey, Spade!" someone yelled from the back. "You get a piece of that diamond?"

"I don't charge for my services," I said, in a gently chiding voice. I made my money years ago as an early employee of Microsoft. I took all my bonuses in stock, and then retired at the age of 31, not as rich as Bill Gates, but rich enough.

"He's a gentleman detective," someone else said from the back, and the entire elevator chuckled.

"Imagine," I said as the doors opened on four, "a gentleman—and a scholar."

I got off, but not before I heard more giggling as the doors closed.

Fannish humor was not the stuff of stand-up routines, but it was usually full of sweet, if not always socially adept, affection.

The room 4708 was on what had been designated by the hotel as a party floor. On these floors, it was okay to have loud conversation all night, to serve beer in rooms, and to talk in the hallways. Other floors, the non-party floors, were for people who actually wanted to sleep during the con, something I hadn't done in the last thirteen conventions I had attended.

Photocopied 8"x11" signs were taped onto the wallpaper, most of them announcing bid parties for other conventions. The signs on 4708 looked professionally done on slick glossy paper. They announced the first annual Literature Con to be held in an ancient Hilton an hour outside of Manhattan. I stared at the signs for a moment, frowning. Anyone with half a brain knew that most of Dinocon's attendees weren't likely to attend a literature con, especially one held all the way across the country. But the posters had another draw besides their slick appearance.

Food.

Come to our bid party, the sign read, *and dine at your heart's content. Award-winning chocolates, Lucinda's World Famous Chili, and gourmet dishes from the farthest reaches of the Solar System. Come to* the *party of the convention. You'll talk about it for the next three lifetimes.*

Curiouser and curiouser. Lucinda was Lucinda Danielle Stanhope, also known as the Martha Stewart of Science Fiction. Lucinda hated media cons, thinking that they ruined "pure" science fiction. Pure science fiction, to her, was anything beautifully written with long treatises on science. She thought plot-driven fiction an abomination, and sf on movies and television beneath her notice.

Although she might have changed that opinion, since her current boyfriend, who had started as Science Fiction's answer to James Joyce, had gotten a job as a story consultant for a major studio. ("A guy has to make a buck," he said to me at the last Worldcon. "Besides, since *Independence Day*, everyone is hot for sf properties.")

She might have changed her opinion, but I doubted it.

I had known Lucinda for a long time. She and I had had a run-in at Con Diego (called Con Digeo by its attendees because of all the typos in the program book) several years back and I had tried, unsuccessfully, to avoid her ever since. Our conversations from that day on had consisted of only two words, uttered in passing.

Asshole, she say.

Bitch, I'd respond.

I sighed, squared my shoulders, and braced myself for the verbal onslaught as I knocked on the door.

Doris answered. She looked grim and shaky. She motioned me inside and closed the door.

The suite smelled of fresh bread, chili, and something foul, something I had never smelled before and wasn't sure I wanted to smell again. We stood in an entry that led to the bathroom on the left, a main room just before me, and a bedroom on the right. The security kid so skinny he was skeletal and a shade of green I'd never seen outside of a blacklight poster, leaned against a faux Louis the Fourteenth table. He had a hand over his mouth and was taking deep breaths, as if to calm his stomach.

"What is it?" I asked.

Doris pointed toward the main room. I lumbered in, cautiously, not sure what to expect. A chocolate pterodactyl hung from the ceiling and flower arrangements that looked vaguely prehistoric stood on every end-table, along with cute little origami triceratops heads. A human-sized tyrannosaurus rex made entirely out of cheese stood on a circular mirror stand in the center of the room. Crock pots filled with chili bubbled on a table leaning against the wall dividing the main room from the bathroom.

"What —?" I started to ask again, and then I saw her.

She was sprawled on the floor, her left hand resting on the glass double doors leading out to the patio. The doors were closed. I cautiously made my way around the cheese dinosaur and the main table, still in the middle of preparations for the night's party, and stopped near her apron-clad torso.

There was no doubt it was Lucinda. She wore a linen pantsuit beneath that apron, and in her right hand she held an apple partially julienned into a stegosaurus. It was her head that was the problem.

It had been stomped flat, crushed into unrecognizability. More gray matter than I would have expected spattered the teal carpet, mixed with more blood than I had ever seen in my life. I swallowed twice, hard, not wanting to repeat the pea soup episode and contaminate the crime scene. Then I cautiously made my way back into the foyer.

"You call the cops?" I asked.

"No!" Doris said. "They'd shut us down."

"Damn straight they'd shut us down," I said. "We have a murderer on the loose here."

The kid moaned and headed toward the bathroom.

I grabbed his arm. "Uh-uh," I said. "Puke in the public restroom. You don't want to contaminate a crime scene."

"Too late," he mumbled, yanked free, and stumbled into the bathroom, kicking the door closed behind him.

"Poor kid," Doris said. "I'm amazed he has any stomach left."

"Listen, Doris, we gotta call the cops." I covered my hand with my sleeve and reached for the black rotary dial on the faux Louis the Fourteenth.

Doris put her hand on mine, forcing the receiver down. "It's Friday afternoon," she said. "Think about what that means."

Eight thousand attendees, all of whom would demand refunds. The hotel, which would sue for breach of contract. The reputation, which would shut down all Los Angeles area conventions for the foreseeable future, not to mention all media cons, not to mention all conventions held in this hotel chain forever.

Millions of dollars, all because Lucinda made someone stomping mad.

"Can't we at least wait until tomorrow?" Doris asked.

Retching sounds echoed from the bathroom. My stomach rolled in sympathy.

"Tomorrow?" I asked. "Don't you remember the party signs that are up all over this convention. For tonight? In this room?"

"Can't we change them to tomorrow night?" she asked. "Then we won't have to refund, and we won't be in breach of contract."

But we would still have the reputation problem, along with another one. "Tampering with a crime scene is illegal, Doris," I said softly.

"Can't you solve this?" she asked. "Can't you solve this before the cops get here?"

"I've never done a murder investigation before, Doris," I said.

"*Please*," she asked. "If we can give them a suspect, they won't shut us down, and Ruth and I can handle the PR problem, at least long enough to save the con."

"You don't care that a woman has been trampled in her own hotel room?"

Doris crossed her muscular arms. "You really need to ask me that, Spade? I wouldn't be so rude as to ask you."

She could have, though. Because I was upset. Lucinda had her points. She made a mean chocolate soufflé, and she knew more about fannish foods than anyone I had ever met. She also had her moments: the charity auction she ran for literacy at Orycon in the early '90s brought in $5,000 more than usual because she browbeat the attendees into spending more money. And she got them to do it by having them buy signed books.

Sometimes I found myself in complete agreement with Lucinda's arguments.

And that terrified me.

I stared at Doris.

"Will you help us?" she asked.

I sighed. "I won't tamper with the crime scene, and I will meet with the police when they arrive. You will call them from this room and you will make sure that no one else enters here. You'll also keep the kid from talking to anyone but me. If I happen to solve this thing before the police arrive, fine. But I won't go any farther than that. I'm not going to let some murderer run loose because you want to hold a media con honoring one of the lamest movies of all time."

"The special effects were cool." The kid had opened the door to the bathroom. He was now a chalk white.

"But the plot sucked," I said. Then I nodded at Doris. "Call. I'm going to snoop a bit. And don't leave until I tell you to. Got that?"

She nodded and reached for the phone. I stopped her. "Cover your hands with your sleeves. And don't touch anything besides that receiver."

She glared at me, but followed my instructions. I prowled into the bedroom, deciding to talk to the kid after his breath cleared up.

Lucinda, not surprisingly, was a neat freak. She had arrived and unpacked, her clothing hanging on her hangers in the walk-in closet. Each item was separated by tissue paper, and her hats were in boxes on the shelf above. Her shoes were lined up below in neat little rows beneath the matching clothes. She had two wigs on the dressing table, one studded with little plastic dinosaurs—the clear brightly colored kind that bartenders used to put in drinks in the mid-sixties. A silver lamé dress hung from the plant hook in the ceiling. Lucinda had planned to go all out on this party, and it surprised me. She had to be doing a favor for someone. Media cons were beneath her—and while she enjoyed fannish cooking, she hated fannish clothing.

I got back into the foyer as Doris hung up the phone. "I didn't tell them it was a murder," she said.

I mentally shook my head. That would be her problem when the cops arrived. It would be better for all of us if I had some idea what had happened.

"Okay, kid," I said to the security boy, "come into my office and talk to me. And don't touch anything."

The kid's color still hadn't returned. He followed me into Lucinda's bedroom and started to close the door.

"Don't touch," I said. We went deep into the bowels of the room, and stopped near the bed. I knew that Doris would have trouble hearing us from this spot because I had had trouble hearing her on the phone.

"What's your name?" I asked.

"Chad," he said. I raised a single eyebrow, Spocklike. I had never met a kid who worked con security named Chad. Or at least, a kid who worked con security who would admit to being named Chad.

"Okay," I said, "I need to know: what made you come to this room in the first place?"

He wiped his mouth with the back of his hand. That stomach of his was amazingly weak. "I was by the flyer table—that was my post—when these fans came down the stairs and told me they'd heard a huge pounding on the fourth floor. They took me to their room on three and I heard it too, like something really heavy was going to crash through the floor. Then I came up here. The door was open, and I let myself in. It was really quiet. I called out to see if anyone was here, and then I saw the food. I went in to grab a snack and —"

He burped, then covered his mouth, swallowing hard. "Sorry," he said.

"It's all right," I said. "Do you know who these fans were?"

"Not by name," he said. "But they have the room below this one."

And were probably preparing for another party since the room below also had to be a suite. I rubbed my chin in proper detective fashion. I had a conundrum. I need to talk to those fans, but I didn't want to leave Doris alone in the room. Nor did I want anyone else to know what had happened to Lucinda.

Then I realized it didn't matter. Doris had been in the room without me already. I had investigated, and I knew how things looked. I had seen everything but the bathroom, and that could be remedied.

I took the kid back to the foyer. "Wait here," I said, and peered into the bathroom. The kid had already contaminated the crime scene—several times—but there didn't seem to be much to see. The bathtub was still maid-spotless and the counter had Lucinda's make-up and nothing else. The toilet seat was up, one of the towels was askew, and otherwise every-thing looked fine. It didn't even smell as bad as I thought it would.

"Okay," I said as I emerged. "Let's find those fans. You wait here, Doris, and don't touch anything."

"Don't worry," she said, looking faintly annoyed at the suggestion.

The kid and I slipped into the hallway. The con was filling up. Two women wearing belly dancer skirts and midriff tops, conversed about the proper navel jewel. Five teenage boys compared tattoos. Three grown men, in Klingon boots and armor, adjusted each other's forehead ridges.

The kid and I took the stairs.

The third floor was filled with people in dinosaur costumes. Some were cheap Halloween masks, while others were full-bore papier-mâché or plastic. The costumes looked heavy, they looked hot, and they smelled of glue. I stared at them, mostly at the feet, wondering what kind of pressure a person would need to drive those hard plastic soles through a skull and crush it.

Then we were in front of 3708. The kid knocked on the door. His hand was shaking.

It was opened by a slender woman whose black hair formed perfect Louisa May Alcott ringlets around her face. She wore a lavender satin shirt with purple satin pants, and the outfit somehow looked perfect on her. Her convention badge was clipped to a tiny piece of cardboard inside her shirt's high pocket, so as not to ruin the satin.

"Hi," she said, looking a bit confused.

"Security," the kid said, glancing at me. "Remember? You asked about the big stomping?"

"Oh, yeah." She was staring at me. Her eyes were lavender, like the shirt. I'd never seen eyes like that in person before. Only in photographs of Elizabeth Taylor. "Who're you?"

"I'm from Ops," I said. "Mind if we come in?"

"Why?" She was asking the kid.

"Because when I went upstairs," he said, "I found —"

I kicked him. He shut up.

"He found that he had a few more questions to ask you," I said. "Mind if we come in."

"No," she said. "I guess not."

She got out of our way, and we stepped into the foyer. It exactly matched the suite above, only here the carpet was brown. Two men sat in the suite's living room. They looked vaguely familiar. They stood as they saw us come in.

"Something wrong?" the first one asked.

He was tall and muscular—those fakey kind of muscles that come from too much health club, and too much low-fat food. His shirt was unbuttoned below the navel, revealing a washboard stomach, and his bare feet looked manicured. His companion wore ripped jeans and a *Star Trek* t-shirt, but unless I missed my guess, his hair had been permed.

Interesting look, for fans. It looked a little too Hollywood, a little too put together, for my tastes. Maybe these folks were slumming.

"You guys with the convention?" I asked.

"What's this all about?" T-Shirt asked. He had his hands on his hips. Same fakey muscles, and he didn't look as if he had ever cracked a book. But, I reminded myself, this was a media con. Folks here didn't have to crack books, even though most of them did.

"Of course we're with the convention," the woman said, and tugged gently on her badge as if to prove it.

"What's your interest?" I asked. "Filking?"

"Excuse me," Manicured asked. His face flamed and he looked insulted.

"Fill-king," the kid said, "not fucking."

Interesting comment, I thought, but I didn't look at him. "Pipe down, Chad," I said. "What are you guys doing at the con?"

"Anyone can come," the woman said, apparently realizing that my questions had more importance than the guys were giving them credit for. "Right?"

"Of course," I said, "but usually people have special reasons for attending. What are yours?"

"We like dinosaurs," T-Shirt said.

"Fascinating," I said in my best Spock voice. No one laughed, even though most fans usually did. My best Spock voice was pretty damn good. "So what's your favorite dinosaur? A plugosaurus or a brontodacdyl?"

"All of 'em," T-Shirt said.

"Hmmm," I said. "Hear you had some noise problems."

"Yeah, man, sounded like weird pounding upstairs," Manicured said. "Like someone was trying to punch a hole in the floor."

"Sounds serious," I said. "Will someone move that chair over here?" I pointed to a square wooden chair that seemed to be the sturdiest thing in the room. T-Shirt moved the chair to the place I pointed to, right next to the balcony doors.

"Spot me, Chad, will you?" I asked as I climbed up.

"Ah, um, ah, you might want me to do that," he said.

"No need," I said, even though the chair was groaning under my weight. I reached up and removed the ceiling panel. Gobs of dust and dirt rained on me, and I had to clear a spider web, but after that I had a pretty good glimpse of the space between the ceiling and the floor above.

"Looks normal," I said, and to my surprise, it did. I put the tile back. "You guys are safe."

"That's it?" the woman asked. "That's all? It sounded wretched up there."

"It was," Chad said. I braced myself on his shoulder and squeezed as I got down. It shut him up again.

"That's it," I said cheerfully. "I hope you have a good con."

"Ah, thanks," T-Shirt said. He was frowning at me.

The kid and I left. The dino costumes flooded the hall. The newer ones looked even more realistic than the earlier ones. Especially the Spiel-bergian velociraptors. All terrifyingly icky except for the guy wearing blue jeans and a tie-dye brontosaurus head. And the inevitable tot dressed as Barney.

One glance at the elevator told me we weren't going back to the fourth floor that way. Too crowded. It also meant the cops wouldn't come up very quickly when they arrived.

"Where to now?" the kid asked.

I didn't answer. I was feeling pretty annoyed with him. Pretty annoyed with the whole thing, really. I wanted to get back to my Ops computer with its lovely numbers and forget I had ever gotten involved with this detecting business.

Even if I was good at it.

We took the stairs and I was puffing by the time we reached the fourth floor. I hadn't had this much exercise in weeks. And I was moving faster than I liked.

Most of the dino costumes were on the third floor. Regular con-goers littered the fourth. None of them looked like the three ringers downstairs.

I shave-and-a-haircut knocked on 4708. Doris answered immediately. "What took you so long?"

I didn't answer. As I came in, I asked, "Did Lucinda know I was coming to Dinocon?"

"How should I know?" Doris asked.

I glared at her.

She sighed, exasperated. "Probably. If she was looking. You would have been hard to miss since your name was in the con-com listing in all the progress reports. Why?"

I had my suspicions. I made my way back into the suite's main room.

"Hey!" the kid said. "What're you doing?"

His voice had gotten increasingly shrill. I ignored him. I made my way to the body, and, just as I remembered, the floor didn't sag under my considerable weight.

I knelt beside the body. The gray matter and blood were drying in a perfect arch.

"Hey!" the kid yelled. "You said no tampering."

"Grab him, Doris," I said through my teeth. He was getting on my nerves. This whole thing was.

I grabbed the right wrist, dislodging the julienned stegosaurus, and felt —plastic. Soft, lifelike, fake plastic.

"Bitch," I mumbled. I half expected the crushed dummy to mumble "asshole" in return. Then, louder, I said, "Doris, did you call 911?"

She didn't answer. I turned. She was frowning at me.

"Doris?"

She flushed. "No," she said. "I called the regular line. I wanted to give you as much time as possible."

Her caution had worked to our advantage. "Call and cancel," I said. "Then break that kid's arm if he doesn't tell you where Lucinda is."

"Lucinda —!"

"Just do it." First time I'd ever understood the sense of a Nike ad.

She twisted the kid's arm up behind his back. Within seconds, he was screaming, "Executive Suite! Executive Suite!"

I got up and walked over to him. "Key," I said.

He handed me a specially marked executive floor key. "Come on, Doris," I said. "Keep a good grip on this kid and commandeer us an elevator."

She did exactly as she was told.

———

On the way up, I explained the whole thing, and the kid wisely said nothing, confirming all my suspicions. I was trying to contain my anger, because this thing had just become personal.

And to think I would have mourned the bitch if that had truly been her on the floor below.

You see, the plan was simple: the execution was hard. Lucky for Lucinda that her boyfriend had his new job in Hollywood and even luckier for her that most special effects guys are also sf nerds. Ironic that she needed media people to tamper with a media con. But Lucinda had always been a bit dim when it came to irony.

And, apparently, detail, at least non-food related detail.

First there was the fannish clothing. No matter what kind of theme party Lucinda gave, she never, ever dressed in fannish clothes. No wigs decorated with little plastic dinosaurs, no silver lamé dress. She might have consented to work a media con, but she would never have given up her stylishly proper clothing. She planned the perfect media party, all right, down to the clothes, forgetting that she would never, ever wear those clothes because, of course, she didn't plan to.

But that wasn't the only detail that bothered me. The three "fans" on the floor below had been extras in a straight-to-video sf release that I'd been watching at home a few nights before the con. I would have made them as non-skiffy folk anyway. All science fiction fans—media and lit alike—know the difference between a real dinosaur and a made-up one.

And then there was Chad, clearly another actor for hire. Except he overdid the vomit bit, and the bathroom smelled as if the maid had just left. Lucinda probably hadn't counted on the strength of my sniffer.

But she had counted on me. In fact, I had been the center of her plan. Without me, it wouldn't have worked. She knew that I knew better than to tamper with a crime scene, no matter how great the temptation. She knew that I had a healthy respect for the authorities and that I would insist on cops being present.

And she knew that the cops would see this for the hoax it was. She would appear at the right moment, blame the convention for overreacting to her little party, piss off the cops just enough to get the whole con shut down. The hotel chain would have been angry, the attendees would have demanded refunds, and the whole cascade effect that Doris had foreseen when she first saw that body would have occurred. Media cons, not just in LA, but all over the country would have suffered, and possibly died.

Lucinda's little stunt would have caused more damage than the murder. It was sabotage, served cold.

———

When we reached the executive suite, Doris made the kid open the door. Lucinda saw him, stood up, and cooed. She was dressed for her act in a white sheath that accented her lightly tanned skin and golden hair.

When she saw us, her eyes widened.

"You bitch," Doris said, blowing my line and letting go of the kid. He started to back away, but I shoved him forward and closed the door behind us.

"Back off, Doris," I said. "She's mine. There won't be any cops, Lucinda. You won't ruin this convention."

"I'm going to see that you're banned from cons forever. I'm going to make sure that your name is taken out of the Fannish Directory. I'm going to —"

"For what? For a little party I planned to throw for some friends?" Lucinda asked. "Don't you think it rather cute? I do."

"You —"

Doris lunged for her, and I caught her, staggering a bit under her power. The kid bee-lined for the bathroom, fear making his intentions real this time.

"Go to Ops," I said to Doris. "Tell them everything is fine. I can take it from here."

"I'm going to get you," Doris said, but she listened to me. She knew as well as I did that strange things happened at sf conventions, and that there was no proving malicious intent here.

Knowing about it was something else.

"Misunderstandings are so tragic, Doris," Lucinda said, blinking her blue eyes guilelessly.

Doris growled and disappeared out the door. I stood in front of Lucinda. "Media cons aren't your style."

She smiled. It was sweet as rhubarb pie. "They're not yours either."

"I don't see anything wrong with people having fun. I'm a bit more open-minded than you, Lucinda. I believe people can enjoy reading and watching movies. I believe there's room in fandom for both."

"You're so naive," she said. "These cons are so anti-literature. They appeal only to the ignorant. People who don't understand real science, or real science fiction."

"I think people who think they guard pure science fiction may not understand real science or real science fiction either," I said pointedly.

"Good god," she said, "a philosophical discussion when I have a party to finish."

"It seems strange to me that you'd put on a party here, Lucinda."

She shrugged. "I thought I'd give these people the opportunity to come to a lit-con and see what they were missing."

"So kind of you," I said.

She smoothed her dress. "We all do what we can in the circumstances provided."

At that moment, I almost told her what tripped her up. I almost told her that it was her lack of scientific knowledge, her lack of understanding of forensic science that had destroyed her. First, the splatter had been too pretty, too uniform. Second, and more importantly, the type of force it took to stomp out someone's brains would have caused damage to the plywood floor. Damage someone of my weight would have felt in loose boards or groaning wood.

But I didn't. Why give her the ammunition? She might try again someday.

"Am I excused?" she asked brightly.

"There is no excuse for you, Lucinda," I said in my best fannish manner, and moved out of her way.

———

The bane of the non-licensed investigator is that we have no real authority. We can't arrest. Worse yet, people with authority often look down their noses at us.

So we are forced to take some matters into our own hands.

Lucinda, misguided as she was, was clever. Who could prove that the panic the kid, Doris, and I felt was anything more than a product of our own imaginations? She would say that she had planned a perfect party, and we had nearly ruined it.

In fact, that night, she did carry off the party with full aplomb. She did change the victim from her clone to that of a lawyer, in keeping with *Jurassic Park* (the movie) tradition, and she did pour ice in the bathtub, but those were the only changes she made. The party was the hit of the convention, and became the talk of sf—both media- and literature-oriented—for years to come. It was, in its own way, the Woodstock of science fiction. Eventually everyone who was anyone claimed they had been there, even if they had been clear across the country at the time.

Everyone who was anyone except me.

You see, I was in Ops, checking the computer records. We had an unexplained power failure just as I was transferring Lucinda's credit card information from her con file into an active file so that we could bill her account. Unfortunately, the accident caused blips in her credit record that cascaded down the system and destroyed her credit rating for the next year. She had to defend and deny and repair, all of which took time away from cons and con parties, and fandom.

And somehow she got it in her pretty little head that this would happen again if she ever attempted to sabotage—even accidentally—a major convention again.

Misunderstandings are so tragic.

But we all do what we can in the circumstances provided.

Murder,
She Workshopped

Kristine Kathryn Rusch

Murder, She Workshopped

Spending six weeks at a writer's workshop in the Midwest would drive an empath insane. Or maybe it would make the empath suicidal. Or homicidal, depending on the emotions swirling around the empath that day.

I think about such things because 1) I am trapped at just such a writer's workshop and 2) I am in the process of divorcing said empath. He's at home, with all our belongings and our cats, while I'm here for week four, when my target finally arrives. Fortunately for me, Said Empath (who shall remain nameless) didn't get the bright idea to clear out our bank accounts until yesterday. I had that bright idea three hours before I started researching my lawyer months ago. All the money once labeled ours is now in several accounts now labeled mine, and no matter how hard Said Empath screams over the phone, he'll never be able to find them.

Empathy works two ways. He can feel all of my emotions when we talk and I can feel all of his. His are extremely powerful. Mine are generally muted, which explains the initial attraction.

It also explains why I do what I do.

I kill people. Well, not people per se. Evil magical creatures that misuse a human form. Lest you think I am insane myself and use this explanation to rationalize my murderous tendencies, let me simply tell you that I have few murderous tendencies. That's why I get the jobs I do. I'm a highly skilled, highly paid assassin who works only once every four to five years.

I also happen to have a 100% success rate.

Which might completely vanish on this particular job, distracted as I am by Said Empath and by the silly workshop itself.

Here's the problem: I'm thinking seriously of retiring and taking up writing as a new career. Secretly, I've always wanted to write.

But if you had asked me—oh, say, three weeks ago—which would be harder, becoming a writer or an assassin who specialized in magical creatures that misuse human form, I would have answered writer every time.

Then I met the first three of my so-called professional instructors. The best thing I've learned at this workshop is this: *If they can become professional writers, then anyone can do it.*

Sure wish I'd known that twenty years and five assassinations ago.

But I wouldn't have ended up here on the campus of a major state university at a program for serious unpublished writers taught by the professionals. Theoretically, I'm here to assassinate someone.

In reality, I'm taking these six weeks to learn how to write.

So I'm a busy little writer bee, handing in a story per week to each new instructor and letting my fellow students shred me in public. At first, I thought I'd get assistance from the instructors, and while the first one was helpful, the instructor for week two was more interested in fomenting discord—which was relatively easy to do, considering most of the students have nothing to do except read about two short stories per night.

The instructors come from different fiction genres and are supposed to give us insights into their various disciplines. As I'm learning, the use of the word "discipline" along with the word "writer" verges on oxymoronic.

That oxymoron seems to apply more than usual to week three's instructor, a has-been award-winning western writer who hasn't published a book in more than a decade. She's subbing for a bigger name who got sick and couldn't come. She's always the sub at this workshop because she needs the money. She doesn't have a lot to teach, except gloom and doom, and so after Discord from the week before, she's only making things worse.

My handlers warned me this would happen. Apparently this workshop has a pattern. By the middle, the inmates—I mean students—have forgotten everything they knew about home and have now become convinced that the workshop is the world.

Weeks Three and Four are when the big blowups happen. Students quit, affairs end, and fistfights occur. One group stripped the least-liked student naked, painted her green, and carried her like an offering to the Dean of the English Department.

That was the year the workshop had to change university sponsors.

I was told to pay special attention starting in week three, because my target would arrive in week four, and she would make sure this workshop was one for the record books.

―――――

My target, Margarite Lawson, writes lurid bestselling novels based on actual crimes. Margarite picks a famous crime, changes the names, maybe even moves it to a new location, and gives it her personal spin. The weird thing about Margarite's books is that the more she published, the more likely she was to have a hand in solving the famous crime. In fact, in the latter five books or so, the famous crime became famous because Margarite was on-site when it happened.

It's become a joke that whenever Margarite shows up, someone is going to die. In fact, my workshop has been nervously kidding each other about this since our first night together. Everyone, that is, except me.

Because to me, Margarite's talent for finding the crime in a given community isn't coincidence. It's part of her unnatural charm.

Margarite arrives on Friday night of Week Three, so that she can confer with the Western Writer before the poor sap leaves on Sunday morning. If all goes according to script, someone on this university campus will die on Saturday.

Margarite will organize the police investigation, handle the media, and solve the case by the following Friday. About two years from now, she'll published a novel about the case.

She'll get wealthier while she's feeding the demon within.

My assignment is simple: I'm supposed to stop her once and for all. If possible, I take her out on Friday night, before anyone else gets hurt.

But after nearly three full weeks undercover in this rather unique circle of hell, I'm not sure I want to prevent anyone from getting hurt. I'm tired of the drama, the petty jealousies, the bickering and the backbiting.

These people need something real to whine about.

And I figure Margarite Lawson is going to give that to them.

————

Nine a.m. Friday morning, the workshop meets as per usual. We have full run of a graduate student dorm that opens into a private courtyard. At one end of that courtyard is the so-called lounge—really an oversized conference room filled with uncomfortable upholstered chairs, flimsy tables, and one extremely loud Coke machine. Laptop users have to make certain the batteries are charged before they arrive, or fight for a seat nearest one of two unused outlets on the only wall without a window. That wall is covered with whiteboards, because—apparently—in university circles, chalkboards have become passé.

My "student" laptop—a battered first-generation iBook—is always charged. Whenever I'm out in public, I carry that thing.

My business laptop stays in my silly little graduate student suite, under lock and key. The laptop is unlike anything anyone around here has seen, except maybe in some of the secret R&D labs around campus. Maybe not even there.

Because this thing is high powered—not just with tech, but with the occasional magical connection. And how to explain magic to the non-believers in my audience? It's simple, really.

Magic slips into the real world. Or the real world slips into the magical world, depending on your point of view. Mine is the point of view of a person who uncomfortably straddles both worlds. I can see the magical, even though I have little magic myself.

I have little magic, but I have access to magic. Thanks to engineers with magic who also happen to design computers, I have at my fingertips the simplest of spells. I also have commonsense non-magical remedies to magical potions, and other such things that occasionally come in handy when dealing with the other side of reality.

In truth, I've only used those things with Said Empath's friends. In my work, I've used the standard gun/knife/whatever's handy to complete the job.

Which is looming.

That's what I'm thinking as I approach my usual chair. It's a wingback with high arms that sits directly across the room from the instructor's chair.

I staked out this chair on day one of the workshop, and although one of my less observant compatriots tried to take it from me on day two, no one will ever try that again.

They say I'm touchy.

I'm just a little protective.

The problem is that I don't look touchy. If you were to walk into our little critique session on this Friday morning, I'm the one you'd ignore. I'm older than most of the class for one thing. I also have cultivated the don't-pay-attention-to-me vibe so essential in my job.

Maybe it's one of my little magics.

If you glanced at me, you'd see a once-pretty woman who allowed time and lack of attention to make her seem faded. But if you looked, really looked, you'd notice a few anomalies. I wear baggy clothes to give the impression of flab, when in truth I have none. I also have a hard time hiding the intelligence in my eyes, so I look through my eyelashes a lot, like an unrepentant Southern belle.

My fellow students have yet to notice these things about me, but the instructor week two, Discord, noticed right off. He never picked on me, even though I was the one who had two (rather mediocre) stories in for critique that week. Instead, he avoided me as much as possible, making him rank just a bit higher in my mind than he normally would have.

Apparently, he became a bestselling thriller writer through observation, not through all that tough-talk he imparted to the other students.

But I digress.

I also arrive at my seat before everyone else, so I can watch them enter. I ignore most of them. They're the background for my two missions. But a handful of people are impossible to miss.

Like our teaching assistant, Raj O'Driscoll. He's a glorified gofer, and not bright enough to realize that should anything go wrong with this workshop, he will get the blame.

Then there is the faculty advisor, Lawrence B. Hallerhaven. Hallerhaven has taken on the job to schmooze with the famous writers. He's terrible at planning and even worse at following through. He leaves all of that to poor Raj, who is spending this morning preparing for Margarite Lawson.

Apparently she made an unusual list of demands before she agreed to come. Raj is trying to meet those demands before her arrival tonight.

All of his running about makes me nervous, and I'm just sitting in my chair, typing random thoughts in my student laptop as the rest of the class arrive.

They're carrying a variety of things: the laptops, hardcopy manuscripts covered with their inept scrawls, and various poisons from lattes to regular coffees to donuts to apples to leftover pizza.

We don't have a lot to say to each other any more except *Shut up* or *Move your ass, I need some room here* or *Were we supposed to read Steve's story for today?*, so there's a lot of rustling without a lot of conversation.

That's okay. It gives me a chance to figure out, once and for all, who is going to die.

That person has to have no redeeming characteristics. This is the person we all love to hate. When that person dies, we're all going to be relieved he's dead. We'll just wonder why someone hasn't killed him sooner.

As the class wanders in, I contemplate the possible candidates.

The three likeliest victims arrive in a clump. These three are miserable and proud of it, because they believe (erroneously, in my opinion) that misery begets book contracts.

First through the door is Hamlet Thorshov who deserves the Most Miserable Person of the Workshop Award just because his horrible parents decided to name him Hamlet. He's an underdeveloped twentysomething of very obvious Russian lineage. His white-blond hair matches the color of his white-blond skin and fails to accent his pale blue eyes. He has somehow managed to find t-shirts that are too small for him, and he wears a watch half the size of his arm.

His watch is where the trouble begins, every single workshop. The damn thing can probably fly an airplane on its own. And he toys with it in the middle of the first critique, pressing buttons as if he were setting the stopwatch for his mid-morning run (if he ever exercised, which he most clearly does not).

No one tries to get him to stop any longer, although two days ago, Carlotta Sternke—one of the other three troublemakers—tried to cover the thing in bubble wrap, just to silence it.

That was probably the only time the workshop cheered for her. Carlotta Sternke was the workshop goat long before we decided to pick on Hamlet.

Carlotta is chubby and shows way too much skin through fishnet stockings, tops that deliberately leave her stomach bare, and leather skirts that are both too short and too tight. Her lips are always covered with black gloss and she outlines her eyes in late season raccoon.

Her hair is black with a white streak that might be deliberate, although with Carlotta, it's impossible to tell. She's as unpleasant as her clothing, with a high-pitched nervous giggle that makes me long for fingernails running along blackboards.

She feels like she needs to police everyone—hence the bubble wrap on Hamlet's giant watch. And the person she loves to police more than anyone else is the third in our nasty triumvirate.

Norman Zell makes a good first impression. He's tall, lanky, and reasonably good-looking. He's embarrassed by the name "Norman," so he insists that everyone he meets call him Zell, which, I have to admit, is an improvement.

The problem is that Zell has the attention span of a gnat and the energy level of a hummingbird. He's in constant motion—either one knee jiggles or an arm or every single finger (and not in unison). In the first week, he managed to sleep with or proposition every woman here (I said no with probably more enthusiasm than I needed to express), and made it clear by the end of the week that he considered every woman who tumbled into his bed to be a conquest.

A conquest that he had the right to write about in Margarite Lawson roman à clef style. Only he wasn't nearly as good at changing the names or the events. The instructor week two actually made Zell stand in front of the group and apologize to everyone.

Zell burst into tears in the middle of his apology and yet somehow didn't command any sympathy. We'd all had enough by then, and even though the tears were probably genuine, they wouldn't change his behavior. And sure enough, by week's end, Zell was sleeping his way through the cafeteria staff, and the first story he turned in this week is titled, "Love in A Time of Meatballs."

This morning, Hamlet, Carlotta and Zell manage to sit equidistant from each other, forming a perfect equilateral triangle. They are getting out the first story for critique when the door opens again, and Margarite Lawson sweeps into the room.

She's taller than I imagined she would be, blonder, and prettier. Or maybe that's just how her human covering manifests itself in person. She wears a gauze lilac tunic over black pants, and manages to appear imposing and charming at the very same time.

I can see the magic flickering off her, sending sparks around the room. And inside that marvelous human form, I see the TrueSelf, spiny, scaly, and moss green—rather like an upright alligator with tusks.

She surveys the room and sees exactly what she should see: Surprise, shock, and dismay. Surprise because she's hours early. Shock because no one picked her up at the airport. And dismay because most of us were looking forward to our last few private hours with our sad-sack western writer.

"Well," Margarite says, "what a motley crew."

She actually licks her lips, but it doesn't look out of place unless you can see those tusks like I can. Everyone else just stares at her, no one more than Raj. I don't have to be an empath to know he's worried about losing his job. Somehow he failed to escort the most important guest writer of the workshop to her accommodations. Never mind that no one told him she'd be early. Never mind that she probably didn't tell *anyone* that she'd be early.

Margarite doesn't seem upset by the reaction to her appearance. If anything, she's probably pleased by it, although she doesn't show that pleasure. She doesn't dare. It would ruin her entire plan.

How do I know her plan? Because if you chart the appearances she's made before a murder, you can see a pattern of twenty-two months between unfortunate events.

The twenty-two months are the tip-off to the fact that she's a chaos dragon. The first part of the name fits—she does thrive (and I mean thrive, as in need it to live) on chaos. The second name is a misnomer given by someone like me who can see the upright alligator in these imposters and somehow mistook it for a dragon.

More accurately, you should probably call her a chaos reptile or a chaos demon—but again, you find yourself in linguistic hell. Since she doesn't have as many powers as the average demon, and she has considerably more than the average reptile.

Still, the bottom line is that every twenty-two months, she needs to snack on the distress caused by the release of a soul. That soul must die by murder most foul, and there must be some kind of investigation in which at least five people are suspects. If the chaos dragon doesn't get her negative emotions within a two-year window, she will waste away.

Unfortunately, for her, she can't overindulge either. The handful of chaos dragons who become police detectives or defense lawyers tend to explode—quite literally. These deaths are usually blamed on bombs or car accidents or, in one rather dramatic case, some weird kind of poison.

The disciplined chaos dragons feast every twenty to twenty-two months, which gives them two to four months leeway should the earlier feeding go wrong. And the disciplined chaos dragon also has a cover story for why she's near so many horrible homicides.

She needs the cover story because the real story is more sordid. The real story is that the actual homicide itself is triggered by the chaos dragon's presence.

In fact, she's probably triggering someone right now. I watch her work, see her make eye contact with half a dozen people in the room, including—not surprisingly—my triumvirate. She doesn't make eye contact with me, for which I am grateful.

Then Margarite smiles. She's seen what she wanted to see. I know this because the reptile within smiles as well. She says, in a voice I'm already beginning to hate, "I just wanted to say hello and envision all of you before I go to my hotel room for my beauty nap."

(She's the only instructor who insisted on a hotel room. Even Bestselling Discord Thriller Writer, from week two, had no trouble staying in graduate student housing for the duration of his instructorly duties.)

Then Margarite waggles her fingers at us, says, "Toodles," and goes out the door into the courtyard. We watch her walk away, except Raj, who scurries after her.

He catches her arm, which makes me wince, and then gestures as he talks to her, probably telling her he needs to come with her to check her into that hotel.

Poor guy. He's always been good and fair to me whenever I've had issues with the workshop (and I've had a few). I don't envy him that moment of contact, which probably sent a small shock through his already-overburdened system.

They disappear through the courtyard's main door. Our sad-sack western writer, still nominally our instructor for the week, sighs, and somehow refrains from commenting. Instead, she holds up the three manuscripts we're to critique today and asks who wants to go first.

———

Class ends a half an hour late, what with book signings and hugs and heartfelt cries of *I thought you were the best instructor so far* (which the other instructors also heard on their Fridays). I go back to my room and make myself a bologna and cheese sandwich, then carry it to the kitchen table where I bring out my other laptop, so I can catch up on industry news while I eat.

I probably should be with the group, eating lunch and gossiping. They'd be surprised, though, because it's not my thing. I have to do my job—my real job—but I can't be obvious about it either.

I figure the murder won't take place until tonight. That gives me most of the afternoon to finish a story and probably the early evening to make sure my weaponry is in the proper state.

I bring a kit with me wherever I go. Different evil magical creatures must be killed by different real-world tools. But you already know that. You've seen it in a variety of stories.

The stories get various elements right, but not all of them. For example, the wooden stake that kills vampires must be made out of the no-longer existent cedars of Lebanon. The silver that kills werewolves must be pure old-fashioned European silver, not the purer, prettier stuff from the Americas.

Chaos dragons are a modern phenomenon, so they die in more modern ways. First, you have to touch the thing with an authentic Bowie knife, preferably one from the 19th century. That makes the human form dissipate. Then you have render the thing immobile, which is a lot more difficult than it sounds because, at this point, you're fighting with a small alligator. It has alligator claws and alligator teeth and in addition, really big tusks.

I've only killed one chaos dragon, which is one more than my colleagues, and even though my handlers like to attribute that to skill, I know that the death was simply luck.

Because there's a third step: You have to remove the tusks or the thing will regenerate. The tusks are pretty simple to remove. You grab one and tug. The tusk comes out easily, like a fake fingernail comes off a hand. But you have to be able to get close enough to tug.

I learned my lesson the last time. I have reptile tranquilizer darts—the large kind used for crocodiles. I didn't use this the last time. Instead, I managed to knock the chaos dragon unconscious.

But, as I said, that time, I was lucky.

This time, I doubt luck will run my way. That's probably the other reason I'm finishing the story.

Because a part of me thinks it might be my last.

I'm done with both the bologna sandwich and the story when someone knocks on my door. I sigh. I thought I'd discouraged knocking during the first week when I made it clear that I wasn't into socializing or making nice.

Still, the knock's pretty insistent. I peer through the window to the left of the door and see Raj standing there, fist up, looking frazzled. Poor guy. I actually feel sympathy for him. He probably spent the last hour with Margarite. I'll wager he returned to a variety of errands for Hallerhaven, and one of those errands includes me.

I pull open the door—

—and dodge the giant arch of a knife.

Raj pushes his way inside, kicks the door closed with his foot, and tries to knife me again. His eyes are glazed, and spittle runs off the side of his mouth.

How had I missed that?

I grab his knife hand and shove it behind his back. He starts kicking. Then he grabs my hair and pulls my head forward. Somehow he spins me, and gets the knife out of my hand. He jabs at my neck and succeeds in sinking the knife into the flesh above my right breast.

It's startlingly painful. I break out of his hair-hold and grab him by both sides of the face. Then I twist.

His neck breaks with an audible snap, and he crumples, clearly dead.

I'm breathing hard. I'm not bleeding much—the knife somehow managed to avoid important stuff like arteries and nerves. But I have a hunch that some muscle has been compromised.

Then I realize I'm thinking like a person in shock.

Maybe because I am a person in shock. I'm injured, but that's not what's causing the shock.

What's causing the shock is that jolt you get when your perception of yourself gets turned upside down.

The goat at the workshop, the person everyone wants to kill, the one who would generate the most suspects if he/she/it died isn't one of the triumvirate.

It's me.

———

I splash cold water on my face to force myself to think clearly. Then I put my magic laptop away and call the police. I try to sound like a damsel in distress, which isn't easy for me.

I say, "I let him in and he stabbed me."

I say, "I think he's dead."

I don't say that I used a technique I'd learned in my assassin training to snap his neck.

The campus police arrive almost immediately, look in my room, and confirm with someone on the other end of their radios that indeed I've been stabbed and there's a dead man in my room. They offer me an ambulance, which I accept as part of my damsel in distress disguise (hoping the whole hospital thing won't take long), and then the real police arrive.

They take one look and start asking questions.

Like, "How did a little thing like you break his neck?"

And, "Where did you learn how to snap necks?"

And, "You really snapped his neck?"

I blink a lot and make my eyes tear up, and say things like after watching many episodes of *Buffy the Vampire Slayer*, I decided I needed a self-defense class, and there they taught us to grab someone by both sides of the face to distract him and then knee him in the groin.

I say he must have turned oddly when I kneed him, because I heard his neck snap.

I say I've never heard that before.

In other words, I lie.

Eventually, the EMTs arrive and haul me away to the university hospital where the emergency room doc X-rays me, pronounces me lucky that nothing much was hurt, and sews me up. Then he sends me out into the wild with a prescription for enough painkillers that I could sell them on the street and still have some leftover for me.

I fill it, but take none of them. That's for later. Instead, I arrive back at my room to find crime scene splatter everywhere (fingerprint dust, Luminal, and a general mess). No one has discovered my magic laptop or my weapons kit. (Thank heavens.) The last of the photographs have been taken, the body has been removed and the room is being returned to me, blood and all.

My classmates have shown up. They actually seem concerned, but more that Raj has gone off the deep-end (and that concern manifests in a "who's next?" kinda way). They try to be solicitous, offering to feed me and comfort me and give me advice on how to take care of a knife wound (as if any of them has ever done that).

Hallerhaven shows up to let me know the university will take care of everything, including my tuition (in other words, *please don't sue us*) and promises me I'll be just fine.

I thank everyone for their kindness and plead exhaustion. Slowly, I get them out of my room and sigh with relief.

Then I wait until the little clump in the middle of the courtyard is gone. While I was being questioned and poked and prodded this afternoon, I got to thinking.

I have screwed up Margarite's plan. She isn't going to get the chaos she wants. In fact, a straightforward stabbing/self defense probably doesn't even register as an energy spike.

I have a few precious hours before she tries to rile up someone else to kill me.

I'm going to have to take care of her now.

And if I do it right, no one will ever blame me for her death.

Of course, doing it right means I can't use the tried and true chaos-demon killing techniques. Doing it right means I do something no one has ever done before.

I don't even know if it'll work.

But I'm going to have to try.

———

The fanciest hotel in town isn't all that fancy. It's basically a mid-level hotel with a Four Seasons attitude and a Holiday Inn budget.

I slip in the front doors, and walk purposefully to the house phone near some potted plants. The nice thing about me, remember, is I'm one of those beige middle-aged women, formerly pretty, that most people see but don't really see.

Of course, the security cameras see me, but most hotels put them in the same locations—facing the registration desk (because of the money), the offices (again, the money) and the entrances and exits. Elevators and stairwells have them too.

No one cares about the house phone, however. I use it to verify that Margarite is here (she is) and what room she's in. I do that by asking for her direct dial phone number. Hotels always put a nine in front of the hotel room number as the direct dial, and they're usually happy to give that out to other guests—or the person who booked the room, namely one Raj O'Driscoll acting on the part of the university.

Apparently, the hotel operator has no idea that Raj is a male name.

Which works to my advantage of course. Margarite's room is on the top floor (as I expected) and is probably one of the few suites in the hotel.

I take the stairs, because it's easier (and more logical) to keep your head down in a stairwell than in an elevator. I'm carrying a purse instead of my weapons kit, having already prepared my tools.

I have my standard equipment inside the purse—a pistol and a couple of knives as well as the Bowie knife in its sheath. I also have the tranquilizer ready to go. Fortunately I learned that the best way to tranquilize an alligator is to use the same tranquilizer needle that vets use on elephants. So I have a few in stock.

I'm as ready as I'll ever be.

Except for the aching knife wound and the slowly growing exhaustion. I might be at more of a disadvantage here than I thought.

I make it to the eighth floor, find the room, and get confirmation that yes, she's in a suite. If I had more time, I'd finesse the room next door or find a maid's cart or something, but I don't.

So I go the old-fashioned route.

I knock.

It only takes a moment for the door to sweep open. Margarite is standing there in a lovely pink negligee, complete with matching pink mules.

I of course see both her and the tusked alligator within, and I have to admit the pink looks a lot better with scaly green than the purple ever did.

She looks surprised to see me.

"We have a problem," I say and walk inside as if I've been invited.

She has no choice except to follow me.

Here's the moment of truth. With one quick movement, I grab the tranquilizer and shove it—not in her neck, like you'd do with most humans—but in that poochy belly of hers.

If she were a real human, that just might kill her, but she's not. And my aim has to be perfect, because I'm trying to drill through the fake human skin into the soft spot where the alligator's jaw meets its neck.

If I miss and survive, I have to go to plan B, where I try to get rid of the human form (which'll be tough because now she's prepared) and then go for the alligator soft spot.

She looks at me in stunned surprise, and then growls. Or roars. Or whatever it is alligators do. I feel the damn tusks clamp down on my wrist —something I hadn't thought of at all. What if she disables my good hand? I'll be damaged on both sides.

I push the plunger and hold it down, praying this stuff works. She starts wailing and wreathing. Her human face changes from pasty white to gold to a sickly green and back again.

Bone snaps and it's not hers. It's mine. My right hand is useless. The syringe falls away.

She keeps digging those tusks into my skin.

I'm not sure Plan B is even possible. I'm not sure escape is possible. I'm not sure how anyone is going to explain this one to the cops.

Then her eyes roll into the back of her head (both sets of eyes in both heads) and she topples over backwards.

Her tusky grip on my wrist, however, gets stronger.

I probably only have a few minutes. I'm trapped by those damn tusks, but I still have one hand free. That it's the hand with the damaged arm is less important than it would have been, say, half an hour ago.

I grab a regular knife, the closest thing I have to the knife Raj used on me, and proceed to use it to slit the alligator within from gullet to gizzard. Then I pull out the tusks.

They still don't come off my wrist. It's like they've adhered on.

But the alligator within has curled up and turned black, and because I've seen it before, I know that means only one thing.

She's dead.

———

I was going to slip out the balcony and rappel down the side of the building, just like they taught us in assassin school, but with one arm disabled and one useless wrist, I'm not going anywhere—at least by rope.

I have to let myself out of the hotel room and slither unrecognizably down the hall.

Not for the first time do I wish assassins of the magical are given their own powerful magic. I have to keep my head down and my movements non-conspicuous like any other hired killer.

And I can't think about the searing pain in my wrist.

I get to the stairwell and stagger down, careful to always look away from the cameras.

All the way, I'm reevaluating my thinking. Maybe I should have killed her the prescribed way. Of course, how do you explain to university and hotel personnel that a famous writer has gone missing and in her hotel room is a dead alligator? It was hard enough to explain that the first time when the chaos demon wasn't famous.

It'd be even tougher now.

No. I used poor Raj to my own advantage. He'll get blamed for Margarite's death (that's why I used the same kind of knife) and the cops'll decide that after killing her, he came after me. Maybe, they'll say, he was going to kill everyone connected to the workshop.

Poor guy. If I could rehabilitate him, I would. But right now, I need a crazy version of Raj, not a brainwashed version. And I have to get back to my room before anyone sees me.

It's not as hard as it seems. As long as I keep my tusked wrist tucked inside my purse, no one looks at me. I walk as best I can back to campus and back to my room.

Once there, I use an all-purpose pair of pliers in my non-dominant hand to try to remove the tusks. It's so hard to do, I almost have to get help. (The question of who is what stops me.) Finally I manage to get the things off, but not before I hear my stitches rip.

The bone is broken, but I can't do anything about that now. Tomorrow I'll go to the hospital, say they overlooked the wrist, and I didn't notice until morning. By then the scrapes will have bruised up nicely, and they'll look more like something you'd get in a fight with a human than, say, a tusked alligator.

I clean the new wound, bandage it as best I can one-handed, then take as many painkillers as I can without killing myself and fall into bed.

When I wake up, it's twenty-four hours later, and Carlotta Sternke is sitting on the edge of my bed.

"I was afraid you were dead," she says in a tone that implies she wasn't afraid at all but was, in fact, looking forward to it. "We cleaned up your floor."

We, it turns out, was Hamlet Thorshov and Norman Zell. Turns out I had misjudged them. What I took for alienation was actually friendship among the most antisocial of writers.

They want to take care of me. I let them discover the wrist and insist on another hospital visit.

Where I get a splint, more stitches in the other side, and another prescription for painkillers.

Which I need, since it turns out that the Triumvirate was being nice to me only because I woke up while they were stealing my pain pills. Or maybe they were being nice to me because they felt guilty about stealing my pain pills.

It doesn't matter either way. I'm not going to report them. I want this workshop to continue.

It looked shaky for a few days, but the school psychiatrists said we'd all be better off if we finished our workshop than if we left now. We agreed. Hallerhaven found someone to take over Margarite's week, and we tried to get back to normal.

Or at least I did.

Because I'm getting out of the assassination racket. In fact, I can't work assassinating even if I wanted to. I'm short-term recognizable. I've been interviewed by all the major networks, asking me why Raj came after me and Margarite. (I don't know! I claimed in my best damsel in distress voice.)

Then I got an idea.

The western writer called her agent because she wants to write the true crime version of what happened.

I can't write the true crime version because it would be too true and too unbelievable.

But I can write the fictionalized version.

If I play this right, I can become the new Margarite Lawson. I know of enough mysterious and unsolved crime scenes (not all of them my own) to keep me in novels for decades. I don't have to go around magicking graduate assistants into forced homicides.

So even with the damaged breastbone and the broken wrist, I'm pecking away at the keyboard. I'm going to learn as much as possible these remaining three weeks.

And then I'm taking the publishing world by storm.

Eating It Too

Kristine Kathryn Rusch

Eating It Too

Her mother had taught her that each meal, each dish made with her own fingers was a gift. *You should cook with your loved one in mind, Sophie,* her mother used to say, *and strive for the best.*

So Sophie had. Each meal was a feast, a gift of love.

Harold ate each with gusto, complimenting her, and never missing a meal.

Two cakes, and a batch of cookies sat on the countertop. A frenzy of baking, Harold would say when he got home. You're the best cook in the country. Too bad you never share it with anyone.

She would smile, as she always did, and say, I share it with you.

All of her ingredients were on the counter, next to the soufflé dish, lightly dusted with sugar. The three egg whites and their tablespoon of sugar were beaten until they formed stiff peaks. The semisweet chocolate and four tablespoons of sugar were melted and cooling in a stainless steel bowl. She had only to beat in the egg yolks. A few more ingredients, a bit of time.

Behind her, the trial of the President played in the background, CNN commentators evaluating this, evaluating that. Last night, some reporter said things had been difficult for the First Family in August, after Hillary learned that Bill had lied.

Sophie remembered the vacation the next day—August 18th, her wedding anniversary, the day before the President's birthday. How the first lady had used her daughter to keep her distance from her husband, how plain it was that Hillary was very, very angry.

Disgraced, not just in private, but in public too.

Like the time that Harold put his arm around Anna Armbruster, and kissed her cheek. The day he had said to his best friend, out of Sophie's hearing he thought, that he had nearly placed all of Sophie's inheritance in private accounts. Divorcing lawyers, he had once said, was one of the most difficult tasks of all.

Almost as difficult, she thought, as divorcing a President of the United States.

Thirteen years he had slept with Anna, starting the month after he and Sophie married. She had thought the marriage had been for love; he had married her for money. All those years, all those meals, for money.

On January 17, the day the presidential scandal broke, she had bought white powdered cleanser with cash at an out-of-town grocery. The warning on the box was plain: poison if swallowed.

On August 20th, she had bought two powdered sugar boxes for the pantry. On September 15th, she had opened them and dumped some of the sugar into her garbage disposal. Then she had mixed the sugar with the powdered cleanser. She had resealed the boxes, using glue she bought with cash and then threw away along with the cleanser tube. She replaced the powered sugar boxes in the pantry, and made a point of cooking no sweets for guests.

She had used a different box for her Christmas baking. She would use "sugar" from the new boxes to sprinkle the soufflé when it was done.

She stirred in the egg yolks, then mixed a third of the egg whites into the chocolate. Carefully she folded the rest of the whites into the mixture, and spooned the whole mess into the soufflé dish.

Then she double-checked herself. Timer set at 25 minutes, the open box of confectioner's sugar beside the stove.

She rinsed out her mixer, then examined the cakes. A white cake, and a marble cake. Harold had a fondness for chocolate soufflé. Her frenzy of baking would last the week, or so she would tell him.

The cakes needed frosting. He loved butter frosting, more than he loved her. He would come home at night, just for dinner, and then return to the office. She had always thought it a sign of his devotion—and it had been. Devotion to her cooking. All the while, living a lie.

She would have forgiven him, if he had loved her. She would have forgiven him, even if he had humiliated her for decades to come, even if her humiliation were part of the historical record, even if it were grounds for impeachment. She would have forgiven him.

But the detective's report made forgiveness impossible.

Damn Oregon. If it had been a community property state, Sophie wouldn't have to do this. But if it had been a community property state, she wouldn't have the excuse.

She poured in the powder and sugar, along with the milk, melted butter, and vanilla. The frosting was gluey, so she added more milk, making a glaze. She'd have to apologize to Harold for the glaze, saying she didn't know why her frosting hadn't worked this time. He wouldn't care. He'd eat piece after piece, and if he didn't like it, he would eat the soufflé, which she would share with him.

After twenty-five minutes, the soufflé was puffed. She dusted it with confectioner's sugar and smiled as she heard Harold's car door slam outside. Just in time.

Dinner already on the table, desserts at the ready. She would have some too, just enough soufflé to get sick, maybe damage her throat. A small price to pay, really, when the net gains were so high. Another inheritance, this time from her husband. A return of her own money. And—perhaps—if this made the news, a suit against the store, or the powdered sugar manufacturer.

She shut off the television. Enough of other people's problems.

The door opened, and Harold came in, looking trim and tailored. "Is dinner ready?" he asked. "I have to go back at seven." Then he sniffed and grinned. "You went on a baking frenzy."

"I did." She smiled at him. "And I thought of you the entire time."

WEDNESDAY, 5:36 A.M

Holmes looked out of place as he crouched on the pavement, staring at the streak of blood. I had already put Vicks on my nose and lit a cigarette. The stench on the side of the road had nearly gagged *me*—a ten-year veteran of homicide and fifteen on the force. The area smelled as if someone had run over a herd of deer three days ago, then left them in the sun. Holmes had merely wrapped a scarf around his face before examining the blood streak as if it contained the secret of the ages.

I had already followed that blood streak. It led down an embankment to a mutilated female body lying in the drainage ditch against the chain wire fence. The killer had been daring this time, dumping the body next to one of the busiest interstates in the area, only yards away from Cabot Hill, Santa Lucia's newest—and ugliest—housing development.

But the location didn't seem to catch Holmes's attention, and neither did the rusted-out 1970 Oldsmobile abandoned on the roadside, with blood on its fender. A member of the forensics unit was scraping off the blood into a plastic bag. The photographer was straddling the drainage ditch, snapping pictures of the body. Three men from the unit were scouring the car, and two other detectives were scanning the roadside looking for other clues.

I was standing beside the squad car listening as Rae Ann, the only woman on the team, hunched over the radio, requesting a few more hours at the crime scene. It would play hell with the morning commute, but Holmes had requested it. And since the department had paid over a quarter of the budget to get the only privately run time travel company to bring the Great Detective to Santa Lucia, it had to honor his requests.

I had been watching him since they brought him into the force twenty-four hours ago. He was thin, of average height, with a hawk nose. I had expected a taller man, and perhaps by Victorian standards he had been. His suitcoat was a bit more tailored than I had expected, but he did wear a deerstalker cap, and he carried a curved pipe which he put away when he discovered that a person who owned something made of elephant ivory was subject to verbal abuse in California.

I had protested Holmes's arrival, but the chief insisted. Our small department had had a running rivalry with the FBI for years, and since there was no actual proof that the murderer was kidnapping his victims and running them across state borders, the chief was doing all he could to prevent FBI involvement. Holmes was merely the ace-in-the-hole, a last-ditch effort to prove to the feds that the homeboys could solve one of their own.

From the moment Holmes arrived, he listened a lot, asked few questions, and asked for information on the era, on California, and on Santa Lucia in particular. I had snorted when they told me that. He may have been the greatest detective that ever lived—although I would wager greater detectives had existed in relative anonymity—but his information was one hundred years out of date. How could a man who had made his reputation by observing the small details discover a twist none of us—good detectives all—had failed to see?

And believe me, we had looked. I had had four hours of sleep a night since the task force was formed a month ago. That's when we realized that Santa Lucia was as much a victim as the mutilated bodies we found. The killer was preying on the rich and famous—two young movie stars, a former child television star, a Princeton football player who was this year's number one draft choice, and the wife of one of the state's most famous senators—a well known sculptor in her own right. Each of his victims was famous enough to make the evening news across the country, and all of the bodies had been found here, in Santa Lucia, even though most of them had disappeared—alive—from somewhere else.

Holmes followed the bloodstain to the crusted grass on the embankment before putting a hand over his nose. Then I nodded. He seemed to have a diminished sense of smell, probably from snuff, or his pipe smoking.

"What the hell you think you're doing, Ned? You too good to scour the crime scene?"

I glanced over my shoulder. Birmar was standing there, his tiny eyes running and his round face pale and greenish. He was a different kind of detective than I was. Holmes had been his idol as a boy and Birmar had been the brains behind calling the Santa Cruz Time Wizards for help in this case.

"I'm working," I said in a tone that brooked no disagreement.

"Looks like you're watching Holmes," Birmar said, but he walked away, his overcoat clinging to his frame like wet sandpaper.

I had been watching Holmes, but I had already surveyed the crime scene. I had been the first member of the team to arrive. My house was a block away. That galled me. I was the spokesman on this case. If the killer was following the press coverage, he knew about me. And even though my address and phone number were unlisted, it wouldn't take a lot of effort for a guy this smart to figure out where I lived.

"Officer Zaleski." Holmes was looking up the embankment at me. "Would you join me for a moment, please?"

I sighed, leaned over, and stamped out the cigarette in the squad's ashtray. Then I approached the embankment, careful to avoid the blood streak. A low irritation was building in my stomach. Whenever this guy wanted a consult, he chose me, not Birmar. And I had better things to do than babysit someone who was wasting more of the department's money than the chief was.

"Do we know whom this unfortunate woman is yet?" he asked. Even with the Vicks and the cigarette, the smell was nauseating. A body, decaying normally, shouldn't smell that strong. "No," I said. "Well," he said. "This one may be exactly what we have been looking for. She does not have much in common with the others." I looked down, reluctantly, holding up all my training as a shield. The body was not a person; it was the king in a chess game, the reason for the fight and no more. But the killer had left her face intact, and the look of horror in her wide blue eyes would haunt me if I let it.

I made myself examine her for the clues Holmes was talking about. Her teeth were uneven and discolored—certainly not the product of million-dollar attention. The remains of the dress she wore showed a store-bought label. Holmes reached down and held out a piece of fabric to me. The cuff of a sleeve. One button was missing. The other had been sewn on rather ineptly.

"Jesus," I said. "Copycat."

Holmes leaned on his haunches and peered up at me from beneath the brim of his cap. "Copycat?" He clearly didn't understand.

I pulled myself out of the embankment. "We got two of these nuts on the loose. One of them is killing for weird personal reasons and the other is reading the press coverage and imitating."

Holmes clambered up beside me, remarkably at ease with his body although he looked as if he never exercised. "Nonsense," he said. "Such a thing is preposterous. The odds of having two killers with the same—"

"It happens all the time," I said. I walked to the squad. Rae Ann's cheeks were flushed. She was fighting with dispatch. "They're already rerouting because of a multicar pileup on 1-5," she said.

"Let me talk to them."

"There is no need." Holmes was standing behind me. "As long as your photographers are finished, we may return to the station. You and I must discuss the way these copycats work."

WEDNESDAY, 11:53 A.M

The last thing I wanted to do was sit at my desk and talk basic criminal theory with a man who had died three decades before I was born. But he absolutely refused to work with Birmar ("I am afraid, my dear sir, that the man does not understand nuance."), and the chief told me my job was on the line if I ignored Holmes. Wonderful. It seemed that the Great Detective needed a foil, and he had chosen me as this century's Watson.

The chief was using his office to brief a new team that would handle a double murder reported to the Gato Apartments. No privacy anywhere. So I took Holmes to my favorite dive, a bar just off Fifth that had been passed over by ferns, gold piping, and neon lights. The place hadn't seen daylight since 1955, and the windows were painted shut. The interior smelled of cigarette smoke layered so deep that the walls were half an inch thicker. The floor was littered with popcorn and sticky with spilled beer. Someone had to be bribing the city health authorities because logically the place should have been closed in its first year.

To my surprise, Holmes said nothing as we walked in. He followed me to a booth and slid in as if we were both regulars. I ordered a light beer and he ordered an iced tea "heavy on the sugar and cream," then smiled at me. "I have grown quite fond of that in the last few days," he said.

I was in no mood for idle conversation. "So you want me to explain copycats."

He shook his head, a slight smile on his narrow lips. "I think I grasp the concept. However, I thought I should let you know that I believe you are wrong."

I felt a heated flush rise in my cheeks. The man knew how to get to me. I had been decorated three times by the State of California for my work, recognized as one of the best detectives in the nation by *The New York Times,* and had been portrayed in a TV movie based on one of my cases.

"Look," I said. "I've investigated more homicides than I care to think about, and I've been on teams that have captured six different serial killers. Someone who doesn't follow the pattern is inevitably a copycat."

"But the pattern was followed," Holmes said. "All the way up to and including the directions of the knife wounds, as well as the advanced odor of decay. Some of the flesh was not hers, and beneath her were the bits and pieces of another corpse. An animal, as in the other instances. In the past the killer has used this technique so that a hidden body will be discovered, and has done so this time. I do not believe you have put these details in the press, have you?"

The cocktail waitress set down my beer, sloshing some of the foam onto the scarred wooden table. Then she put down a glass of iced tea for Holmes, followed by a pitcher of milk and a bowl of sugar. With a sarcastic flourish, she produced a spoon and handed it to him, scooped my five dollar bill off the table, and left.

"No," I said reluctantly. "We haven't."

"In addition, there was a small print from an—athletic shoe—and it had come from the opposite direction away from the car. I think you will find that the killer splashed the blood on the bumper as a way to lead us astray. The blood streak was a similar ploy, for it is too even and straight to have been caused by a body dragged to the edge of the embankment. The killer walked through the embankment in the pre-dawn hours, walked from one of the side streets, carrying the body with him. Since the incline from the road is so steep, I would doubt that anyone saw him."

I took a sip of the beer. My hand was shaking. I had noticed those things, but had not put them together. Holmes was right. I guess some details didn't change over the span of centuries.

"I believe," Holmes said, "that if we discover who this woman is, we will have found our killer."

WEDNESDAY, 2:33 P.M

We sent the victim's fingerprints and photograph to crime labs nationwide. We gave her picture to the press, who published it nationwide, then we hired a temp to monitor the phone calls.

Holmes was amazed by some things: the amount of data we had at our fingertips; the way that information could travel across country in a matter of seconds. Of course, he expressed that amazement with calm, letting us know that such changes were logical extensions of the era in which he had lived. He also told me privately that he believed such intellectual ease had made us lazy.

Birmar thought the remark funny. I didn't. Holmes wasn't making any points with me at all.

By this point in the investigation, we had eight different psychological profiles on the killer. The profiles assumed the killer was male and strong (which seemed obvious, given the football player), deficient in social skills and with a deep-seated hatred of famous people. Holmes disagreed with all of the experts on all of the points but two. He conceded that the killer had a hatred of the famous, and that the killer was strong.

We had returned from the bar after a lunch of burgers, heavy on the grease. I had had the one beer and Holmes had downed four cups of tea, making him jittery. When we returned, we were summoned to the chief's office, along with Birmar, for an analysis of the case.

The office smelled of reconstituted air and old gym socks. The chief kept his workout clothes in his filing cabinet—"that way no one will snoop," he would say slyly—and never opened his windows. His desk was littered with papers, and a computer hummed continually on the edge of a nearby table. The chief sat in an overstuffed chair behind the desk. Holmes and Birmar had taken the only remaining seats. I leaned against the closed door, arms crossed in front of my chest.

The chief had gone over the newest psychological profile—which said nothing different from the others—and then asked for our opinions.

"I would disagree with your experts," Holmes said. "It would seem to me that our killer is quite socially adept. After all, he managed to get close to people who are continually surrounded by others—and in the case of the—stars—are heavily guarded. No, this is a person who has enough resources to be able to travel great distances quickly and unseen, a person with the ability to get close to the unapproachable, and a person with ties to Santa Lucia."

The chief and Birmar were watching Holmes as if he were god. I was beginning to resent the sound of that resonant accented voice. I had already figured out the Santa Lucia part—that seemed obvious—and I had told the chief about my theory that the killer had a job that attached him to the famous. I had missed Holmes's third point, and I shouldn't have. Maybe Holmes was right: maybe my access to technology was making me intellectually lazy.

"It's got to be a private plane," I said. "He brought three of the victims in from the East Coast in less than two days."

"I'll call the airport," Birmar said.

The chief shook his head. "Our killer would be too smart to land in Santa Lucia. We need to check the airports that handle small planes. Get some help on this, Birmar. Get the logs from all the airports within a day's drive from here."

Birmar blanched. "Sir, I don't believe he would drive all the way here from, say, Utah."

"One must never let one's own preconceptions interfere with an investigation," Holmes said.

I stared at him. He looked perfectly at ease, sitting in a plastic chair, his feet outstretched, the chief's computer humming from the table beside him. No wonder Holmes was not ruffled by being leaped into the future. When he was involved in an investigation, he checked his expectations of the world at the door.

Holmes looked at me. "What type of job would a man need to get close to the famous?"

I shrugged. "Journalists get passes. Police, security guards, hairdressers, drivers, caterers—there's a whole list of support personnel that could get inside any citadel as long as they know how to open the door."

"Yes," Holmes said, steepling his fingers, "but that door must be the same for each of these unfortunates."

"We already have a team investigating the links between our victims."

Holmes smiled. "We will find nothing yet. Until we know the name of our final victim, our killer has us at a disadvantage."

I deliberately uncrossed my arms, and let them drop to my side. "What makes you say that?"

"We have all assumed the killer is male," Holmes said. "It wasn't until this very moment that I realized we are looking for a woman."

Wednesday, 3:15 P.M

I was very glad that Rae Ann wasn't in the office with us—or any of the other women in the department for that matter—since Holmes spent the next half hour explaining that the "fair sex" can be quite brilliant. He relayed his experiences with one Irene Adler and, while he implied that she was an exception to most females, he assumed that each century must produce at least one similar mind. Only this mind, the one we were seeking, was diabolically fiendish.

The thing which convinced him that our killer was a woman was the shoeprint. Holmes claimed he had been turning the pattern over and over in his mind while we talked. Forensics had confirmed that the shoe was a bargain brand, bought at a discount shoe store, and that it was a male size four. Holmes said he had watched footwear for the next day and noted that many of the female officers preferred men's tennis shoes to women's. No men wore a size four, but a number of the women did.

"That's not proof!" the chief snapped. "That's supposition. Besides, serial killers are always men."

Holmes sighed. "I understand that you have a lot of data on these killers. But there is nothing to prevent a woman from using these techniques for her own gain. There are several other things that point to a female hand. The victims were clothed, not naked, as seems to be common in these cases. And, while she seems to have done a lot of lifting — which I believe possible for the women I have seen since I have come here—the method of murder, the knife attack, relies more on surprise and a victim's abhorrence of knives than any need to physically overpower someone. The knife, by the way, is an angry weapon, often chosen by people who have kept a great deal of fury buried inside for a long time. A woman's weapon, if you will, since women are trained not to express their feelings." Then Holmes smiled. "That much, at least, has not changed between our time periods."

Holmes leaned back in his chair and pressed his steepled fingers against his lips. He spoke softly, as if he were speaking to himself. "In fact, I would suppose that a number of the unsolved serial killings you have in this nation are unsolved simply because you are unwilling to admit that the fair sex is as capable of atrocity as we are."

At that comment, I turned my back on the discussion and left the office. Holmes's contempt for our methods sent an anger through me that was counterproductive. He had worked on a handful of cases in Victorian London, a city with a population half that of Santa Lucia, Santa Cruz, and San Jose combined. Murder was a parlor game then, and the only serial killer, the infamous Jack the Ripper, had never been caught. If I had remained in the room, I would have said all of those things.

Instead, I went to my desk, took deep breaths, and thought. The precinct was nearly empty, with most of the department working on various cases, and another group handling the Gato Apartment murders. In the background, a phone rang incessantly. Behind bubble glass at reception, a uniformed officer argued with a woman about wasting the department's time searching for a lost cat. One of the dispatchers, a slender woman with black hair, wandered out of the radio room, and poured herself a cup of coffee.

I wished there was more noise. I thought better when I had to screen out distractions.

I hated to acknowledge that Holmes had a clarity of vision which I lacked. That our killer was a woman made sense. It would explain the two anomalies to our statistical analysis: the football player and the senator's wife. A young man in his early twenties could be lured anywhere by an attractive woman—and not feel threatened by her. The senator's wife with feminist leanings simply needed her sense of sisterhood invoked.

That made our search easier. We weren't looking for hairdressers or caterers or even journalists, which had been my initial bet. We were looking for someone who fit more into the profile of a person who owned a private plane. Someone who would have contact with all of these people and yet remain anonymous. A driver. For short promotion tours, a lot of studios and publicists relied on a handful of people who were screened to drive the famous about. Most preferred women because women were perceived as nonthreatening. A driver with a private plane could be on call in several communities, under several aliases.

I went over to the departmental computer, mounted and chained onto a desk in the middle of the room (someday maybe the department would spring for individual computers for all of us—a more cost-effective solution than hiring the Santa Clara Time Wizards) and pulled up the victim files. They didn't go into the kind of depth I wanted, so I went into the newspaper logs instead, looking for any recent mention (before the murders, of course) of the victims' names.

The door to the chief's office opened and closed. I heard footsteps behind me and knew who they belonged to. I wasn't surprised when Holmes pulled up a chair and sat next to me. He watched as article after article scrolled by on the screen.

"Are you finding anything?" he asked.

I nodded. The football player had been to three different cities so that he could meet the owners of the team that had picked him and get wined and dined separately by each. Both movie stars had been on promotional tours for films they had just completed, and the senator's wife had been accompanying her husband on a junket around his home state.

"Finding the driver who handled all of these shouldn't be hard," I said. "The companies should have résumés on file complete with photographs. But it is not illegal for someone to use an alias—as long as they're using the correct social security number." I grinned at Holmes's look of confusion. I wished I could see that look more often. "But," I said, "even if we show the link, we still don't have enough to hold up in court."

Holmes leaned back in his chair. "I do not understand the fear with which you all seem to view your legal process," he said. He had heard enough about it—I had heard the chief warn Holmes twice not to mess with evidence or interfere with forensic procedure—but I thought he had been ignoring the warnings until now. "But I do agree that we need more information. A case is not closed until we understand the motivation for our killer's actions."

I had had enough. Too little sleep, too much coffee, and too many lectures. My patience snapped. "First of all, this is not 'our' killer. Secondly, I have worked on cases in which the killer's only motive is a hatred of the color yellow. Thirdly, real life is not a murder mystery. Here, in the 1990s, we rarely tie up all the loose ends."

"Loose ends," Holmes said softly, "are a luxury a stable society cannot afford to have."

Rae Ann's arrival saved me from replying to that. She held out a fax, the cheap paper curling into a small roll. "We found her," Rae Ann said. "Our latest victim. Kimberly Marie Caldicott. A housewife from Bakersfield, California."

"Bakersfield?" I said. I frowned. Bakersfield. Holmes had to be wrong. A housewife didn't fit into this scenario.

"Does she have any ties to Santa Lucia?" Holmes asked.

Rae Ann nodded. "Born and raised here. Graduated from Santa Lucia High in 1970. Homecoming queen, valedictorian, and voted most likely to succeed. Teenagers aren't good at predicting that sort of thing though. Who'd've thought she'd've ended up a divorced secretary, mother of two?"

"She doesn't fit the profile, Holmes," I said. "I think we really have to entertain the idea of a copycat and look for information leaks in the department."

Holmes shook his head. "You are overlooking the obvious, my friend. Before we assume two killers with the same strategy, we must investigate this as a related death. My dear—" he looked at Rae Ann—"answer a question for me. I assume the items you mentioned in reference to Kimberly were honors."

Rae Ann nodded. "That's the top of the heap in high school."

Holmes smiled. "Then we need to find out who got stepped on in Kimberly's rise to the top. We need to find the young lady who came in second."

Friday, 4:10 P.M

The Santa Lucia high school annual had only one picture of the salutatorian from 1970: her official graduation photo. Lorena Haas was a pie-faced girl with coke-bottle glasses and a mid-sixties bouf-do, the kind of bookish intellectual girl who sat quietly in the back of a room and remained unnoticed even after twelve years with the same classmates. A few of them remembered her, and used words like quiet, shy, and moody. Only one classmate kept in touch, and she claimed Lorena lived back east, and drove a taxi for a living.

"Lorena may have hated Kimberly," the classmate said, "but there's no way she woulda killed her." Holmes had smiled at that. "Jealousy," he had said to me, "is, perhaps, the most destructive of human emotions."

Whatever the motive, the evidence against Lorena Haas was mounting. Within a day of looking at the annual, we had found Haas's pilot's license, matched her voice prints to airline logs, and through that tracked her various aliases. We even had enough evidence to tie her to each victim — she had chauffeured all of them in company limousines.

The discovery put the remains of the investigation in the FBI's purview, although the Santa Lucia Police Department Special Homicide Unit would always receive credit for solving the case. The FBI found Lorena in a D.C. suburb, living under the alias Kim Meree. They brought her to San Francisco on Friday morning, for an interview, before they officially charged her with the crime.

Holmes insisted upon seeing her. The chief had had to negotiate for that. Finally, Holmes's fame had prevailed. Holmes was going to be able to speak with Haas alone.

Holmes insisted that I accompany him. I was tired of being his Watson. Ever since Holmes arrived, I had played second fiddle. I really didn't care why Lorena Haas had murdered a bunch of celebrities and her high school rival. I had already been assigned to a murder/suicide that had been called in this morning—easily solved, of course—but the kind of case that generated a pile of paperwork. I was still protesting as we climbed the steps of the FBI building in San Francisco, where they were holding her for questioning.

"We've got enough to make a case, Holmes," I said. "There's no reason to talk to this nut."

I had been making the same argument all day. Holmes had brushed it off before, but this time he stopped at the top of the stairs and looked down at me. On this afternoon, he appeared taller, and I suddenly realized what a striking presence he really made—in any century.

"My dear sir," he said, "one must always discover if one's suppositions are correct."

"And if they aren't?" I asked.

Holmes looked at me gravely for a moment. "Then we solved the case by luck and happenstance, not by intellect."

I sighed to myself. "She's not going to confess anything, Holmes. She's too smart for that."

"I don't need a confession," Holmes said. "Merely a confirmation."

He pulled open the door and went in. I followed him. I would be so glad when he was gone. That patronizing tone, as if he and he alone saw the details of the universe, grated on me so badly that I tensed each time he opened his mouth.

The inside of the building had a dry metallic dustless scent. Our footsteps echoed on the tile floor, and the people we saw—all wearing suits—did not meet our gaze as we passed. We passed door after door after door, all closed as if hiding secrets we could never be privy to.

When we reached the designated room, Holmes took the lead, and had the agent show us directly to the interrogation area. Before we went in, we were instructed that our entire conversation would be taped.

A guard stood outside the interrogation room. The guard nodded at us as we went in, as if memorizing our faces. The room itself was white, except for the one-way glass on the back wall. Even the table and chairs were white. Lorena Haas stood in front of the glass, peering at it, as if by doing so she could see the people hidden behind. She turned as the door closed behind us.

Although I had seen recent photos, I was unprepared for her physical presence. She had come far from her coke-bottle glasses days. Contact lenses had made her eyes a vivid blue. She had shoulder-length blonde hair, high cheekbones, and a small upturned nose. She moved with a litheness of an athlete. She could easily have carried those bodies. If I hadn't known, I would have matched the 1970 Kimberly Caldicott graduation photo with the 1990s version of Lorena Haas.

"I'm not talking to anyone without a lawyer," Haas said. She had the flat nonaccent most Californians specialized in. She leaned against her chair instead of sitting in it, and she kept gazing at Holmes as if he were familiar.

"I merely wanted to meet you," Holmes said, and stuck out his hand. "I am Sherlock Holmes. I am sure you read about my involvement in the case."

She didn't take the offered hand. "Oh, yeah," she said. "The world's greatest detective. I suppose I should be honored. Well, I'm not. People like you, they make their way by focusing on the inadequacies of others."

Then her gaze met mine. Those intense blue eyes sent a shudder through me that I couldn't hide.

"You must be Ned Zaleski. The newspapers mentioned you, too. You were the one who led the investigation until Mr. Holmes came and took it all away from you." Her words had an accuracy that hurt. I had never mentioned my displacement to Holmes as a problem, but I had resented it. More than I ever expressed.

She smiled, slowly, as if we shared a secret, and I remembered that morning, so long ago it seemed, when Holmes took his first action on the case. The last body had been discovered near my home. And until that point, I had been the focus of the investigation, the cop made famous by Lorena's work.

She knew. She saw. And worse, she understood. *Jealousy,* Holmes had said, *is, perhaps, the most destructive of human emotions.*

Lorena Haas had allowed jealousy to destroy her. Who would know what remark one of her famous passengers made that set her violent emotion free. But once freed, it led her back to Santa Lucia, to her home, the place where coming in second had destroyed her life. It didn't matter that Kimberly Marie Caldicott had not succeeded. What mattered was that in high school, Kimberly Marie had become a symbol of everything Lorena could not have.

A symbol she killed over and over again with the weapon of anger. A knife. Holmes had been right again. Without asking her a single question, he had managed to confirm both her guilt and her motivation.

He was right, and I despised him for it.

Lorena's smile grew and I had to look away.

Holmes half-bowed to her, ever the English gentleman. "I thank you for your time," he said, and knocked on the door. A guard let us out of the room.

I said nothing to Holmes as we walked back to the car. My skin was crawling and I was deeply thankful that he was scheduled to leave with the Santa Cruz Time Wizards the following morning.

When he returned to his home, he would not remember me. But, like Lorena with Kimberly, I would always remember him.

Friday, 6:05 P.M

It should have ended there, but it didn't. As I dropped him off at the chief's house for a celebratory dinner that I was not planning to attend, a voice pierced through the static on my police radio, announcing a body had washed ashore from the Santa Lucia River. The body was that of a young girl, missing for two days, and she had obviously been strangled.

As the dispatch fed the information, I imagined the scene: the bloated, black-faced body, tongue protruding, the neck a mass of welts and bruises washed clean of evidence by the river herself. A homicide unrelated to any other that would probably go down in the books as unsolved.

Holmes was watching me. "Loose ends happen," he said, "only when we permit them to exist." My mouth worked, but I said nothing. Who had appointed him my teacher, anyway? I was just as good as he was.

He took his pipe out of his pocket and then pulled out a pouch of tobacco. "What Miss Haas failed to realize," he said, "is that such jealousies prevent us from seeing ourselves clearly. She already had the perfect revenge: a good income, several jobs that put her in touch with something your society values. She had an interesting life, but instead, she constantly compared herself to an imaginary figure from the past."

My jaw was clenched. After this evening, I would never see the man again. Yelling at him would do me no good.

He filled his pipe, and put it in his mouth, then shoved the tobacco in his pocket. Then he reached out a hand. I shook it, more out of a desire to get rid of him than courtesy.

"I am quite sorry," he said, "that I will not be able to take my memories of you back to Baker Street. You have one of the keenest minds I have ever encountered."

Then he let himself out of the car, and walked up the sidewalk to the chief's house. The face of Lorena Haas rose in my mind. History would never record what the young Kimberly Marie Caldicott had thought of her. Perhaps Kimberly looked at her with respect and admiration, or perhaps she had noted, once too often, a talent that went unused.

I could follow Lorena's path, and make Holmes a hated icon on which I could blame all my inadequacies. Or I could move forward.

I glanced out the car window. Holmes stood on the steps, his pipe in his mouth, his cap pulled low over his forehead. I nodded once to him. He nodded back.

Then I wheeled the car onto the road, picking up my mike and reciting my badge number. I would go to the river, with no preconceptions, and forget about technology. I would look for details, and I would open myself to nuance.

I never wanted to see Holmes again, and there was only one way I could make sure that happened.

I had to stop relying on suppositions, experts, and computers. I had to sharpen my own mind, and think for myself.

Nutball Season

Kristine Kathryn Rusch

Nutball Season

In my business, nutball season starts on Halloween, and goes to about Christmas. Oh, you get your occasional Friday-the-thirteenth run on the precinct, and you gotta pray you get every full moon off, but the real serious wackos don't seem to surface until about the last week in October, and they don't disappear until New Year's Day. What they do the rest of the year, I haven't the slightest. But up until then, they're harassing me and mine, or folks just like us all over the country.

Every year, I got my favorite nut story. But last year's I don't talk about much. Because I ain't sure exactly who the nut is, me or the geezer what started it all.

You see, he walked into the stationhouse a shade before midnight on December twenty-third, wearing a red Santa suit, and looking pasty and tired, that kinda tired we all get when we pull too many shifts in a row. The house was empty that night. The desk sarge was handling some crisis, the dispatch was doing his nails, for godssake, and most everyone else was either at their own homes or doing their beats.

Me, I was at my desk. I'd stopped in the precinct after a collar to finish up some paperwork before going home to macaroni, cheese and tuna, my specialty. Not that I minded. It was better than Cindy Lou's meatloaf surprise, which I missed even less than I missed her. So I wasn't really in a hurry to leave

—even though soaking up the camaraderie of the stationhouse at that time of night was kinda like trying to sleep in a rooms-by-the-hour motel.

The old guy came in as I was typing the last part of my report. He sat down in the metal chair before my desk, leaned over the files like he owned the place and said, "Excuse me."

I held up my hand, signaling he should wait until I was finished, hoping someone else would come into the barren house and the old guy would trot off to them. No luck.

"Excuse me," he said again. "Where do I go to file a complaint?"

I knew I wasn't gonna get rid of him as easy as I wanted so I said, "A complaint about what?"

"Mrs. Billings. She plans to shoot me if I land on her roof tomorrow night."

Now to understand that sentence, you had to know that the next night was Christmas Eve. And since it was Christmas Eve, and he was an elderly guy with a long white beard dressed all in red, it was pretty clear who he was gonna impersonate.

At least, that was how I thought of it at that moment. But I wasn't being quick on the uptake. I didn't think about the implications of asking this guy a question. Which I did.

"Does this Mrs. Billings have a child?"

"Well, of course," the old guy said in his precise way, and I realized then and there that I should have kept my mouth shut because I was buying into his fantasy.

Of course, my mouth hadn't stayed shut, and now I was in deep, and I tried to fix it, I really did. I told him, you know, that maybe he could wait a day or stay off the roof or just plain get outta town.

He looked at me like it was sixth grade again and he was Sister Mary Catherine trying to explain Algebra.

"You simply do not understand," he said. "I cannot stay out of town. I must come, and I must arrive on that night. I cannot change that. Too many children will be disappointed."

"Listen, bub," I said. "I know it's Christmas and all, but you know, kids really can't tell time. They won't notice if Santa arrives on Christmas Eve or the day after."

"They'll notice," he said in that precise way of his. It was his manner of speaking that really got me to look at him. He didn't sound like he was from around here.

I know, I know, I don't exactly sound Upstate either, but you can tell I do belong in New York. This guy sounded kinda English, but kinda like Katherine Hepburn too. You know. Cultured.

And the voice didn't quite suit him either. I mean how do you expect a guy dressed like Santa to sound? Me, I'd think all deep voiced and jolly. But no one'd think jolly about this guy. They wouldn't even think fat. This guy was big, but he was all muscle. His eyes weren't twinkling. They were that hard steel gray that some beat cops get after too many long days. And his beard wasn't snowy white. It was a yellowish silver, the yellow probably being tobacco stains from the pipe clenched tightly in his thin mouth.

"Take it from me," I said to him, "when I was a kid, there was this guy next door who worked for PhilcoFord. This was in the days when companies really cared about their workers, you know? And his guy's kid, he was my age. The company Santa drops by every year, not just to this guy's house, but to ours too, and he always came on a Sunday, but I don't really notice, you know—"

"Not until thirteen year-old Michael Trent pointed it out to you. I know," the geezer said. "He got coal in his stocking that year."

The hair on the back of my neck stood out. The moment was a bit too *Miracle on 34th Street* for me. Now, there coulda been a thousand explanations for him knowing that—I mean I told that story a hundred times —but how he knew he'd get me that night, I couldn't figure.

I decided to ignore the geezer's last comment.

"Anyway," I said. "The point is—"

"That the children don't notice, but they do. They have an internal sense of what's right and what's not, particularly when it comes to Christmas. And that's at the heart of my dilemma."

"How's that?" I ask.

"She has a child. A boy of three. He's a good boy, too, and doesn't ask for much. Her neighbors' children have all grown, and they visit their grandchildren on the holidays, so her son is the only child on the block.

Logic dictates that I skip the house, but I simply cannot. In the centuries that I have been doing this work—"

Those hairs rose again. I was gonna have to get them trimmed.

"—I haven't skipped a single child. At least, not a single child who met the criteria."

I didn't want to ask about criteria. I didn't want to know the details. I was sure the old guy would give them to me.

"Mr.—"

"Kringle."

"Yeah, right. Listen, we can visit the lady, ask her to stop threatening you, but without proof or an incident there ain't much we could do. Now you can get yourself a lawyer, and have some judge order her to stay away from you, but even that won't do no good when you go visit her house, don't you see? Maybe there's some other way you can get the presents to the kid."

He stared at me for a moment, and I got the sense, even though he was too polite to say it, that I just didn't get it.

"I have proof," he said softly.

"You do?" For all his complaints against this woman, he never once said nothing about proof. "Well lessee it."

He gave me photocopies—dozens of them—all letters, all from different children, all return addresses right here in our little burg. As he passed the copies to me, he stuck his finger on the top letter and hit it with such force that the sound echoed through the empty precinct.

"Right—" tap "—there."

I glanced at the top letter. It was from a nine-year-old girl. It said that she heard Mrs. Prudence Billings say she'd shoot Santa if he landed on her roof. The little girl, she was writing to warn Santa, and to tell him it was okay if he skipped her this year because she'd rather he'd be safe.

The kid was probably trying to guarantee free presents for life.

Then I thumbed through the letters. They were all versions of the same thing: the kids had heard this Prudence Billings say she'd shoot Santa.

What a great woman. Jeez. What was she doing telling children them things?

"You need a lawyer, Mister," I said, handing the letters back to him.

"But that doesn't solve my dilemma," he said. "I need to go to her house."

"Like I said, get someone else to deliver," and I leaned back in my chair thinking about her poor kid. Imagine having a mom who didn't let you believe in Santa, who didn't let you have that one night when you thought anything was possible, when you actually believed some fat bastard who had flying reindeer could squeeze himself into a space barely wide enough for a broom and give you your heart's desire?

"I can't get someone else to deliver," the geezer said, sounding kinda forlorn. "This isn't a task that can be handed from person to person."

I was feeling a bit bad now. I mean, everyone's entitled to their own delusions if they didn't hurt nobody. But the guy wanted to waste police time on something that wasn't ever gonna happen, and I had to let him know that we didn't send squads chasing after every elf in the bushes, metaphorically speaking.

But then on the other hand, they teach you at the academy to listen to these nuts on the offsides that even nuts sometimes know something what might be true.

So I got to thinking I had this guy figured out, so I leaned forward and I said, "Pop, I know it's tough when families don't get along, and it ain't fair your daughter keeping you away from your grandson, but you know, the kid ain't gonna hold it against you if you get a friend to bring him his toys this year. The kid is gonna be a might upset if his mom takes out the deer rifle and pops you one. I mean if those're your options, you gotta know which one I recommend."

He got up and his voice went all deep, just like I was thinking it shoulda been, except it still wasn't jolly, and he said, "I *hate* going to the established authorities. They never believe me. Why can't you people have an open mind for once?"

The dispatch, he looked up from his nails, and the desk sarge who had come back in from wherever the hell he'd been looked at the old guy throw a fit right in front of me, a very cultured fit, but a fit all the same, and I knew what the sarge was thinking, he was thinking there goes Mantino again, pissing off some citizen.

I'd already heard the lecture about my melancholy state, about the way I should maybe get some help now that Cindy Lou was gone, only the lecture probably wouldn't go that way. It probably would be a bit harsher since Cindy Lou'd been gone nearly six months and my mood hadn't improved much. It was that empty house, you know, the starter, with two bedrooms the size of a closet, and the one empty as a grave, what was supposed to be for the first little Mantino way back when me and Cindy Lou actually liked each other. I'd been spending those last six months thinking, not about Cindy Lou because me and her we weren't right, but about family and how some people want one and never get it and how some people get one and never want it.

All this went through my brain in like a split second, while the geezer's using his elegant voice to broadcast to the whole house how I failed him. So I got up, and I said, not so loud that the sarge could hear, but loud enough to shut up the geezer, "If you got the magic that can make reindeer fly, how come you can't land on a roof without some wacko with a shotgun seeing you?"

The geezer sighed and got back in his chair. The desk sarge looked down, the dispatch went back to his nails, and all was right with the world.

Momentarily.

"The magic works like this," the geezer said. "Anyone who believes in me can see me."

I said, "Look, from what I can see in them letters, she don't believe in you."

"You haven't read closely enough," the old man said. "She believes strongly enough to see me as a threat to the entire civilized world. Unfortunately, she is probably the person who believes in me the most of all the adults in all the world."

He had a point. He had a delusion, she had a delusion, and it was shared and there was a gun mentioned, and I probably shoulda been taking this whole thing a lot more seriously than I had been.

"Okay," I said. "Whatta you want me to do?"

"I want you to go see her," he said, "and make her promise not to shoot me tomorrow night."

"You think that much hate is going to keep a promise?" I ask.

"She's a fanatic, isn't she?" he said. "She should keep a holy vow."

Right. Like I could extract a holy vow from a woman who hated Santa Claus. But it wasn't the hardest thing I'd ever had to do on this job.

So like an idiot, I agreed.

————

Christmas Eve, my shift started at noon, and since I didn't have a family, I was thinking maybe I'd work late, and then pick up some hours Christmas Day. I wasn't lying to myself that one day was like another; I knew Christmas was special. I just figured if I worked through it, I wouldn't notice.

When I was a kid, the festivities started with the whole advent season. The second the decorations went up in church, they'd go up at home. My mom did the advent calendars and the whole nine yards, and it made December something else. I'd felt the lack ever since I moved from home —it wasn't the same after I'd left, and it got worse after she died—but it was never so bad as on Christmas and Christmas Eve.

I probably shoulda gone to midnight mass. I had it in my head I'd do it when I got off work, but I wasn't sure I wanted to see all them folks and their families in the red velvet and the fake fur coats, and me coming in in my uniform. I didn't figure it'd look right, you know?

And that's what I was trying not to think about as I drove up to this Prudence Billings' house. She lived in one of them ritzy areas of town— you know, those colonial houses with the columns and the eight miles of lawn before you even get to the front door. Santa had not just his choice of roofs, but he had his choice of chimneys here.

I didn't like her even worse than I didn't like her before, and that was before I got outta the squad.

I walked up that long sidewalk alone, noting that whoever shoveled didn't do a fine job as there was still a thin layer of ice that cracked beneath my boots. Someone had salted the steps, and the salt had melted through the ice, but no one'd bothered to kick the ice away, which I did, just as a courtesy.

Then I rang the bell.

The door opened and there was this kid wearing a pair of red shorts and a Santa hat, and grinning like there was no tomorrow. In that face, I saw every devil that ever walked and I knew that the geezer lied.

This kid wasn't good, he was hell on wheels, and I was just about to give him flight.

I caught him with one arm as he was about to sail into the snowy depths of the yard.

"Hey, kiddo," I said. "You ain't dressed for winter."

"Don't care," he said, struggling against me.

I wrapped my arm around him, lifted him off the ground and stepped inside with him. The hallway was one of them all wood jobbies with a staircase going up the side. The banister was covered in pine boughs, and there were ornaments hanging every which way.

"Miles?" a woman's voice shouted from above.

"He's down here," I said, hoping I didn't give her too much of a start. "I caught him going out the door."

I heard someone running across the floor upstairs, and then this girl peeked around the banister. Only it took me a half second to realize that wasn't no girl. That was a woman about my age who managed not only to keep her figure, but to keep lines off her face as well. Only her eyes told me she'd seen more of the world than any twenty-year-old ever could.

"And you are?" she asked, like someone in a uniform stood in her entry every day of the week.

"Name's Mantino, ma'am," I said with as much dignity as a man could muster when a three-year-old was squirming over his left arm, and kicking him perilously close to his private parts. "I'm with the police."

"I would hope so," she said. "Would you mind closing the door? It's got to be at least 20 degrees out there."

"Eighteen, ma'am," I said mostly because she had me a bit flustered. I didn't expect a person named Prudence Billings to look like this, kinda like a ballet dancer only without the ugly feet.

"Miles," she said, "where did you get that hat?"

The kid froze like he'd been dipped in ice, and truth be told, I kinda did too. I only heard one other woman on earth use that tone, and it was my mother back when I knew she'd caught me at something but good. My backside was twitching, and I would wager Miles's was too.

Still, he lifted his head over my bicep and grinned that Ain't-I-Cute? grin. "Got it at school," he said.

"Well, take it off," she said. "You know we don't allow that rubbish in here."

"Ma—"

"Miles."

He looked up at me and whispered, "Sorry but I gotta go now," and squirmed his way outta my arm. Then he tossed the hat at me like I gave it to him, and took off like a bat outta hell in the opposite direction. From that way, I smelled Christmas cookies, so I was wagering he was off to the kitchen to torment some poor housekeeper.

The lady sighed and came down the stairs. She was barefoot like I said, and her toenails were painted red and green and decorated with sprinkles that accent the colors. When she stopped on the landing, I noticed she wasn't quite as tall as I was. I figured when she was standing flat-foot on the floor she wasn't even gonna come up to my shoulders.

"What can I do for you, officer?"

I was twisting the red hat around in my hands like it was mine. She held out her hand for it, and I gave it to her. Her fingernails were long and painted just the same way. She didn't wear any rings.

"Prudence Billings?"

"Yes," she said.

I glanced at the hallway, lowered my voice, and then said, "I got some geezer come to the stationhouse last night saying you've been threatening Santa Claus."

She laughed. The sound was like a series of bells ringing on a starry night. "I have been."

I nearly took off my hat and started twisting it in my hands. "You said if he landed on your roof, you'd take a shotgun after him?"

"I said it to anyone who'd listen, Officer."

"Did you mean it?"

She looked at me, and I got the sense that this woman didn't do nothing she didn't mean. "Why do you ask?"

"Like I said, we gotta complaint—"

"Yes, I know. But not many folks would follow up on it. After all, my threat is only good if some man dressed in a red suit has his flying reindeer land a sleigh on my roof. In fact, I won't really do anything unless he slides down my chimney. I don't plan to sit on the lawn with the gun in my lap."

"Good thing," I said, "since it ain't something the neighbors would appreciate."

She laughed even though I was serious. So I got just a tad more serious.

"You gotta license for that shotgun?"

Her smile didn't just fade, it vanished like it never was, and I knew I had a lady who knew nothing about guns at all. A lady, a gun, and a kid. I didn't like how this was shaping up.

"'Fraid you gotta give it to me." I figured I'd keep it for the next few days, and the geezer wouldn't got nothing to worry about. By then maybe she'd rethink the whole gun-owning business. And if she didn't I'd give her a stern lecture when I got back on gun responsibility.

She stood on the landing, and said, "If you take the gun, will you protect me?"

"Seems to me that's a husband's job, ma'am," I said.

She looked up at me, and anger flared in her pretty eyes. I kinda liked the spark.

"Well, seeing as I don't have a husband, I'm relying on either myself or the police for protection."

"Protection from what, ma'am?"

"Santa Claus."

I sighed. I couldn't help it. "You know, ma'am, seems to me there's a lot more to worry about in this world than a man in a red suit who lands on your roof."

"You don't see it my way."

"No, ma'am. I always thought Santa was one of those guys who brought a little joy in the world, if you know what I mean, ma'am." I was treading lightly here because while this broad was one of the most beautiful creatures I'd ever seen, she was probably some religious nut, and I wasn't in the mood to argue the religious implications of jolly ole St. Nick.

"He doesn't always bring joy," she said.

"No, he don't. Sometimes he misses kids. But the fire department and us, we do what we can to make sure them kids get something."

"To keep up the myth." Her voice was rising. I knew then I'd made some kinda mistake.

"Well, you know, it's kinda nice to have something to believe in."

Then I winced, thinking she'd launch into the Jesus lecture, you know, the putting Christ back into Christmas thingie.

"No, it's not," she said, and I looked at her. I mean really looked at her.

This lady was scared.

So I said, "Tell me why you're doing this. It ain't natural to have something against Santa Claus."

"I'm trying to protect my son."

She *was* a loony. I sorta let the sigh out this time. "Lady, Santa leaves presents. I ain't never once heard a story where he traded 'em for the kids."

"That's not it," she said. "You saw him." And at first, I'm thinking she meant Santa Claus. Then I realize she meant the kid.

"Yeah," I said. "He's a pistol."

"Exactly." She came the rest of the way down the stairs and I was right. She didn't come up to my shoulders. But she smelled like roses, all delicate and fragile. "Miles is just like my brother."

"Is that a good thing, ma'am?"

"Not in this case. You're new to town, aren't you, officer?"

"Been here more'n two years, ma'am."

She shook her head. "When he was little, my brother fell off that roof and died. Broke his neck, which was probably for the best or so they tell me, since we didn't find him until Christmas morning. By then he was frozen stiff."

I didn't like how this was going. "I'm sorry to hear it, ma'am."

"He was seven. He was up there to watch Santa land." She swallowed. "My son is just like him. I don't want him to get wrapped up in the Santa myth. I'm afraid he'll do the same thing, and then I'll lose him too."

Her voice broke a little, and I put a hand on her shoulder. She didn't seem to mind.

"Look, ma'am," I said, feeling for her, knowing that we all go a little crazy over the things that hurt us most. "Your son ain't your brother—"

"I know," she said, "but I worry. And I think the best thing is to let him know that Santa isn't real, so then he'll avoid the whole thing. And he would be able to if the town didn't buy into this. I tried to prevent them from doing so, but it didn't work. Everyone still talks about Santa, and you've seen what it does to my son. He's got his Santa hat, and he's ready to show me that I'm wrong."

"Well, I think you are, ma'am," I said. "Santa ain't about materialism, not really, if you think about it. He's kinda a cherished cultural whatchamacallit—"

"Icon," she said.

"Yeah, whatever," I said. "He's one of them. Not because he brings us stuff, but because we think he does." That didn't come out the way I wanted it to so I took a deep breath and started over. "What I'm trying to say is this guy is okay to believe in because he's like pure good, you know. How many other examples do we got of someone who spends his whole year making stuff for others, then gives it all away in one night—to everyone, no one left out?"

"That's not how it works."

"Ain't it?" I said. "I been on various police forces for the last twenty years, and in all that time, I never seen a kid get missed by Santa, even if the Santa was a Toys for Tots program."

"If Santa was real," she said, "my brother wouldn't be dead."

"Ah, lady." I wanted to crouch down, face her at eye level and talk to her like a kid, because that's what she was sounding like. Some little teeny kid. "How old was you when all this came down?"

"Three," she whispered.

You didn't have to be no rocket scientist to figure out who she was protecting here, and it wasn't that underage demon in the red pants munchin' cookies in the kitchen.

"Look," I said, "You give me your shotgun, and I'll come back here when I'm off duty. I'll make sure Miles stays in his room, and Santa stays outside."

She raised her head. Her eyes were wide, and I thought I'd never seen anything so pretty in my whole life.

"You'd do that?" she asked. "Why?"

"Let's just say I think every kid needs a little guaranteed joy once a year, and three's too young to have it snatched away from you. Besides," I smiled at her. "I met your kid. He seems to me to be the type who'd go to the roof to prove to you that Santa *does* exist."

"I've been worried about that," she said. "I just hoped if I talked about it enough, the whole town would forget about this nonsense."

"It ain't nonsense, and no one'll forget," I said. "We all remember what it's like to be a kid and having that hope on Christmas Eve. We ain't gonna give it up, and we ain't gonna deny our kids the same thing."

"Do you have kids, officer?" she asked.

"I ain't found the right woman to have them with," I said.

She put a small hand on the side of my face. "Some woman doesn't know what she's missing," she said. Then she went upstairs, and brought me the gun.

———

I worked my regular shift, got off around eight, and flew outta the stationhouse. The dispatch, he made some crack about me having a date, and the whole group laughed like it wasn't possible, but I didn't say nothing. I just drove to the Billings place, hoping I wasn't too early. As it was, they was waiting for me.

Prudence Billings opened the door when I pulled up out front and motioned me inside. The pistol was wearing feet pajamas and his Santa cap, and holding a plate of cookies. I was thinking this kid wasn't gonna sleep for two weeks, judging by the brightness in his eyes.

"Miz Billings?" I'd changed into jeans and my heavy winter coat, figuring I was spending the night outside, waiting for the jingle of tiny sleigh bells.

"Priddy," she said.

"Ah, beg pardon?"

"Call me Priddy," she said. "Everyone does." Then she grinned. "It's better than Prude."

"Much," I said, thinking it seemed more accurate too. The house was looking nice. There was a tree in the living room, and white lights on the evergreen boughs on the stairs. The place was fairly bursting to be festive, and I figured it wouldn't take a lot of work to get Priddy Billings to start celebrating in a way that'd satisfy the kid.

"I got cookies for you, Mister," the pistol said.

"Thanks," I said, and took one. It was a sugar cookie with a bit too much frosting, but it had a sweet lemony taste like the ones my mom used to make. The taste of Christmas, sure as I breathed.

"It's officer," Priddy was saying to the kid. "Officer Mantino."

"Actually," I said, "it's Nick."

She grinned. "How appropriate," she said.

I guess it was. I never thought of it that way. "Well," I said, "what's the plan?"

"The plan is to get Miles to bed, and then I'll hold down the inside while you guard the outside."

"Seems fair," I said. "You ready to sleep, sport?"

"I'm not gonna sleep," he said. "I'm gonna show Mom that Santa's coming."

Priddy closed her pretty eyes.

"Well," I said, crouching down to be at his level. "You ain't gonna do that by staying awake."

"Why not?" the kid asked.

"You don't know?" I said. "Santa don't come to houses where kids are awake."

I thought Priddy's mouth was gonna fall off her face. I guess she hadn't thought of that one. It was a simple solution to her problem. Keep the kid awake all night and Santa wouldn't show up. Too late now. I'd spilled the beans.

"That true?" the kid asked.

"Scouts honor," I said, holding up my hand.

"You was a scout?" he asked.

"Eagle," I said, not lying.

"Wow," he said. "You know, I wanna be a scout."

"*Miles*," Priddy said in that voice again.

"Ah, Mom," he said, but started up the stairs anyway. Halfway up, he stopped. "You wanna read to me, Mister?"

"Officer Mantino has done enough." Priddy marched past me and went with the kid. "He'll be guarding the house tonight, so you say thank you."

"Thank you," the kid said. "Merry Christmas."

That last was a little forlorn, so I grinned at him. "Merry Christmas, sport."

Then he trudged the rest of the way up the stairs. She followed. I wandered into the living room, wondering if she really wanted me to snoop that far into their lives. The tree was big and green and smelled like pine heaven. Under it were more presents than I'd received since I'd grown up, all in that shiny wrapping paper that reflected the lights.

The lady wasn't loony. She was just fighting something she shoulda dealt with long ago. She'd mixed up believing in Santa with the death of her brother, and then with the growing up of her kid. I was really glad now I got the shotgun outta the house. I wasn't looking forward to a night in the snow, but I figured it was a small price to pay for what I hoped was a chance to take Priddy Billings to dinner—when the holidays was over and she turned back into a normal person again.

It took her a while, but she finally came down the stairs. I was back in the hallway by then. She put a finger to her lips and led me into the kitchen. In there, I saw the remains of a Christmas ham. She handed me a bag filled with sandwiches and a thermos of coffee.

"Sorry to send you out on a night like this."

I shrugged. It wasn't a bad night. Just cold. "I volunteered."

"You're a nice man," she said.

"I got my moments."

"You think I'm crazy, don't you?"

That's one of them trick questions. If I said yes, I doomed this friendship for life. If I said no, I'd be lying. "I think you got issues," I said.

"You're polite too," she said.

I set the bag and the thermos on the table, then pulled my gloves outta my pocket and put my wool cap over my ears. "I'd better get out there."

"You think he'll come this early?"

"Priddy." I liked the way the name sounded when I said it. "I don't think he'll come at all, but I think we should be vigilant now, just in case."

"Good point," she said, and went back upstairs. She stopped at the kitchen door. "Thank you, Nick."

"You're welcome," I said, and let myself out the back.

———

I wasn't gonna hide. I thought the worst thing I could do was wedge myself behind some bush and freeze to death, making Priddy relive her Christmas horror, and giving the kid a bad fright too. I had this all figured. In my car were a few things that a sales clerk assured me a three-year-old boy would like. I was gonna give 'em to Priddy around dawn, before the kid was up. I figured it was up to her to say whether the stuff came from me, a stranger, or Santa, a made-up stranger.

Maybe by then, she'd be willing to acknowledge Santa. If we made it through the night without him, that is. And I figured we would. First, you know, adult common sense said there was no such thing as Santa. But if there was, no self-respecting Santa would show up when people were looking for him. But I did figure there was a chance the geezer would come, and I kinda wanted to head him off at the pass. Maybe sometime in the next year, him and Priddy would resolve whatever differences they had. Maybe I'd still be around to help 'em do it.

So that's what I was thinking. I trudged around the yard, wearing a hole in the snow that probably wasn't doing the lawn any good. I watched the neighbors lights go out one by one, and I sucked down too much coffee and had to wait until one whole side of the neighborhood was dark before getting rid of some of it.

I think it was long about one a.m. when I got the bright idea to get the ice off Priddy's sidewalk. It was too late to use a shovel—that scrape-scrape-scrape would wake up the dead—so I decided to use my boot.

I was working my way from the porch to the road when I saw something move on the roof. I let out a four-banger blue alarm cuss that woulda sent me packing if Priddy heard it, and stepped back for a better look.

Damned if the geezer wasn't there, in his red suit and red hat, and looking jolly. Behind him was reindeer—at least some kinda deer—hooked onto a sleigh that was made of dark wood with red trim. It had curled runners, and the back end was piled high with toy sacks.

The geezer held up his mittened hand and waved at me. Then he hoisted himself onto the chimney, and I started cussing again. I mean, what was I gonna do to stop him, pelt him with snowballs? By the time I got to the back door, the geezer'd disappeared through the chimney and I was praying to every god I could think of that Priddy hadn't hid another weapon where I couldn't see it.

I slid through the back door, and tracked sludge on the linoleum. I slammed open the swinging doors, hurried through the decorated hallway, and stopped in the living room.

There he was, crouched beside the tree, laying train tracks—bright yellow and blue PlaySkool® train tracks with a big fat engine just perfect for a three-year-old. He set a kid-sized basketball hoop on the antique chair beside the fireplace, and put a small basketball beneath it. Then he turned around and pointed at me.

"I expect you to make sure he uses this," the geezer said in that prim tone of his.

"Me?" I said, looking behind me, thinking maybe Priddy was there. But she wasn't. I could hear her light step on the floor above. "Hey, you didn't tell me the whole story."

"But I do want to thank you," the geezer said. "I didn't see a shotgun."

"I got the shotgun," I said. "But she has a legitimate gripe. Her brother died on Christmas Eve. He fell off the roof. You got magic. How come you didn't do nothing?"

The jolly left the geezer's face. Suddenly it was like he was eighty years older than he'd been before.

"Magic has limitations," he said. "Mine is limited to this kind of joyfulness. Do you know how many little children ask me to get their mommies and daddies back together or to put an end to war? I can't. I don't have the power."

"You got the power to grab some kid who's sliding off a roof," I said, and there was a bit of force behind my words. You know, if this guy was who he said he was—and he had to be, didn't he?, I seen the deer—then I'd been idolizing him for some time. I coulda caught a kid with one hand, and pulled him to safety. This geezer coulda too.

"No, I don't," he said. "And you know why."

"The hell I do," I said.

He squinted at me.

"Because," he said, "I don't come to houses where people are awake."

"I'm awake."

"Yes, I know," he said. "But I asked you for help. It's a slightly different circumstance. And I wouldn't be here if Miles weren't sleeping. Soundly."

"So you didn't come at all that night, the night the kid died?"

"Ask Miss Billings," the geezer said, looking over my shoulder.

I turned. She was behind me, looking small. Her eyes were bright with unspent tears. They reflected the tree lights.

"You didn't come, did you?" she said in that little kid voice. "There were no special presents under the tree. I remember now. I hadn't thought of that. It hadn't seemed like Christmas that day. You didn't come because I was awake. I was waiting for my brother to come back to bed. Oh, God," she said, and her voice broke. "I killed him."

"No," I said.

"No," the geezer said at the same time. Only he went on. "It was one of those things that magic doesn't have a solution to. I'm so very sorry."

We were silent for what seemed like forever, waiting to see what Priddy would do. Finally, she blinked and one of the tears fell. Then she looked at the tree.

"Are those for Miles?" she asked.

"Yes," the geezer said.

"Wait," she said, and disappeared around the corner. I was hoping that she didn't go to do something stupid, but I didn't stop her. It was between her and the geezer now.

"You coulda told me," I said.

"You had to discover it for yourself," the geezer said.

"Why?" I ask.

He smiled. "Because I can't do anything without making a gift out of it."

"A gift?" I say.

He nodded, and then Priddy came back into the room. She was carrying that plate of cookies that Miles had out for me, and a glass of milk.

"We need to follow the tradition," she said.

The geezer took one of the cookies, and ate it. He grabbed the rest of the cookies and shoved them in his pocket—"for the reindeer," he said around the food—all except one, a Santa whose red suit was a bit too pink. He bit the head off it, and left it and a bunch of crumbs on the plate. "A tradition," he said and swallowed. He took the milk from Priddy, drank it all, and handed her the glass back. His mustache was dripping.

He looked at Priddy. "I'm glad this is finally settled."

"Between us it's settled," she said. "But it'll never be all right."

That sad look was back on his face. "My dear, things like this are never all right. But we do learn how to go on living, despite the pain."

"I guess we do," she said.

Then he smiled at her. "There is a gift for you here, too," he said. "If you only see it."

She looked at the tree. I was watching him. He put a finger alongside his nose, gave me a nod—and just like in the damn poem—up the chimney he rose.

Priddy looked back at me.

"He's gone," she said.

"Yep," I said. Then I cleared my throat. "I guess you won't be needing me no more."

She put a hand on my arm. "It was kind of you to give up your family time to help us."

I shrugged. "Ain't got family no more, ma'am. So it was no bother at all."

She looked at me, like she was seeing me for the first time. "Then I insist you stay. We have a guest room, and a Christmas turkey that's too big for Miles and me."

"I couldn't," I said. "It's a family day."

"It's no bother," she said. "Really. You helped us. I'd like to repay you." Then I grinned. She meant it. She really did. "I got stuff for Miles in the car."

"You were going to be Santa," she said.

"I think it's important," I said.

She glanced at the chimney.

"I guess it's important," she said, "even when we don't admit it."

"Especially then," I said.

———

Now I wouldn'ta told you all this except in the context that we been discussing nutcases. You see, the next morning, over Priddy's protests, I went out on that roof, and there weren't no sleigh marks or footprints or hoof prints. There wasn't no soot on Priddy's polished floor neither, and later I found a receipt for one basketball hoop, child-sized, by the cookie jar in the pantry.

I woulda thought Priddy was humbugging us all with them threats while celebrating like everyone else did if I hadn't come down with a humdinger of a cold from standing outside for too long on an icy December night. Priddy brought me her housekeeper's famous chicken soup and she took care of me during that awful week.

We've become something of a thing, you know, me and Priddy, and the guys at the stationhouse think it's funny; some woman from old money hooking up with a guy like me. But they don't know that we have lots to share, her and me. I'm the one who believes in stuff; she's the one who needs to. She's the one with the family; I'm the one who needs one. Stuff like that.

We're gonna make it official next Christmas season, but we're getting a new house. Something between my starter and her colonial, something that's just ours. It'll have a roof, but nothing too high, so if the kid gets adventurous—and he won't, not while I'm around—he won't get killed if he slips off.

I just keep thinking about the geezer, you know? I keep thinking maybe we should invite him to the wedding. After all, he's the one what brought us together. And I wonder if we send a wedding invite to that North Pole address the kids use, if he'll get it, and if he gets it, will he show?

Then I think about what I'm worrying about, and I check to see if it's a full moon or something. You know. Nutball season.

Because there's a part of me that's still embarrassed I believe in the old guy, even though I do. Since he was right. He gave all three of us a gift that night.

He gave the kid Christmas and he gave me and Priddy each other.

And that's enough to make anyone believe in Santa—even nutballs. Like me.

Doubting Thomas

Kristine Kathryn Rusch

DOUBTING THOMAS

Tommy Ulrick discovered the scam when he was six. He remembered everything about the night clearly: the winter dampness in the air, the smell of wood smoke mixed with ocean, waking on his flannel sheets with an urgency that seemed only to happen in childhood. He slipped out of bed and hurried to the bathroom—one of those herky-jerky emergencies where he jiggled all the way, holding himself, and praying he'd arrive on time.

Which he did, just barely. He remembered the relief, and as the relief grew, so did his chill. Someone had left the large bathroom window open, letting the December cold inside, allowing people on the street below to see his most private moment.

He glanced out—still too compromised to pull the window closed— to see if anyone was watching. The neighborhood Christmas lights were off, the houselights were off, even the few porch lights that stayed on late were off. Only the streetlight broke the darkness, casting pools of pale light through the thin fog.

He was safe. No one could see him. He shook himself off, tucked himself back inside his flannel pajamas, reached to close the window— and froze.

There was movement on the roof of the house across the street.

Well, not a house, actually. It was too big to be a house. It was the Sutter place, which his mother used to call, "the only bona fide mansion on the Central Oregon Coast." Later when he learned the history of it, when he was older and into such things, he discovered that his mother had been wrong –there had been other mansions, just none as visible, none quite as centrally located as the one on the street below their little two-bedroom ranch.

Still he struggled, trying to get the window closed, the wind blowing against him, plastering the ice-cold snap buttons against his bare chest. Somehow the battle became him against the window, and he was losing.

Then he saw the movement again. And what had looked like shadows became three men dressed as Santa Claus, dark sacks against their backs, struggling with the dormer on the side of the house.

He watched, horrified, as they tugged it open. Then they disappeared inside, one by one, none of them looking up at him, none of them noticing.

Then, from inside, white-gloved hands pulled the dormer closed.

———

Oh, Tommy did all the right things. He woke his parents, who called the police. His dad stared out the bathroom window a long time, as if he could see something different. Tommy stared too, pointed out the sleigh on the front lawn, saying it hadn't been there when he saw the men, but his dad just ignored him.

So did the police after they arrived. They walked around the Sutter place, saw no evidence of false entry, saw nothing out of the ordinary, and said so. They came up to Tommy's house, listened to his story, and told his parents not to let him watch so much television.

Then they left.

Tommy's mom made him use the bathroom one more time before he went to bed. No one had closed the window and as he looked out on the mansion below, he saw that the sleigh was gone.

Only this time, he didn't tell anyone. He snuck back to bed, pulled the covers to his chin, and shivered for the rest of the night.

———

Christmas was never the same after that. Tommy made sure there were no Santa Claus decorations in the house. He wouldn't sit on the Santa man's lap at the mall, and he wouldn't watch any Santa shows on television. He told his parents that he didn't believe, and they seemed saddened by it, but they thought it understandable.

After all, the Sutter place had been robbed that night. Apparently the police had arrived too late to do anything about it. Tommy had seen something. Turned out the dormer window was askew. There was even a bit of extra ash in the fireplace that next morning, and men's shoe prints tracking all over the house.

One of the police officers came by to apologize and to take Tommy's statement again. The theory was that the men had used the Santa Claus outfits as a ruse to get into the house, figuring they could pose on the roof like Christmas decorations if a car went by.

Brilliant, the police called it.

Humbug, Tommy would have said to himself if he had known the word then. Complete and total humbug.

He had seen the dark side of Santa, and was never ever going to be the same again.

———

Childhood lost, cynicism found. Outwardly Tommy Ulrick was the same as all the other little boys of his age, unless someone mentioned Santa Claus. It got so bad that his parents used to warn people not to use the name. At Christmas, he became sullen and fearful, and there didn't seem to be anything anyone could do about it.

His parents thought he would grow out of it. It was a phase, they said, brought on by a traumatic childhood event, and, as Tommy got older and realized that his attitude toward the Jolly Old Elf was socially unacceptable, he stopped talking about it.

Instead, he turned inward. He studied. He learned everything he could about the enemy, and what he saw he didn't like.

It was, he came to understand, the biggest fraud ever perpetrated on the public. A round-cheeked old man masquerading as a saint who gave toys to children, all the while using those children to hide his own greed. In fact, the old man used his scam to teach greed.

In Tommy—now Thomas—Ulrick's life, Christmas ceased to be about love and peace and goodwill toward all men. Instead, it turned into a holiday about stuff. Who bought the most, who spent the most, who got the most. Even people who belonged to other religions gave into the Christmas frenzy. They treated it as a secular holiday, so their kids wouldn't be left out of the stuff-getting.

It was, Thomas realized, a shameful thing.

And when he turned thirty, he'd finally had enough.

———

Later, he figured, everything culminated that year. His parents had died in a car accident the year before. He'd taken a leave of absence from his big city reporter's position—a forced leave of absence: reporters are supposed to do everything they can to get a story, but apparently "everything" did *not* include breaking a few minor privacy laws. His third fiancée left him just like all the others had when she realized that he hated Christmas. Apparently his fiancées could tolerate different religions, different attitudes toward money, but not a bah-humbugish attitude toward Christmas.

It was, he discovered, the ultimate deal-breaker.

So on Christmas Eve of that year, he sat down at his kitchen table, in his comfortable two-bedroom ranch style house in the Portland suburb of Beaverton, and, like he used to do when he was starting an article, made a list.

1. *Adults all acknowledge there is no Santa Claus.*
2. *Children are encouraged to believe in Santa Claus.*
3. *Santa doesn't give gifts. Parents do, thus perpetuating the myth.*
4. *From Halloween on, people see Santa Claus on the streets, and think nothing of it.*
5. *People decorate their homes with Santa Claus iconography, making it easy for fake Santas to hide.*

6. *The only thing that people do when they see a Santa is give him something. (Does the Salvation Army really still exist? Do they sanction those little red change boxes? Is this a direct part of the scam or is this something else encouraged by the Evil Santa Brigade?)*
7. *Was the lump of coal more than a metaphor? Perhaps, in the early years, the Santa thieves left only a lump of coal when they cleaned out a house.*
8. *Naughty or nice. Who's to determine? Based on what criteria?*
9. *Robberies increase supposedly because houses are more vulnerable. People in the holiday spirit aren't as vigilant.*
10. *Fires increase. Arson to cover up robberies?*
11. *More people commit suicide during the holidays than at any other time of the year. Real suicides? Or more cover-ups—killed when they discover someone who isn't supposed to be in the house?*
12. *Was Clement Moore in on this?*
13. *How long has this been going on?*

Thomas stopped, chilled to the bone. One man against a centuries-old tradition of duplicity and thievery.

He had to stop this. But how?

———

It came to him as he woke up the next morning. There had to be a grain of truth to everything in the myth.

He sat up, his frayed cotton sheets pooled around his waist. He was willing to believe that the original Santa thieves went down chimneys, just like the stories. A roof was a great access point for a robber, and a hundred years ago, children used to climb into chimneys to clean them. Skinny children, but children nonetheless. He didn't believe that fat old men slid down chimneys—but that was the impossibility that made the idea seem so ludicrous. Better to go back to the truth.

And he would wager that a lot of Santa's Helpers went through the front doors too.

He rubbed his hands together. He felt like he was finally onto something.

He got out of bed, and grabbed his robe, sliding it on as he made his way to the kitchen. He didn't believe that Santa operated from the North Pole—too cold, too remote, too impractical—but he would wager that there was a hideout. It didn't have to be very big—not like the factory portrayed in all those stupid Christmas movies. After all, Santa wasn't making toys. He was stealing stuff.

The hideout had to be a place to run to, a place to hide, a place to split up the wealth, like the Hole-in-the-Wall of Western Outlaw lore.

And if he found the Hole in the Wall, the hideout, he found the bad guys.

He had the power to stop this scam once and for all.

———

It was easier than he thought. It just took time.

After all, he had data from thirty years of collecting. His newspaper training made him an excellent sleuth. He searched for robberies, fires, and suicides, throwing in a few surprise deaths from heart failure and a couple of thwarted attempts.

He made a cybermap and marked out all the hits in the United States for the last fifty years, searching for a pattern—and what he found terrified him. If his assumptions were true, and he had no reason to think they weren't—then he was dealing with something so large that he could barely contemplate it.

Every state got hit, every county, every town—and in the right statistical proportions. In fact, that's what gave the plot away. The statistics were too perfect. No cluster of suicides in Denver in any one year, for example, or no extra fires in San Jose. Apparently the statisticians hadn't noticed that every city had just about the same number of robberies, deaths, and fires in the weeks before Christmas. The ever-so-slight variations came from what he would consider to be unconnected events—gang killings, insurance fraud arson, and the robberies caused by non-affiliated thieves (whom, he noted, usually got caught).

He expanded his search to include Britain and Western Europe, and found fewer incidences there, although those too were statistically perfect. Going back a hundred years, he found higher incidences in England; he figured that was probably where the scam originated.

Thomas spent weeks analyzing the information and figured that the hideout was in the United States where the pickings were good. There were probably several sub-hideouts, but the main one—if he were the guy planning all of this—had to be centrally located.

Unless...

He paused, hands over the keys, as inspiration struck again.

All those greeting cards, posters, t-shirts. *Images* everywhere of Santa in a swimsuit and loud floral-print shirt, lounging in a beach chair on the sand, chubby ankles crossed while he stared at a pristine ocean. Those pictures never depicted Santa on a Hawaiian beach or relaxing on California's sultry sands.

Santa was always in Florida, generally Miami Beach, and he was always grinning at the camera.

Taunting someone—taunting Thomas—to find him.

Thomas scanned the Florida information. The farther south he went, the more evidence he found—in the lack of evidence, of course. Fewer Christmas fires (statistically attributable to the warm weather, the lack of heaters, the fact that Christmas trees didn't dry out as quickly), fewer suicides (statistically attributable the advanced age of the population; if they lived that long, they wouldn't throw what was left away), and surprisingly, given the wealth of the area, fewer robberies (statistically attributable to the fact that most people traveled *to* Florida during the holidays; fewer vacant homes). Heart attacks were up, but they didn't fall into his mathematical model because very few of those were a surprise, again given the advance age of the population.

He went to his hardcopy cabinet and pulled one of his many Santa souvenirs out of the postcard file. Santa, wearing sunglasses five times too big, a red-and-orange checked shirt a size too small, and matching orange shorts which revealed pale hairy legs, waved out of the image. *Wish You Were Here,* said the red lettering across the top.

"I will be," he promised the Jolly Old Elf. "Soon."

———

For some reason, the thievery began again in Gainesville. Orlando was safe —maybe because Santa liked it there, or spread out his Florida vacation spots–but anything north of Gainesville was as fair as the rest of the western world.

He spent the months before Christmas studying the maps, searching for patterns. He finally found them. Simple, elegant, and difficult to see. The thieves worked in an alphabetical or numerical pattern by street name. Each state was assigned a letter or number, and then the pattern shifted clockwise from year to year. In other words, if Main was the "A" street in the first year, the next year it would be the "Z" street. The pattern worked the same with numbers.

Once the state's number or letter had been assigned, the thieves picked the exact street according to housing prices and the quality of the neighborhood. Then they probably staked a few houses out. It sounded like a lot of work, but it wasn't.

If he was right, that year Florida was the "D" street and the "30th" state. Gainesville was a number town—there were a lot of thirties. Southwest thirties, thirties with streets, thirties with avenues. Thomas scanned all the possible thirties and came up with what he considered to be a jackpot—30th Terrace, an area where the homes were worth half a million or more with lots of acreage, right in the middle of the city. Right smack in the center of that region was a house that had been owned for a couple of decades by the same people, philanthropists by their profile, who didn't believe in home security systems.

He did a bit more research, discovered that the home's owners boarded their dog and canceled their newspaper delivery every year just before Christmas. He didn't even break a sweat to find out that information. He imagined the Santa Stealers had all of this down to a science.

On December 18, he had lunch with fiancée number three—for old times sake, he said—and told her he was going out of town. He gave her a key to his safe deposit box, and told her to open it if he wasn't back by the first of the year.

She looked at him as if he were crazy, which was how she had been looking at him for the last year or more. But she agreed, which was all that mattered.

Then he flew to Orlando, rented a black sports car, and drove to Gainesville.

———

He hadn't done a real honest-to-god stakeout in nearly five years. Back when he was young and hungry, he got a lot of his information just spying on people. The older he got, the more he used legal information obtained through records, and then as he learned his way around computers, he found more and more fascinating things illegally.

But this was no longer a computer sort of case. This required diligence, wakefulness, and quick-thinking.

He slept during the day at a cheap hotel on the highway and watched the empty house at night. No neighbors nearby to report him, no big dogs to bark. By December 22nd, he was beginning to think the house was too perfect, or his research suspect. He hadn't seen hide nor hair of a sleigh or eight tiny reindeer or anything else near the target house.

But he knew that these Santa Bandits struck all the way through December 25th. He just had to be patient.

And finally, at 4 a.m. on the morning of December 24th, his patience paid off. He was keeping himself awake by making condensation rings on the driver's side window, when he heard a car engine, a sound he hadn't heard after midnight in this neighborhood since he started his vigil.

He slumped down in the sports car's bucket seat, and watched as a dark colored late model minivan with its lights off pulled into the house's long gravel driveway. When he was sure the occupants could no longer see his car, he grabbed his binoculars and climbed over the shifting column to the passenger seat. There he leaned against the dash and watched.

A chill ran up his spine, and for a moment, he touched his six-year-old self.

Instead he focused on the movement he saw on the empty house's roof. Three men, just like he had seen twenty-four years before, dressed as Santa, carrying black bags over their shoulders—empty bags. The men balanced precariously on the steep roof, climbing to its peak. Then the first man reached over and pulled open a window that probably led to an attic. He slid in, head first, as if he were diving into a pool.

The other two followed.

And Thomas, his six-year-old self still closer to the surface than he wanted the boy to be, slipped out of the car to pee.

———

Less than an hour later, the men emerged the way they entered, full bags over their shoulders. They slid down the back roof, presumably to the van, which he hadn't been able to see.

Then, lights out, it left the driveway.

Thomas waited until it was nearly a block away before he started the rental. He followed, his lights out too, keeping a discreet distance.

The van's lights came on at the end of 30th Terrace, and from then on all driving was normal. Thomas tailed them, mentally congratulating himself for a) practicing that skill a lot before and b) renting a sports car. He was able to keep up.

As he drove, he called 911 and reported the break-in.

Step one of his plan.

Just as he expected, when they hit the highway, they headed south. But they didn't go to Miami, like he expected.

Instead, they went to Orlando, where the waiters sang, men dressed like giant mice, and make-believe was part of the air.

His enemy was craftier than even Thomas thought. He should have known that Miami Beach was a ruse. It was the Florida part with the grain of truth to it.

When they finally stopped, he felt a surge of disappointment. He couldn't help himself. He had been hoping for something interesting, something unique.

Instead, they pulled into a strip mall in one of the outlying areas of Orlando, where the rents were cheaper and the businesses cheesier. They drove around back and he followed, but he knew where they were going. He didn't have to be a rocket scientist to figure that one out.

The biggest store on the strip. It had a candy-cane striped door, giant toy soldiers guarding either side. Decorated Christmas trees stood in front of each window, and a couple of plaster elves looked like they had just finished painting the store's name on its sign: *The Christmas Cottage*.

But that wasn't the biggest giveaway. The biggest giveaway were the Santa statues—all three of them. On the roof.

———

Thomas had his video camera, his microcassette tape recorder, and a digital camera with a telephoto lens. As he got out of the car, he called 911, said he saw some suspicious activity at the Christmas Cottage, and that he was getting out of his car to investigate.

The dispatch urged him not to, of course, but he hung up, as if he were a zealous citizen. Which, he supposed, he was.

He left the digital zoom in the car, clicked on the microcassette recorder, and headed toward the back. The sun was just starting to come up, sending pale yellow light across the flat Florida landscape.

As he expected, the van was parked directly behind the Christmas Cottage. The store's back doors were open, and no one was in sight.

He slipped inside. The back of the store was bigger than he thought, almost a store in and of itself. There was an assortment of boxes, all of them clearly merchandise, some open with ornaments or tinsel hanging out. But an open storage door on the left side revealed items that didn't belong in a Christmas store.

He moved toward it as quietly as he could. Voices were coming from the storefront, talking amiably, as if someone were telling a story. Probably relating the events of the night.

When he got closer to the storage door, he stopped and made sure he was in shadow. He needed a place to hide if the thieves came back. He found the perfect spot behind a man-sized box, and set to work.

With shaking hands he raised the video camera to his right eye. Mentally, he cataloged as he went: coin collections, artwork, and jewelry—so much jewelry that his entire body felt numb. Then there were silver—from flatware to pitchers, the antiques (all small enough to carry), and the occasional high-end television.

He was nearly done with a white-gloved hand grabbed his wrist, pulling the camcorder down.

"Ho, ho, ho," a deep voice said with more cheer than seemed appropriate to the situation.

Another hand took the camcorder away. Thomas started to protest, but stopped. He was busted. He had to think clearly now.

He turned slowly, and tried not to let his surprise show.

The man standing behind him was no more than five feet tall, with white hair down to his shoulders and a fluffy white beard. He was wearing a red suit with real fur, and shiny black boots. He ho-hoed again and his stomach jiggled, just like that infamous bowl full of jelly. He had an unlit pipe in his bow-shaped mouth, and his blue eyes did twinkle merrily—at Thomas's expense.

All of the images of Santa were on the mark—if one ignored the height problem.

"Little Tommy Ulrick," the man said. "I wondered if you would be a problem."

"H-How do you know who I am?" Thomas asked.

The man tsk-tsked. "Tommy, of all people, you have to ask? I'm Santa. I know everything."

"Yeah," Thomas said, blessing his own forethought in having the microcassette recorder running. "That's why you have to steal for a living."

Claus—or whoever he was—sighed. "Ah, an explanation man. Somehow I would have thought you had it all worked out, Tommy."

"Thomas. And all I want to know is why."

"Not how? Not all the particulars?"

"No," Thomas said. He finally had control of his voice again. "Only why."

Claus's twinkling eyes narrowed. "I wouldn't have figured you for a true believer."

"I'm not," Thomas said. "I'm a reporter. I have a Need to Know."

Claus made a rude sound. "A need to spy, you mean. Which I would have thought that incident when you were six cured you of."

"Naw," Thomas said. "Just made me even more curious. So. Why do you do it?"

Claus sighed. "I hate this part."

His friends came through the doorway. They were even shorter. Even though they were wearing jeans and ratty Marlins t-shirts, they looked like Santa's elves. Which they probably were.

"Another one, Boss?"

"Whatcha gonna do this time?"

Claus ignored them. Instead he stared at Thomas. "Look, I'll split the loot with you fifty-fifty if you just don't ask for the explanation."

"Too late," Thomas said. "I already did."

One of the elves laughed. "Gotta tell him, Boss. Don't you just hate those magic rules?"

"How much time do we have?" the other elf asked.

"If he called 911, maybe ten more minutes."

"Plenty of time, Boss."

"Someone trained you, right?" Thomas asked. "This is like a world-wide scam that's been going on for centuries. The original Santa was, what? a real Fagan? A man who trained his cohorts from childhood?"

"I am the original Santa," Claus said.

This time it was Thomas's turn to make the rude noise.

"I *am*," Claus said. He turned to the elves. "I really do hate this part."

"Get it over with, Boss," the first elf said, then crossed his arms and leaned against the wall. "I'm keeping an ear out for the coppers."

"Pigs," the other elf corrected.

Thomas frowned at them. Coppers? Pigs? Was their slang really out of date? Or were they faking it just for him?

"You figured it out," Claus said. "You know that part of the myth is true, and part of it is convenient. Well, I'm just a jolly old elf. Really."

"More like a leprechaun," the elf said.

"Or even that Coyote character," the other elf said.

"A trickster?" Thomas asked. That part he hadn't figured out.

Claus put one finger beside his nose and pointed at Thomas with the other hand. Thomas ducked, as if he expected something magical to happen to him.

Claus chuckled, a deep rolling laugh that seemed to fill the room. "You *do* believe."

"I know something was up," Thomas said. "I figured out your theft pattern. I know about your units. I even figured you were in Florida."

"But you don't know why, and it bothers you." Claus let his fingers drop.

"Yes," Thomas said, if he could keep the trio talking, they'd stay here until the cops arrived. Then he'd have everything on tape. "If you have magic, why steal?"

"Magic requires belief. A few people still believe, but for the most part, rationalists have taken over. About the time Claus started, don't you know."

Thomas did know. He just hadn't put it together.

"So," Claus said, "if I can get people to believe in a jolly old elf for part of a year, why then, I have a bit of my powers. Not all, any more. Just enough."

"But why use them to steal?"

Claus frowned. "An immortal has-been needs a way to maintain his lifestyle."

"At the expense of people's homes? At the expense of their lives?"

"Oh, crap, Boss," one of the elves said. "This is a live one."

Claus continued to ignore them. "Mistakes happen," he said. "The deaths are always regrettable."

"Regrettable?" Thomas's voice rose. Then he cleared his throat, too late, of course. They'd probably already heard the panic.

"I think I hear sirens, Boss," one of the elves said.

"Me too." The second elf's ears—which really were pointed—started to twitch.

"You go," Claus said. "I'll handle this guy."

"Boss, we're going to need a new hideout," the first elf said.

"We'll worry about that later. Just go."

They scurried out the back and closed the double doors. After a moment, Thomas heard the van start.

Claus was smiling at him. It wasn't a nice smile. "I have so many options. I could let those cops you called find you here with the loot. I could kill you. Or I could make use of you."

"You'd make me a part of your thieving band?"

"Don't be silly," Claus said. "You wouldn't last a year. I can see through to Naughty and Nice, and you got waaaay too much Nice in you. That's probably why you searched me out, even though you say it's for the story."

He squeezed Thomas's wrist just a little harder. For an old man, he was very strong.

"Story," Claus muttered. "I wish I could use you for the story. But times have changed."

"Is that what the elves were alluding to? Someone else has caught you?"

"You'll kick yourself when I tell you." Claus grinned. His teeth were pointed, almost fanged. Thomas wondered how he ever found this face pleasant.

"Clement Moore," Thomas said softly.

"Twas the Night Before Christmas. Same day, different year. Different century." Claus tilted his head, looking thoughtful. "Didn't have computers then. We weren't as accurate in knowing who'd be home and who wouldn't be. *He* had children I could threaten. You keep losing your fiancées."

"You know that?"

"My mind is full of useless information, all of it relating to goodness or badness. You'd think magic would be great—and it probably would if someone got the stuff of stories, you know, the ability to make things disappear, being able to fly things across a room. But no. I get stupid talents. Seeing people while they sleep. They lay in one position for a while, sigh, and roll over. Nothing exciting there. And the naughty and nice stuff? Good for the occasional blackmail, but nothing more."

Claus rolled his tiny eyes. Thomas strained to hear those sirens. But he couldn't, not yet. How good were those elven ears?

"I'd like to pat you on the head and tell you to write a nice poem, filled with *my* lies, of course, and a little bit of the truth," Claus said. "But these days, the myth-making machine is self-generating. Who'd've known what a boon television would be?"

"Who'd've known?" Thomas asked. He swallowed, wondering if he could shake himself free, and get out those double doors before the Jolly Old Elf caught him. Probably. It would be worth a try.

"So," Claus said, "I think I'll just let you go."

Thomas had been concentrating so much on escaping that he almost missed what Claus said. "What?"

"I'm letting you go." Claus dropped Thomas's wrist like it contaminated him. "Toddle on."

"But they'll catch you."

"No, they won't," Claus said, going to the storage area, dropping and locking the door.

"I'll tell," Thomas said.

"Of course you will." Claus grinned. "But who's going to believe you?"

———

No one, it turned out. Not the cops who showed up, only to be greeted by the big man himself ("Sorry to bother you, officers. We got an early morning shipment and this man was worried."), not Thomas's old editor ("Tom, I say this only as a friend. Counseling. Lots of counseling.") and especially not fiancée number three ("Don't ever call me again. Ever!").

In the end, there was nothing he could do. Oh, he called and reported a few break-ins before they occurred, but that only got him brought him to the attention of the police –and not in a good way. And then he tried to warn potential victims, which only made his police surveillance worse. He soon figured that if he continued along this path, he would soon be arrested for the crimes himself.

And to make matters worse, every January, he got a postcard from Florida—that year's Santa postcard, which always had the happy *Wish You Were Here!* on the front. On the back was just a scrawled number.

That first year he had no idea what the number meant. But the second year, after he mapped the robberies, he knew.

Total profits, after expenses, of course. Never less than ten million dollars. Tax free.

The old guy could have quit years ago. But he didn't. He wasn't doing it for the money. He was addicted to the belief.

And Thomas, whom everyone doubted, understood why.

An Incursion of Mice

Kristine Kathryn Rusch

An Incursion of Mice

Here's what I know: You can't have a crime without an explosion.

I know this from my vast study of crime, criminal behavior, and detective work.

I do this study from my couch in the basement. Sometimes I sit on the large recliner, usually resting on a blanket in the lap of one of the servants. I prefer the male servant because he caters to me. The female servant feeds me, but doesn't brush me or coddle me.

She claims that I am convinced that I am the center of the universe.

As I understand the universe—and granted, I understand it less than crime and criminals—it has no center. She means that I am self-involved and self-centered.

I am not. I have never claimed to be the center of any universe.

The servants have a variety of names for me, which they believe are mine. Those names are not mine, although the four cats in my pride have adopted one of them for me.

They call me Wall T.

I prefer to think of that as my street name—if I ever went to the street and/or needed a name. I prefer remaining inside.

In an earlier life, one I do not discuss, I was a show cat. I had several names, all delineating my lineage, which is old and storied and Quite

Upstanding. I won many awards. I am "stunning" and "good humored" and "one of the most beautiful males ever witnessed" especially when I've had a proper bath, blow-dry, and brushing.

My first servant knew how to tend me, but felt that my mission in life was to show my beauty to the world. I let him take me to shows, introduce me to other cats, and make a Good Impression. Then, he died of a terrible wasting disease, and the people who came for him tossed me outside.

I lived on the street, hooked up with a scruffy orange male who never shared his name, and who had a soft spot for clueless beauties. He taught me the ways of street cats. I would have thrived, I'm sure, but he believed I needed servants.

So he found me these.

I'm unable to convince the servants of a proper routine. They do not know that breakfast starts at 7:30, that second breakfast occurs at 10, and that lunch follows shortly thereafter. They believe in kibble treats left out all day, and the occasional soft meal.

They do not believe that cats should be bathed and blow-dried. They had to be convinced about brushing.

But they have no interest in shows and ribbons and awards, at least for me, although they have discussed my past history. They honor it. They call me "retired."

I would step back into the ring if need be, but I prefer my study of crime and criminals and all-around bad behavior.

I prefer my couch, and my reputation. Not as a show cat, which does not impress the others in the pride. But as a street cat.

As Wall T.

I might be pretty, but I'm not soft.

And I'm smarter than anyone gives me credit for.

———

It started with a mouse incursion.

Why mice thought they could invade this household is beyond me. Yes, we live near a wooded area, and yes, the house is huge, with enough room for the entire pride (plus more, if I were to allow it, which I will not). But we patrol.

My second in command, a beautiful silver-and-gold girl we call M, handles household organization. We all lived on the streets at one point, but she arrived here, young, battered, pregnant, and alone, mostly feral like my orange friend, and after healing, she made it her duty to make certain that our home is perfect.

In my research, I have learned that such types are often called anal or obsessive-compulsive. The human experts recommend therapy. I have found that an obsessive-compulsive has her uses—and one of them is making certain the household runs on time—or as close to on time as it can with recalcitrant and somewhat stubborn servants.

M set up the patrols and commands them. Each cat (aside from me, of course) has an assigned area of our home, and each must maintain that area.

M handles the kitchen, and she is the one who found the first mouse. She guarded it until I could see it. She left it in the able paws of King, who is the only other male in the pride. He predates me in this location, but simply does not care for command (nor does he do it right).

King watched the mouse for thirty seconds before smashing it beneath his left paw. The mouse tried to scamper away, but King scooped it in his mighty jaws, and with one single crunch, killed our only witness.

At the time, we were unconcerned—although M was furious. She had curtailed the witness, cordoned it off, and maintained its imprisonment until she was relieved of sentry duty. Then she came to me to discuss the interrogation, only to discover there would be none, thanks to King's impulsive and somewhat reckless behavior.

I believed interrogation, particularly of a rodent, a complete waste of time. In the olden days, before kibble and delicious soft food, rodents were considered little more than food. Once kibble and delicious soft food became the diet of choice for rich cats, the makers of such delicacies never included rodent, believing it tainted the palette.

I agreed and, frankly, still shudder at the thought of that hairy, flea-infested body inside King's mouth, the squirty warmth of blood and bitter taste of mouse-flesh. Yes, I've eaten mouse in my street days, and I've lived to tell of it.

But I am here to tell you that Fancy Feast, in all flavors, is ever so much better.

I digress. (Although, honestly, when is a culinary discussion ever a digression?)

I did not discipline King. It's not my place, really. Besides, he was doing his duty as he saw it, and I cannot argue with that. M knew better than to argue with a male, although she glared at him angrily. He is such a laid-back creature, and he is so used to M, that I doubt he even noticed.

We knew, however, that we faced an incursion later in the day, when the second mouse appeared. Our lame and slightly crazy female, Diva, found him.

I tend to write off her disposition. She is a tortoise shell, and we all know that torties are born crazy. Plus a car smashed her hind leg when she was barely six months old. She arrived in this household post-surgery, paranoid, angry, and addicted to pain meds.

I learned a word for her condition in my nightly research. Or rather, an acronym: PTSD.

If anyone were to kill anyone, it would be our Diva, and it wouldn't be her fault.

But murderous she is not. She saw the incurring mouse, and screamed, slapping it until it retreated.

M put 24-hour guards on the entrance, and I thought the problem over.

Of course, the servants, late to the game as usual, found the mouse body we had conveniently left near the door, and panicked. Servants are so useless. They don't take guidance. They overreact to everything.

At least they tossed the body outside.

M saw that as charity—the starving street kittens would have extra meat tonight—but I knew it for what it was. Wealthy cats throwing away perfectly good food. Even my old street buddies wouldn't eat that thing. Someone else's kill? Rodent doesn't taste good in the first place. Charity rodent tastes particularly foul.

The servants called more servants, the ones who kept us and the house "pest" free, and they had some kind of consultation about the whys and wherefores of mice, whether or not we had an "infestation" and if that was even possible with five cats running the house.

The servants contended that we were lazy and pampered, ignoring, of course, who killed the mouse in the first place, and said the house could have been infested for years.

If I didn't like the servants so much, I would have fired them on the spot. I would not run a household infested by mice.

No self-respecting cat would.

Shortly after the extra servants put out mousetraps that would not injure the paws of our Diva (who never paid attention to do-not-touch instructions), M came to me.

—*I have been thinking about this*, she said. *The servants might not be wrong. Food has disappeared at an alarming rate.*

My tail dipped. I hadn't noticed a decrease in the food supply, and said so.

M sat out of the reach of my paws. She tilted her lovely head and said, *I thought perhaps you were indulging a bit too often, Wall T.*

She blamed *me* for the food disappearing? I ate my share, of course, and my share included bits of everyone else's—after they had tasted a bit first, so that I knew it wasn't poisoned—but I did not overeat, much as I subscribed to the idea that no cat could be too rich or too fat.

—*I have access to all the best treats*, I snapped. *Why would I feel the need to sneak food?*

She raised her head. She had a superior little expression that she usually used on the others, not on me. Only this time, she did use it on me.

—*I never said you sneaked anything, Wall T. I didn't think to monitor who was taking the food. Only that the servants had to refill our bowls more often than usual.*

I had noticed that too, and blamed Sweetie, the newest of our tribe. She had spent a year outside, abandoned by the boyfriend of the servant who pampered her. When she entered our household, she did so after much consideration. Sweetie was a thinker, but if M hadn't already had firm paws on the household, Sweetie would run it all with an iron claw.

—*I am now thinking that mice have been stealing our food*, M said.

I wanted to slap her with fury. Theft? In our house? By *mice*? She was impugning my catness.

—*You're wrong*, I said.

—*I'm not so certain.* Sweetie sat near the food bowls. She'd been watching the servants argue over the mice, but now she turned her attention to us.

She was a beautiful black and white cat with long hair that she kept in order. I tried to convince her to command the male servant to brush her, but she preferred the female, and she wasn't all that certain human touch was something to be invited regularly.

—*Have you seen the weather?* Sweetie asked.

I didn't pay attention to weather. Now that I did not leave the house for shows, I had no need to brace myself against cold. On the street, I had found the weather to be my enemy.

I preferred indoor weather. Gray days, with rain pelting the windows, were great for sleeping. Sunny days, with warmth filtering through the glass, were great for sleeping. All days, indoors, had the perfect weather.

—*No,* I said, with a tail switch that implied weather watchers were stupid. *Why would I?*

—*We've had snow and ice and wind and storms and cold, cold air for weeks now,* Sweetie said, her paws touching before her. She did haughty very, very well.

She had spoken of this snow before. I had never experienced it, although I did take a look at it after she moved in. On the night she joined us, she said it wasn't because we looked handsome or pampered or even happy. It was because she remembered how warm and dry felt. And six inches of snow (which fell near her outdoor food bowls) reminded her that life could be better.

—*Who cares about the weather?* I snapped.

—*You should.* King sauntered in and sat beside Sweetie. *Because you let a major crime occur on your watch.*

—*My* watch? I said, my tail switching even more. *You're King of the house.*

He wrapped his tail around his front paws. He did that when he was feeling particularly self-satisfied.

—*I've heard you,* he said. *You've told everyone you're in charge, but you'll let me believe that I am. So I let you run things for a while.*

I had no idea why that statement made me shiver. But it did.

—*No crime occurred,* I said.

—*Mice have been stealing food for weeks now, Wall T.*

—And you didn't stop them? I asked.

—When M got involved, I couldn't watch any longer, he said. *You don't make the women work extra hard because you're blind, Wall T.*

—Blind? I snapped. *I'm not blind. I run a tight household.*

—Is that why M does all the work? King asked. *Why Sweetie makes sure that the Diva doesn't damage herself in her midnight crazies? Why I have to inform the servants when it's mealtime and someone in the pride needs medical attention?*

—None of that happens, I said. *I would know.*

They all watched me, all except Diva, who was sleeping without dreams in her favorite corner. When she achieved dreamless sleep, we indulged her, because she had nightmares much too often.

Plus, her testimony would be tainted by her paranoia.

I was certain.

—I would know, I said again.

Sweetie sighed and walked past me. M gave me a sad little glance and headed toward the kibble.

Only King remained.

—The servants will prevent the mice from coming in. They were starving, you know. Those mice. That's why they stole food. They're not used to the weather you claim you don't need to know. He made a little snorting sound. Disgust.

I bristled. He had no right to snort at me.

—A major crime on your watch, King repeated. *Fortunately, it was one we could afford. Or I would have stopped it sooner.*

He snorted again. The hackles rose on the back of my neck.

—You couldn't even bring yourself to sniff the body, he said. *You are a pathetic excuse for a tom.*

Only I wasn't a tom. And neither was he. We had somehow given consent for life-saving drugs, and while under, the servants went crazy and removed our tomness.

Had we still had our tomness, we would have fought it out. King had lifted his left paw, which he had dubbed The Paw Of Doom one catnip-strewn night. He would use it on me and we would have to fight to establish dominance.

Or I could see if he would run things better. Clearly, he liked the taste of rodent. He believed in paws-on governance. He would waste good sleeping time in pursuits such as window-watching, mouse-trap guarding, and servant-tending.

I thought of raising my own paw of doom. But honestly, I'd never seen the need to name my body parts.

I sighed, and stood with the incredible poise and dignity I had learned at a hundred cat shows.

— *Well*, I said, *if you think you can do better...*

I let the last of it hang. He understood.

I went down the stairs to my couch. I preferred study anyway.

But it wasn't until I had curled up with an *NCIS* rerun (that a lazy servant was sleeping through) that I realized I should have argued at least one point.

No major crime had occurred.

Yes, there had been a dead body, but not a murdered one. And the theft wasn't a theft at all, since it occurred under the watchful gaze of King.

King had mischaracterized the events. They did not constitute crime.

I know crime better than I know anything else (except, perhaps, cat shows).

Crimes, you see, have patterns.

First, a body gets discovered. Then a human investigates. Cars chase. Someone tries to escape on foot. A criminal gets slammed into a wall and sometimes dies.

And in the middle of it all—usually halfway through—there is an explosion, whether it's caused by car on car or car into a wall or a bomb under a hood or a lucky gunshot into a propane tank.

We had no explosion. Ergo, we had no crime.

Unless you consider a planned coup a crime.

King allowed the theft. King allowed the mice to invade our domain. King convinced the women that I was unfit for leadership. And when the moment was right, King took my leadership and crushed it beneath his mighty paws, like he had crushed the mouse and left it for the servants to find.

King would say this is all political, like the newscasts the servants watch daily, as if the news makes any difference at all. He would say that politics and crime have nothing to do with each other.

And since politics rarely involves car chases or explosions, he might have a point.

All I know is this: It requires more study.

So I shall spend some time on my couch, investigating.

Because that's what I do best.

The Poop Thief

Kristine Kathryn Rusch

THE POOP THIEF

"Okay, this is just weird."

The voice came from the back of the store. It belonged to my Tuesday/Thursday assistant, Carmen. High school student, daughter of two mages, Carmen had no real talent herself, but she was earnest, and she loved creatures, and I loved her enthusiasm.

"I mean it, Miss Meadows, this is weird."

Oddly enough, weird is not a word people often use in Enchantment Place. Employees expect weird. Customers demand it. What's weird here is normal everywhere else—or so I thought until that Tuesday in late May.

"Miss Meadows...."

"Hold on, Carmen," I said. "I'm with a client."

The client was a repeat whom I did not like. I'm duty bound at Familiar Faces to provide mages with the proper familiars—the ones that will help them augment their talents and help them remain on the right path (doing no harm, avoiding evil, remaining true to the cause, all that crap). I do my best, but some people try my patience.

People like Zhakeline Jones. She was a zaftig woman who wore flowing green scarves, carried a cigarette in a cigarette holder, and called everyone "darling." Even me.

I called her Jackie, and ignored the "It's Zhakeline, dahling." Actually, it was Jacqueline back when we were in high school and then only from the teachers. The rest of us called her Jackie, and her friends—what few she had—called her Jack.

Whenever she came in, I cringed. I knew the store would smell like cigarettes and Emerude perfume for days afterwards. I didn't let her smoke in here—Enchantment Place, for all its oddities, was regulated by the City of Chicago and the City of Chicago had banned smoking in all public places—but that didn't stop the smell from radiating off her.

Most of my creatures vacated the front of the store when she arrived. Only the lioness remained at my feet, curled around my ankles as if I were a tree and Zhakeline was her prey. A few of the mice looked down on Zhakeline from a shelf (sitting next to the books on specialty cheeses that I'd ordered just for them), and a couple of the birds sat like fat and sassy gargoyles in the room's corners.

Nothing wanted to go home with Zhakeline, and I didn't blame them. She'd brought back the last three familiars because the creatures had the audacity to sneeze when they entered her house (and silly me, I had thought that cobras couldn't sneeze, but apparently they do—especially when they don't want to stay in a place where the air is purple). We were going to have to find her something appropriate and tolerant, something I was beginning to believe impossible to do.

On the wall beside me, lights shimmered from all over the spectrum, then Carmen appeared. Actually, she'd stepped through the portal from the back room to the shop's front, but I'd specifically designed the magical effect to impress the civilians.

Sometimes it impressed me.

Carmen was a slender girl who hadn't yet grown into her looks. One day, her dramatic bone structure would accent her African heritage. But right now, it made her look like someone had glued an adult's cheekbones onto a child's face.

"Miss Meadows, really, my parents say you shouldn't ignore a magical problem and I think this is a magical problem, even though I don't know for sure, but I'm pretty certain, and I'm sorry to bother you, but jeez, I think you have to look at this."

All spoken in a breathless rush, with her gaze on Zhakeline instead of on me.

Zhakeline smiled sympathetically and waved a hand in dismissal. Bangles that had been stuck to her skin loosened and clanked discordantly.

"This hasn't really been working, Portia." Zhakeline said with a tilt of the head. She probably meant that as sympathy too. "I've been thinking of going to that London store—what do they call it?"

"The Olde Familiar." I spoke with enough sarcasm to sound disapproving. Actually, my heart was pounding. I would love it if Zhakeline went elsewhere. Then the unhappy familiar—whoever the poor creature might be—wouldn't be my responsibility.

"Yes, the Olde Familiar." She smiled and put that cigarette holder between her teeth. She bit the damn thing like a feral F.D.R. "I think that would be best, don't you?"

I couldn't say yes, because I wasn't supposed to turn down mage business and I could get reported. But I didn't want to say no because I would love to lose Zhakeline's business.

So I said, "You might try that store in Johannesburg too, Unfamiliar Familiars. You can see all kinds of exotics. But remember, importing can be a problem."

"I'm sure you'll help with that," she said.

"Legally I can't. But you're always welcome here if their wares don't work out."

The mice chittered above me, probably at the word "wares." They weren't wares and they weren't animals. They were sentient beings with magic of their own, subject only to the whims of the magical gods when it came to pairings.

The whims of the magical gods and Zhakeline's eccentricities.

"I'll do that," she said. Then she turned to Carmen. "I hope you settle your weirdness, darling. And for the record, your parents *are* right. The sooner you focus on a magical problem, the less trouble it can be."

With that, she swept out of the store. Two chimpanzees crawled through the cat doors on either side of the portal holding identical cans of Febreze.

"No," I said. "The last time you did that we had to vacate the premises. Or don't you remember?"

They sighed in unison and vanished into the back. I didn't blame them. The smell was awful. But Febreze interacted with the Emerude, leading me to believe that what Zhakeline wore wasn't the stuff sold over the counter, but something she mixed on her own.

Without a familiar, which was probably why the stupid stuff lingered for days.

"Miss Meadows." Carmen tugged on my sleeve. "Please?"

I waved an arm so that the store fans turned on high. I also uttered an incantation for fresh ocean breezes. (I'd learned not to ask for wind off Lake Michigan; that nearly chilled us out of the store one afternoon). Then I followed Carmen into the back.

Walking through the portal is a bit disconcerting, especially the first time you do it. You are walking into another dimension. I explain to civilian friends that the back room is my Tardis. Those friends who don't watch *Doctor Who* look at me like I'm crazy; the rest laugh and nod.

My back room should be a windowless 10x20 storage area. Instead, it's the size of Madison Square Garden. Or two Madison Square Gardens. Or three, depending on what I need.

Most of my wannabe familiars live here, most of them in their own personal habitats. The habitats have a maximum requirement, all mandated by the mage gods and tailored to a particular species. Each bee has a football-sized habitat; each tiger has about a half an acre. Most creatures may not be housed with others of their kind, unless they're a socially needy type like herding dogs or alpha male cats. The creatures have to learn how to live with their mage counterparts—not always an easy thing to do—and its best not to let them interact too much with other members of their species.

Theoretically, I get the creatures after they complete five years of familiar training (and yes, you're right; very few familiars live their normal lifespan. Insects get what to them seems like millions of years and dogs get an extra two decades; only elephants, parrots, and a few other exceptionally long-lived species live a normal span).

That day, I had too many monkeys of various varieties, one parrot return who'd managed to learn every foul word in every language known to man (and I mean that) during his aborted tenure with his new owner, several large predatory cats, twenty-seven butterflies, five gazelle, sixteen North American deer, eight white wolves, one black bear, one grizzly return, one-hundred domestic cats, five-hundred-sixty-five dogs, and dozens of other creatures I generally forgot when I made a mental list.

Not every animal was for sale. Some were flawed returns—meaning they couldn't remember spells or they misquoted incantations or they weren't temperamentally suited to such a high-stress job. Some were whim returns, brought back by the mage who either bought on a whim or returned on a whim. And the rest were protest returns. These creatures left their mage in protest, either of their treatment or their living conditions.

All three of Zhakeline's returns had been protest returns although she tried to pass the first off as a flaw return and the other two as whim returns. It gets hard for a mage after a few rejections. Eventually she gets a reputation as a familiarly challenged individual, and might never get a magical companion.

And if she goes without for too long, she'll have her powers suspended until she goes through some kind of rehab.

Fortunately, that's never my decision. I'd seen too many mages fight to save their powers just before a suspension: I never want all that angry magic directed at me.

Carmen was standing on the edge of the habitats. They extended as far as the eye could see. My high school assistants didn't tend the habitats the way that civilian high school assistants would tend cages at, say, a vet's office. Instead, they made sure that the attendants that I hired from various parts of the globe (at great expense) actually did their jobs.

Each attendant had to log in stats: food consumed, creature health readings, and how often each habitat was entered, inspected, and cleaned. Then they'd log in the video footage for the past day—after inspecting it, of course, for magical incursions, failed spells, or escape attempts.

Carmen had called up our stats on the clear computer screen I'd over-laid over the habitat viewing area. She zoomed in on one stat—product for resale.

I frowned at the numbers. They were broken down by category. The whim returns and most of the protest returns were listed, of course, along with byproduct—methane from the cows (to be used in various potions); shed peacock feathers (for quills); and honey from the bees that had convinced the mage gods to make them hive familiars, not individual familiars.

Those bees only went to special clients—those who could prove they weren't allergic and who could handle several personality types all speaking through their fearless leader, the sluggish queen.

"See?" Carmen asked, waving a hand at the numbers. "This week's just weird."

I didn't see. But I didn't have as much experience with the numbers as she did. And, truth be told, I didn't think her powers were in spell-casting. I believed they were in numerology—not as powerful a magic, but a useful one.

"I'm sorry," I said, feeling dense, like I often did when staring at rows of facts and figures. "What am I supposed to see?"

She poked her finger at one of the columns. The lighted numbers vanished, then reappeared in red.

"Available fertilizer," she said. "See?"

I stared at the category. Available Fertilizer. Our biggest seller because we undercut the competition, mostly so we could get rid of the crap quickly and easily.

"There's no number there," I said.

"Zero is a number," Carmen said with dripping disdain that only a teenager could muster.

"E...yeah...okay." I knew I was stammering, but the big honking noth-ingness made no sense. "The assistants haven't been cleaning the habitats?"

She pressed the screen, drawing down the earlier statistics. Cleanings had gone on as usual.

"So what happened to the fertilizer?"

"I have no idea where the fertilizer went," she said. "I'm not even sure it came out of the cages. I mean, habitats."

I had planned to give her a tour of the back, but I hadn't yet. So she always made the "cages/habitat" mistake, something she'd never say if she actually saw the piece of the Serengeti plain that Fiona, the lioness who liked to sleep under my cash register and Roy, the lion who supposedly headed her pride, had conjured up to remind themselves of home.

Cleaning the habitats was a major job, especially for the larger animals, and usually required extra labor. Entire families came in for an hour or two a night to clean grizzly's mountainside, especially during blackberry season.

I moved Carmen aside, pressed some keys only visible to me, and looked at several of the previous day's vids in fast motion. Habitat cleaning happened in all of them.

Habitat cleaners weren't required to log in what they cleaned unless the item was marketable which poop generally was. Animal poop that is. There's never a big market for insect poop.

Animal poop (ground up into a product called Familiar Fertilizer) had a wide variety of uses. Mages bought it for their herb gardens. In addition to being the Miracle Grow of the magical world, it also made sure that wolf's bane and all the other herbal ingredients of a really good potion, magical spell, or "natural" remedy was extra-powerful. Some mages vowed that anything fertilized with familiar poop could be safely sold with a money-back guarantee—especially (oddly enough) love spells.

"Must be a computer glitch," I said and stabbed a few more buttons.

"Let me." Carmen got to the correct screens quicker, without me even asking. She knew I wanted to check all that basic stuff—how many pounds of poop got ground into fertilizer at the nearby processing plant, how many pounds of fertilizer got shipped, and how many of our magical feed-and-seed brethren paid for shipments that arrived this week.

Each category had a big fat zero in the poundage column.

"I don't like this," I said. "You just noticed this?"

I tried to keep the accusation out of my voice. It wasn't her job to keep track of my shipments and my various product lines. She was a high school student working two days a week part-time after school.

I was the person in charge.

"I was going over the manifests like you taught," she said. "I let you know the minute I saw it."

Which was—I checked the digital readout on the see-through computer screen—half an hour ago, one hour after Carmen arrived.

Pretty dang fast, considering.

"I mean, everything was fine on Thursday."

Thursday. The last day she worked.

My lunch—an indulgent slice of Chicago pan-style pizza—turned into a gelatinous ball in my stomach. "Can you quickly check the previous four days?"

"Already on it." She pressed a few keys.

I watched numbers flash in front of my eyes—too quickly for my number-challenged brain to follow. I could have spelled the whole thing, looked for patterns, but I had Carmen. She was better than any magical incantation.

"Wow," she said after a few minutes. "Those animals haven't pooped since Friday."

The gelatinous ball became concrete. I reached for the screen to look at health history, then stopped. A few of those creatures would have died if they hadn't pooped in three days. Some internal systems were less efficiently designed than others.

Still, I had her double-check the health records just to make sure.

"Okay," she said after looking at health records from Thursday to Tuesday. "So they all have normal bowel readings. What does this mean?"

"It means that your parents are right," I said.

"Huh?" She looked at me sideways, all teenager again. She hated hearing that Mom and Dad were right.

"Magical problems become bigger when they are allowed to fester."

"This is a magical problem?" she asked.

"The worst," I said.

She continued to stare at me in confusion, so I clarified.

"We have a poop thief."

———

You find poop thieves throughout magical literature. Heck, you even find them in fairy tales.

Of course, they're never called poop thieves. They're "tricksters" who steal their victims' "essence." They're evil wizards who rob their enemies of their "life force."

Most scholars believe that these references are to sperm, which simply tells me that magical scholarship has been dominated too long by males. (Those inept male scholars don't seem to be able to read either; a lot of the victims are women who are, of course, spermless creatures one and all.)

The scholars are right in that "life force" and "essence" are often composed of bodily fluids. Some (female) scholars have assumed that this essence is blood, but blood is a lot harder to obtain than the simplest of bodily fluids—pee.

Pee, though, is like all other water. It seeps into the ground. It's difficult to get unless someone pees into a cup or a bottle or a box. (Or unless you've magicked the chamber pot—and there are a few of those stories as well [Those Brothers Grimm didn't like the chamber pot stories, and so kept them out of the official compilation.])

Poop, on the other hand...

Poop, actually, on either hand is a lot easier to obtain.

Poop, like pee, blood, and yes, sperm, is a life essence. Even in its nonmagical form it has magical powers. It gets discarded only to be spread on a fallow field. The nutrients in the waste material break down, enriching the soil which is often used to grow plants—plants which later become food. The food nourishes the person who eats it. The person's body processes the food into energy and vitamins and all sorts of other good stuff, and the leftovers become waste yet again.

Most of the non-magical have no idea the power held in a single turd.

Hell, most of the magical didn't either.

But the ones who did, well, they were all damn dangerous.

And I'd already lost too much time.

———

It seemed odd to call Mall Security at a time like this, but that was the first thing I did. Mine wasn't the only store with magical creatures.

If someone was stealing from me, then maybe he was stealing from the pet store down the way, the organ grinder monkey show just outside the food court, and the various holiday setups with their real Easter bunnies and Christmas reindeer and Halloween bats. Not to mention all the working familiars accompanying every single mage who walked into the place.

I let Carmen talk to Security. She was young enough and naïve enough to think they were sexy. She had no idea that most of them were failed magical enforcers or inept warlocks who'd been demoted from city-wide security patrol to Enchantment Place.

I stayed in the back room, bending a few rules because this was an emergency. Anyone who took that much poop had a plan. A big plan—or a need for a lot of power.

At first, I figured this thief simply wanted the magical support of a familiar without actually getting a familiar. Magical crime blotters were full of minor poop thieves who stole rather than get a new familiar of their own. They'd mine someone else's familiar, using the poop as a tool with which to obtain the magic, and no one would notice until that familiar got sick from putting out too much magical energy.

Maybe what we had here was a more sophisticated version of the neighborhood poop snatcher.

Which made Zhakeline a prime suspect.

But Zhakeline's magic had always been shaky at best, even when she had a familiar. That was why she looked so exotic and had so many affectations.

She had to appeal to the civilians who think we're all weird. She mostly sold her small magic services to them. If she predicted the future and was wrong or if she made a love potion that didn't work, the civilian would simply shrug and think to himself *Ah, well, magic doesn't really work after all.*

But the magical, we know when someone can't perform all of the spells in the year-one playbook. Zhakeline barely passed year one (charity on the part of the instructor) and shouldn't have passed from that point on. But that happened during the years when telling a kid that she had failed was tantamount to murdering her (or so the parents thought) and Zhakeline got pushed from instructor to instructor without learning anything.

Which was one of the many reasons I didn't want to give her another familiar.

And that was beside the point.

The point was that Zhakeline, and mages like her—the ones who needed the magical power of familiar poop—didn't have the ability to conduct a theft on this massive scale, at least not alone.

And even if they tried, they'd be better off going to the back yard of a mage with a canine familiar. There was always a constant poop supply, and it provided enough power—consistent power (from the same source) —so that the thief might become a slightly less inept mage, for a while, anyway.

Next I investigated my assistants. Most had no magical powers of their own, but had come from magical families. They knew that magic existed —and not in that hopeful *I wish it were so* way that a civilian had, but in a *this is a business* way that led them to peripheral jobs in the magical field.

They worked hard, most had a love of animals, insects or reptiles, and they often had a specialty—whether it was cooking the right kind of pet food or calming a petulant hyena.

I couldn't believe any of the assistants would be doing something like this because they would have to be working for someone else.

The nonmagical don't gain magic just by wishing on a powerful piece of poop.

I scanned records and employment histories. I scanned bank accounts (yes, that's illegal, but remember—emergency. A few rules needed to be bent), cash stashes and (embarrassingly) the last 48 hours of their lives. (Which, viewed at the speed of an hour per every ten seconds, looked like silent movies watched at double fast-forward.)

I saw nothing suspicious. And believe me, I knew what to look for.

Although I wished I didn't.

———

You see, I got this job, not because I have a particular affinity with animals or I'm altruistic and love pairing the right mage with the right familiar.

I got it because I have experience.

I know how to look for mages heading dark or mages who should retire or mages who mistreat their magic (and hence their familiars). I know how to take care of these mages quietly, efficiently, and with a minimum of fuss.

It didn't used to be this way. In the past, places like Familiar Faces existed on side streets and had just a handful of creatures, few of them exotic. Only in the last few years have the mega stores come into existence at high-end malls like Enchantment Place.

And even though we're supervised by the rules of the mage gods like all other familiar stores, we're run and subsidized by Homeland Security —Magical Branch.

(Not everyone knows there's a Homeland Security—Magical Branch, including the so-called "head" of Homeland Security. Hell, I even doubt the president knows. Why tell the person who's going to be out in four or eight years one of the world's most important secrets. Knowing this crew, they'd probably try to co-opt the Magical Branch into something dark. Better to keep quiet and protect us all.

(Which I do. Most of the time.)

My job here is to watch for exactly this kind of incursion. Technically, I'm supposed to report it, and then wait for the guys with badges to show up.

But I didn't wait for the guys with badges. I doubted we would have time.

(And, truth be told, I did want the glory. I was demoted to this position [you guessed that already, right?] for asking too many questions and for the classic corporate mistake, proving that the boss was an idiot in front of his employees. I'm a government employee and as such can't be fired without lots and lots of red tape [even in the magical world], so I was sent here, to Chicago where I grew up, to Enchantment Place where I have to put up with the likes of Zhakeline with a smile and a shrug and a rather pointed [and sometimes magically directed] suggestion.)

I toyed with rewinding time in all of the habitats—another no-no, but it would have been protected under the Patriot Act, like most no-nos these days. But rewinding time takes time, time I didn't really want to waste looking at creatures moping in their personal space.

Instead, I did some old-fashioned police work.

I went back out front where Carmen was still flirting with some generic security guard (and the mice were leaning over so far to watch that I was afraid one of them would fall down the poor man's ill-fitting shirt) and beckoned the lioness, Fiona.

She frowned at me, then rose slowly, stretched in that boneless way common to all cats, and padded through the portal ahead of me.

When I got back to the back, she was sitting on her haunches and cleaning her ears, as if she had meant to join me all along.

"We have a poop thief," I said, "and I think you know who it is."

She methodically washed her left ear, then she started to lick her left paw in preparation for cleaning her right ear.

"Fiona," I said, "if I don't solve this, something bad will happen. You might not get a home of any kind and none of the other familiars will be of use to anyone. You might all have to be put down."

I usually don't use euphemisms, and Fiona knew it. But she didn't know the reason that I used it this time.

I couldn't face killing all these wannabe familiars. And it would be my job to do so. I'd get blamed for the theft(s), and I'd have to put down the creatures affected. It was the only way to negate the power of their poop.

She put her newly cleaned paw down on the concrete floor. "You couldn't 'put us down.'" She used great sarcasm on the phrase. "It would set the magical world back more than a hundred years. There wouldn't be enough of us to help your precious mages perform their silly little spells."

"Which might be the point of this attack," I said. "So tell me what you saw the last few days."

And why you never said a word, I almost added, but didn't.

"I'm not supposed to tell you anything. I'm not even supposed to talk with you."

Technically true. Familiars are only supposed to talk to their personal mages. But I get to hear and every one of them speak when they come into the store to make sure they really are familiars and not just plain old unmagical creatures looking for a free hand-out.

But Fiona had spoken to me before, mostly sarcastic comments about the store patrons. I'd tried pairing her up with a few, but she always had an under-the-breath comment that convinced me she and that mage wouldn't be a good match.

"I haven't seen anything," she said.

"What have you heard, then?" I asked.

"Nothing," she said. "The system is working just fine."

That sarcasm again, which lead me to believe she was leaving out a detail or two deliberately, hoping I would catch it.

Damn lions. They're just giant cats. They toy with everything.

And at that moment, Fiona was toying with me.

"But something's bothering you," I said.

"Not me so much." She picked up that clean right paw, turned it over, and examined the claws. "Roy."

Roy was the lion to her lioness. He wasn't head of the pride because there was no pride. We knew better than to get an entire pride of lions into that small habitat. No one would ever be able to see their individual natures—and no mage was tough enough to get that many catly familiars.

"What's bothering Roy?" I asked.

"Ask him."

"Fiona…"

She nibbled on one of the claws, then set her paw down again. "There was—oh, let me see if I can find the phrase in your language—an overpowering scent of ammonia."

"Ammonia?"

"And a very bright light."

"An explosion?" I asked. Fertilizer mixed with the right chemicals, including ammonia, created the same thing in both the magical and the non-magical world.

A bomb.

Only the magical bomb made of this kind of fertilizer didn't just destroy lives and property, it also cut through dimensions.

"It's not an explosion yet," she said. "He claims he has a sixth sense about things. Or did he say he can see the future? I forget exactly. But it was something like that."

"Or maybe he just knows something," I snapped.

"Or maybe he just knows something." She sounded bored. "He does say that because he's king of the jungle, the wannabes tell him things."

Which was the most annoying thing about Roy. He really believed that king of the jungle crap. Too much Kipling as a cub—or maybe too many viewings of the *Lion King*.

"I should really send you back to the habitat until this is resolved," I said to Fiona.

She hacked like she had a hairball, a sound she (sort of) learned from me. She thought it was the equivalent of my very Chicago, very dismissive "ach."

"I'd rather be out front, watching the floor show," she said.

And I sent her back out there because I had a soft spot for Fiona. Technically, I don't need a familiar. I have more than a thousand of them.

But if I did need one, I'd pick Fiona.

She knew it and she played on it all the damn time.

I waited until she was through that little curtain of light before I stepped through the hidden door into the habitat area.

It was always surprisingly quiet inside the habitat area. The first time I went in, I expected chirping birds and chittering monkeys and barking dogs—a cacophony of creature voices expressing displeasure or loneliness or sheer cussedness.

Instead, the area was so quiet that I could hear myself breathe.

It also had no smell—unless you counted that dry scent of air conditioning. The animal smells—from the pungent odor of penguins to the rancid scent of coyote—existed only in the individual habitat.

Just like the noises did.

If I went through the membrane on my left (and only I could go through those membranes—or someone I had approved, like the assistants), I would find myself in a cold dark cave that smelled of rodent and musty water. If I looked up, I'd see the twenty-seven bats currently in inventory.

We were always understocked on bats. Mages, particularly young ones raised in Goth culture, wanted bats first, wolves second, and cats a distant third. I'd given up trying to tell those kids to get some imagination.

I'd given up trying to tell the kids anything.

If I went through the membrane on my right, I'd slide on polar ice. Here the ice caps weren't melting. Here, my six polar bears happily fished and scampered and did all those things polar bears do—except that they didn't attack me. They didn't even bare their fangs at me.

I stopped between the two membranes and frowned. Whoever took the poop hadn't taken it from inside the habitats. It was simply too dangerous for the unapproved guest.

Hell, it was often dangerous for the assistants. I'd had more than one assistant mauled by a creature that didn't like the way he was looking at it.

And the poop was not registered as collected either. So whoever had taken it had spelled it out between gathering and delivery into the outside system.

I walked between dozens of habitats, trying to ignore the curious faces watching me.

I did feel for the wannabes. They were like children in an old-fashioned orphans' home. They hoped that someone would come to adopt them. They prayed that someone would come to adopt them. They were afraid that someone had come to adopt them.

And the only way they would know was if I brought them out of the habitat to the front of the store. (Except in the case of the dangerous exotics or the biting/stinging insects. In those cases, the mage had to enter the habitat without fear. *That* rarely happened either.)

Finally I got to the Serengeti Plain.

Or what passed for it in Roy and Fiona's habitat. It was kind of an amalgam of the best parts of a lion's world minus the worst part. Lots of water, lots of space to run, lots of space to hide. A great deal of sunshine and never, ever any rain.

I slipped through the membrane and, because of my past experience, paused.

The first step into Roy's world was overwhelming. The heat (about twenty degrees higher than I ever liked, even in the summer), the smell (giant cat mixed with dry grass and rotting meat from the latest kill), and the sunlight (so bright that my best sunglasses were no match for it—and as usual, I had forgotten any sunglasses) all made for a heady first step into this habitat.

More than one assistant had been so disoriented by the first step that Roy was able to tackle, stand on, and threaten the assistant in the first few seconds. After you've had several hundred pounds of lion standing on your chest, with his face inches from yours—so close you could see the pieces of raw meat still hanging from his fangs—you'd never want to go back into that habitat either.

Unless you're me, of course. I expected Roy to scare me that first time. I didn't expect him to catch me off guard.

So when he did, I congratulated him, told him he was quite impressive, and warned him that if he hurt a human he'd never graduate from wannabe to familiar.

And from that point on, he never jumped on me again.

But he always snuck up on me.

On this day, he wrapped his giant mouth around my calf. His teeth scraped against my skin, his hot breath moist and redolent of cat vomit. He'd been eating grass again. We were going to have change his diet.

"Hey, Roy," I said. "I hear you have a sixth sense."

He tightened his jaw just enough that the edges of those sharp teeth would leave dents in my flesh—not quite bites, not quite bruises—for days. Then he licked the injured area—probably an apology, or maybe just a taste for salt (I was instant sweat any time I came into this place).

Finally, he circled around me and climbed a nearby rock so that he would tower over me. If I weren't so used to his power games, he'd make me nervous.

"It's not a sixth sense," he said in an upper-class British accent. That accent had startled me when we were introduced. "So much as a finely honed sense of the possible."

"I see," I said, because I wasn't sure how to respond. I hadn't even been certain he would talk to me, and he'd done so almost immediately.

Which led me to believe the king of the jungle was more terrified than he wanted to admit.

"You realize I am only speaking to you," he said with an uncanny ability to read my mind (or maybe it was just that finely honed sense of what I might possibly be thinking), "because great evil is afoot, and I have no magical counterpart with which to fight it."

I almost said, *It's not your job to fight it,* but I didn't. I didn't want to insult the poor beast. Instead, I said, "That's precisely why I'm here. I figured you know what was going on."

"Bosh," he said. "Fiona told you. She has a thing for you, you know."

"A thing?" I asked.

"She wants to be your familiar." He opened his mouth in a cat-grin. "She doesn't understand—or perhaps she doesn't believe—that you have hundreds of us and as such do not need her."

I nodded because I wasn't sure what else to do. And because I was already thirsty. I'd forgotten not just my sunglasses but my bottle of water as well.

"Well," I said, "you do know what's happening, right?"

"Oh, bomb-making, dimension hopping, familiar murder—all the various possibilities." He laid down and crossed his front paws as if none of that bothered him. "And just you here because you seem to believe that you can save the world all by your own small self."

"With the help of your finely honed sense of the possible."

"That too." He tilted his massive head and looked at me through those slanted brown eyes.

My heart rate increased. Occasionally I still did feel like prey around him.

"Well?" I asked.

"Have you ever thought that your culprit isn't human?"

"No," I said. "Demons don't care about familiars. Only mages do."

"Really." He extended the word as if it were four. "Humans generally ignore scat, don't they?"

"Generally," I said. "We try not to think about it."

"And yet those of us in the animal kingdom find within it a wealth of information."

"Yes," I said. "But the amount of power it would take to complete this spell tends to rule out anything that isn't human."

He made the same hairball sound that Fiona did. They were closer than they liked to admit.

"You humans are such speciest creatures. It doesn't help that the mage gods allow you the choices and we have to wait until you make them. It leads me to believe that the mage gods are human—or were, at one point."

I wasn't there to discuss religion. "You're telling me, then, that your finely honed sense of the possible leads you to the conclusion that a familiar has done this."

"I didn't say that."

"A creature then. A magical creature of some kind."

He slitted his eyes, the feline equivalent of yes.

"But you have no evidence," I said.

"I have plenty of evidence. Consider the timeline. It took you forever to discover this theft, and yet no bomb has exploded. No one has made threats, and no mage has suddenly gained unwarranted power."

"That's not evidence. That's supposition."

He lifted his majestic head. "Is it?"

"So who do you suppose has stolen the poop—and why?"

He rested his head on his paws and continued to stare at me. "That's for you to work out."

"In other words, you don't know."

"That's correct. I don't really know."

"But you're not worried."

"Why should I worry? From my perspective, removing the scat is a prudent thing to do."

I hadn't expected him to say that. "What do you mean?"

He heaved a heavy, smelly sigh. "I'm a cat who lives in the wild. Think it through."

Then he jumped and I cringed as he headed right toward me. He landed beside me, chuckled and vanished through the tall grass.

He'd gotten me again. He loved that. He'd probably been planning to jump near me through the entire conversation, his back feet tucked beneath him and poised, even though his front half looked relaxed.

He wasn't going to give me any more. He felt he didn't need to.

Cats in the wild.

Cat poop in the wild.

Hell, cat poop in the house. Cats were all the same.

They buried their poop so no one could track them.

The problem wasn't the poop thief.

The poop thief was protecting the wannabes from something else. Something that tracked through scat.

Something that wasn't human.

I swore and bolted out of the habitat.

I needed my research computer, and I needed it now.

———

Very few things targeted familiars—or perhaps I should say very few non-human things. And I'd never heard of anything that targeted wannabes, because a wannabe's power, while considerable, wasn't really honed.

Wannabes were, for lack of a better term, the virgins of the familiar world.

And nothing targeted virgins (not even those stupid civilian terrorists. They got virgins as a *reward*).

145

So when I got out of the habitat, I had the computer search for strange creatures or things that targeted virgins. I got nothing.

Except the search engine, asking me a pointed electronic question:

Do you mean things that prefer *virgins?*

And I, on a frustrated whim, typed *yes.*

What I got was unicorns. Unicorns preferred virgins. In fact, unicorns would only appear to virgins. In fact, unicorns drew their magic from virgins.

But the magic was pure and sweet and hearts and flowers and Hello Kitty and anything else treacly that you could think of.

Except if the unicorn had become rabid.

I clicked on the link, found several scholarly articles on rabies in unicorns. Rabid unicorns were slightly crazed. But more than that, they had no powers because no virgin (no matter how stupid) was going to go near a horse-sized creature that shouted obscenities and foamed at the mouth.

That was stage one of the rabies. Unlike rabies in non-magical creatures, rabies in unicorns (and centaurs and minotaurs and any other magical animal) manifested in temporary insanity, followed by darkness and pure evil.

The craziness, in other words, went away, leaving nastiness in its wake.

Minotaurs, centaurs, and other such creatures attacked each other. They stole from the nearest mage—or enthralled him, stealing his magic before they killed him.

But unicorns...

Unicorns still needed virgins.

And the only solution was to steal the powers of wannabe familiars.

Provided, of course, that the unicorn could find them.

And unicorns, like most other animals, hunted by scat.

———

I wish I could say I got my giant unicorn-killing musket out of mothballs and carried it through an enchanted forest, hunting a brilliant yet evil unicorn that wanted to devour the untamed magic of wannabe familiars.

I wish I could say I was the one who shot that unicorn with a bullet of pure silver and then got photographed with one foot on its side and the other on the ground, leaning on my musket like hunters of old.

I wish I could say I was the one who cut off its horn, then snapped the thing in half, watching the dark magic dissipate as if it never was.

But I can't.

Technically, I'm not allowed to leave the store.

So I had to call in the Homeland Security—Magical Branch anyway. I could have called the local mage police, but I wasn't sure where this unicorn was operating, and HS-MB had contacts worldwide.

They found four rabid unicorns all in the same forest, somewhere in Russia, along with a few rabid squirrels (probably the source of the infection) and a rabid magical faun that was going around murdering all the bears for sport.

The unicorns died along with the squirrels and that faun. The poop reappeared in my computer system, and went back through the normal channels. That week, we made double our money on magical fertilizer, which was good since we'd made none the week before.

All seemed right with the magical world.

Except one thing.

I dragged Fiona to her habitat so I could confront both her and Roy.

They usually didn't spend much time together. They blamed it on not really having a pride, but I knew the problem was Fiona. She hated having to hunt for him, then watch him eat the best parts.

She hated most things about feline life and once muttered, as yet another well adjusted young mage took a domestic cat as her familiar, that she wished she were small and cute and cuddly.

She had to fetch Roy. He wasn't going to come. He hadn't even attacked me as I entered the habitat—probably because Fiona was with me.

I waited as he climbed to the top of his rock, then assumed the same position he'd been in before he jumped at me. Only this time I was prepared. I had my sunglasses and my water bottle.

I also stood a few feet to the right of my previous position, a place he couldn't get to from the top of that rock.

Fiona sat at the base of the rock, beneath the outcropping, in the only stretch of shade in this part of the plain.

"You want to tell me how you did it?" I asked when Roy finally got comfortable. He sent me an annoyed look when he realized that I had stationed myself outside of his range. "You knew that there was a rabid unicorn after wannabes, and you somehow got the entire group at Familiar Faces to cooperate with you, all without leaving your habitat."

Then I looked at Fiona. She had left the habitat. She left it every single day.

The tip of her tail twitched, and she tilted her head ever so slightly, her eyes twinkling. But she said nothing.

Roy preened. He licked a paw, then wiped his face. Finally he looked at me, the hairs of his mane in place, looking as majestic as a lion should.

"I am king of the jungle," he said.

This is a plain, I wanted to point out, but I didn't for fear of silencing him. Instead I said, "Yet some of the other familiars don't live in habitats like yours. The snakes, for example."

He yawned. "The unicorn wasn't after them."

"But the animals?" I asked.

He closed his great mouth, then leaned his head downward, so that his gaze met mine. "The Russian Blues are refugees. You didn't know that, did you?"

I got two domestic cats—purebred Russian Blues. Most purebred cats aren't familiars—they have the magic bred out of them with all the other mixed genes—but these Blues were amazing. And pretty. And not that willing to talk, even when they knew it was the price of gaining a mage.

"Refugees?" I said. "They were adopted before?"

"Their mages murdered by the new secret police for being terrorists. I thought you checked all of this out."

I tried to, but I never could. Animal histories weren't always that easy to find.

"They'd heard rumors about something rabid getting into an enchanted forest somewhere in deepest darkest Russia. Then some young familiars—what you call wannabes—withered and died as their powers were sucked from them over a period of months."

He tilted his head, as if I could finish his thought.

And I could.

"So the Blues suspected unicorns," I said.

"There were always rumors of unicorns in that forest," he said, "but of course, none of us had ever seen them. For normal unicorns, you need virginal humans. None of us had encountered abnormal unicorns before."

I did the math. The Blues had arrived last Thursday, which was the last day Carmen had worked before Tuesday, when she discovered the problem.

"You went into protect mode immediately," I said.

"It is my pride, whether you admit it or not."

I didn't admit it, but I understood how he thought so. He needed a tribe to rule, so he invented one.

"I still don't understand what happened. You don't have the magic to make other animals' poop disappear."

"But they do," he said.

"I know that." I tried not to sound annoyed. He was toying with me again. I hated being a victim of cat playfulness.

"So how did you tell them what to do?"

He opened his mouth slightly, in that cat-grin of his. Then he got up, shook his mane, and walked back down the rock. He vanished in the tall grass, disappearing against its brownness as if he had never been.

"He could tell me," I said.

"No, he can't." Fiona hadn't moved.

I let out a small sigh. He hadn't been toying with me. She had.

"You did it," I said.

"Me and the bees," she said. "They're creating quite a little communications network with those hive minds of theirs. They send little scouts into the other habitats every single time you go from one to the other. The ants too. You really should be more careful."

I felt a little frisson of worry. I had had no idea. I didn't want the bees to get delusions of grandeur. I already had to deal with Roy.

"You told them to spread the word."

She nodded.

"And you told them how the animals could hide their poop."

She inclined her head as regally—more regally—than Roy ever could.

"Why?" I asked. "You had no guarantee of a threat."

"This is the biggest gathering of the Hopeful on the globe," she said. "Of course we are a target."

She was right. I sighed, took a sip from my water bottle, and frowned. This entire event had opened my eyes to a lot of scary possibilities, things I had never considered.

We were going to have to rethink the way we handled waste. We were going to have to protect the poop somehow, and I didn't want to consult HS-MB about that. They'd have to hold hearings, and the wrong someone could be sitting in.

I didn't want us to become a magical terrorism target, nor did I want us to be a target for every rabid unicorn in the world.

I would have to set up the systems myself.

"You need me," Fiona said, "whether you like it or not. You can't have pretend familiars. You need a real one."

She was making a pitch. Cats never did that. Or they only did so if they believed something was important.

"Why here?" I asked. "I've found you some pretty spectacular possible mage partners, and you've turned them down."

She wrapped her tail around her paws and stared at me. For a moment, I thought she wasn't going to answer.

Then she said, "This is my pride. Roy might think it his, but he's a typical lion. He thinks he's in charge, when I do all the work."

She raised her chin. That tuft of hair that all lionesses had beneath looked more like a mane in the shade than it ever had. It made her look regal.

"Well," she added, "I'm not a typical lioness, content to hunt for her man and to feel happy when he fathers a litter of kittens on her only to run them out when they threaten his little kingdom. I don't want children. And I want to eat first."

"You can do that with other mages," I said.

"But I won't have a pride. Don't you see? I'm the one who spoke to the Blues. I'm the one who keeps track of those silly mice—even though I want to eat them—and I'm the one who calms the elephant whenever she has the vapors. No one credits me for it, of course, but it's time they should."

No one, meaning me. I hadn't noticed, and Fiona was bitter. Or maybe she just felt that I wasn't holding up my end of the bargain.

"Besides," she said, "it's hot in here. Can we go back to the air conditioning?"

I laughed and stepped out of the habitat. She followed.

"I'll petition the mage gods," I said.

"I already did." She was walking beside me as we headed toward the front room. "They said yes. I put their response under the cash register."

We went through the portal. The mice were having a party on top of the cheese books. One of the snakes was dancing too, trying to come out of its basket like a charmed snake from the movies. The dance was a bit pathetic, since the snake was the wrong kind. It was the tiniest of my garden snakes.

They all stopped when they saw me. I looked toward the mall's interior. The customer door was closed and locked and the main lights were off. The closed sign sat in the window.

Carmen had gone home long ago.

I went to the cash register and felt underneath it. Some dust, some old gum—and yes, a response from the mage gods, dated months ago.

"You took a long time to tell me this," I said to Fiona.

She wrapped herself around the counter. "You should clean more."

Come to think of it, a few months before was when she really started muttering her protests out loud. In English. She was doing everything felinely possible except blurting it out that she was now my familiar.

I had never heard of a familiar picking a mage.

Although that wasn't really true. The familiars always made their preferences known. I knew how to read the signs. For everyone, it seemed, but me.

"Do you regret this?" Fiona asked quietly.

"Hell, no," I said. "Your brilliance averted a major international incident and saved the lives of hundreds of familiars."

"Don't you think that makes me deserving of some salmon?"

I almost said *I think that makes you deserving of anything you damn well please,* and then I remembered that I was talking to a cat. A large, independent-minded, magical cat, but a cat all the same.

"Salmon it is," I said and snapped a finger. A plate appeared with the thickest, juiciest salmon steak I could conjure.

I set it down next to her.

"Next time," she said, "you're taking me out."

"Restaurants don't allow animals," I said. "At least, not in Chicago."

"I wasn't talking about a restaurant," she said. "I meant a salmon fishery or perhaps one of those spawning grounds in the wild. I heard there's a species of lion who hunts those grounds."

"Sea lions," I said. "You're not related."

She chuckled, then wrapped her tail around my legs, nearly knocking me over. Affection from my lioness.

From my familiar.

However I had expected my day to end, it hadn't been like this.

Carmen was right. This day had been weird.

But good.

"So are you going to promise to take me to a fishery after the next time I save lives?" Fiona asked.

"I suppose," I said, wondering what I had gotten myself into.

Fiona licked her lips and closed her eyes. The mice started dancing all over again, and chimpanzees came out of the back to see what the commotion was.

After a weird day, a normal night.

And I found, to my surprise, that I preferred normal to weird.

Maybe I was getting soft.

Maybe I was getting older.

Or maybe I had just realized that I was a mage with a familiar, a powerful smart familiar, one I could appreciate.

One who would keep me and my animals safe.

One who would rule her pride with efficiency and not a little playfulness.

I could live with that.

I had a hunch she could too.

SCHEDULING CONFLICT

KRISTINE KATHRYN RUSCH

SCHEDULING CONFLICT

"Detective Riley Scott?" The female voice on the other end of the line was rich and throaty, the kind that usually sent shivers through him.

But this morning, nothing sent shivers through Riley Scott. He stared blearily at his full coffee mug. The coffee had some kind of oil slick floating on top. He wasn't sure if that was from the coffee or the mug itself. When was the last time he'd rinsed the thing out?

"Hmmm?" he said into the phone pressed between his shoulder and his ear. If he moved wrong, the cord would catch his hand and he'd knock that full mug over, like he'd done last week. How come this rich and throaty female voice hadn't called on his cell?

"I'm the person who robbed the National Bank and Trust. I'd like to turn myself in, but I have a rather full schedule. How does your week look?"

"Huh?" He sat up, snapped his finger at his partner Dave across the desk, and sideways nodded at the phone.

Dave picked up his own phone, pressed a few buttons, and made sure the techs were figuring out where this call was coming from.

The woman on the other end of the line chuckled. "I'm not going to repeat myself, Detective. Except to ask you about your schedule."

"Looks like I got a bank robbery to investigate," he said, wiping the sleep out of his eyes.

Half the people in the squad room—that would be two detectives and a crime scene tech—looked at him. He must have spoken louder than he thought.

"And nothing else? My, my, my. You're living the life of Riley."

He hated that joke. He'd heard it since he was a little boy, mostly from his family, most of whom were old enough to remember what the phrase "The Life of Riley" actually meant.

"Check your calendar. I'll call back. Ta."

"Wait!" he said, but she had already hung up.

Dave folded his meaty hands and leaned across the partner's desk, nearly knocking down fifteen files someone had thoughtfully stacked on the only empty space. "Disposable cell. We can trace what tower actually took the call, but that's about it."

"Get someone on it." Riley sipped the coffee, then wished he hadn't. The oil slick was some kind of soap. Maybe he had tried to wash the stupid mug out and forgot about it. "You and I have to head to the National Bank and Trust."

"Why?"

"I hear they were robbed this morning."

———

The National Bank and Trust stood in the center of downtown. One square city block of granite, built around the turn of the last century, with ornate cornices, recessed windows with gold bars, and several oak doors that didn't meet current bank security standards.

Riley let himself in through the main doors, still stamped FIRST BANK AND TRUST in gold leaf—no one tried to change that after all the various mergers and conglomerations—and sniffed the familiar scent of century-old dust that every granite building in the once-prosperous downtown still had.

Customers stood in line on the marble floor, held in place by a red velvet rope attached to waist-high gold stands. The bars in front of the tellers' windows were open, and conversation hummed. Security guards stood at all the entrances, looking calm.

"What the...?" Dave asked.

Riley shrugged. "Maybe that's why nothing was reported to dispatch."

"You think they don't know about it?"

"Anything's possible," Riley said, including the fact that the call might've been a hoax.

"May I help you?" One of the guards came over and spoke in a low voice. Apparently the two detectives looked suspicious.

Dave flashed a badge. "Any problems this morning?"

The guard frowned. "What kind of problems?"

"Where's the manager?" Riley asked, not wanting to have this conversation in front of a roomful of bank patrons.

"Over there." The guard nodded at a row of offices, neatly hidden down a corridor. Old-fashioned banking at its best.

Riley thanked him and headed down the hall. As he approached, the door at the end opened. Just like Riley expected, the guard had called ahead.

The manager was a slender, wispy man who looked like the scrawny version of the schmuck in James Thurber's cartoons. Riley sighed. Elderly parents, maiden aunts—all of his personal references were forty years out of date.

"May I help you?" the manager asked.

By this time, Dave had caught up. Rather than let him blurt out his stupid questions, Riley nodded toward the office. "Let's go in there."

The manager nodded, told his secretary not to disturb him, and led them into a square room with red carpet. The walls were covered with flocked wallpaper, but the furniture was solid mahogany. Every bank manager from the beginning had apparently used this office, and none of them had bothered to remodel it.

The manager sat down. Riley and Dave did not.

"We got a report this morning of a bank robbery," Riley said.

"Where?" the manager asked.

"Here," Dave said. "Some woman confessed."

"Who?"

"We didn't get her name," Dave said, and Riley wanted to smack him. Dave's attention to detail of late had been worse than awful.

But Riley couldn't say much. Dave had covered for him during his divorce; Riley could cover for Dave through the same kind of trauma.

If he didn't kill him first.

"Then how do you know the complaint is accurate?" the manager asked.

"We don't," Riley said, taking over the interview. "We figured it wasn't legit when no one set off the silent alarms. But we sent some uniforms over immediately to circle the place, and make sure nothing looked wrong. Then we came over as soon as we could to see if anything subtle is happening. It's not, is it?"

"What?" the manager asked.

"Something subtle," Riley said. "Some kind of embezzlement, the loss of one major item. You know, something that doesn't require guns and masks."

The manager's eyes widened. He pressed a buzzer on the side of his desk. The secretary opened the door and leaned in.

"Have the department heads check the morning's accounts," he said, "and make sure we haven't had any threats."

"Threats, sir?" she asked.

"Of any kind," he said. "And send Baxter in here."

"Yes, sir." She closed the door.

"Baxter?" Riley asked.

"He's been here since he graduated from college in 1950 or something like that. He's our unofficial historian."

"Historian?" Dave asked.

"And gossip," the manager said. "We keep him on even though he should have retired ten years ago because if anything's going wrong, Baxter seems to find out about it first."

The door opened a second time, and a portly elderly man stepped in. He wore a three-piece suit, decorated with a pocket watch, and his shoes shined. *Now he*, Riley thought, *was the picture of a bank manager.*

The real manager explained the situation. Baxter pursed his lips, and then nodded slightly.

"We haven't had a robbery here since 1995," he said.

"1995?" Riley didn't remember that, but then he had been working Vice those years. He used to envy the regular detectives who got normal crimes, like bank robberies and murders. Vice, he used to think, was ruining his marriage.

Turned out that Vice had nothing to do with it. Most of that ruin happened because of his surly attitude and the fact that he suspected he hadn't really loved Karen in the first place.

"Oh, yes," Baxter said. "It was a minor thing and our fault, really. We kept too much cash in the tellers' tills. The robber followed the Hollywood model—note on a deposit slip, cash where he could see it, etc.—and somehow managed to avoid the dye pack. We lost, I believe, ten thousand dollars, but it cost a great deal more because our insurers required that we update our security. Even though we are an old-fashioned institution, we do have excellent security."

It didn't look excellent to Riley, but he was no expert.

"No one's tried anything in the last few days?" he asked.

"We would have reported an attempted robbery," the manager said.

"What about talked about it?" Dave asked.

"Again, we have to report," the manager said. "You don't joke about robbing banks while inside a bank."

"No employees with sticky fingers?" Riley asked.

The manager's face turned red, but Baxter shook his head. "Our last one of those occurred in 1988. That young lady was quite good at taking five from one account, twenty from another, and she always chose accounts that were in disarray. It took us nearly a year to catch her. I never understood why she stuck around to get caught, but *c'est le vie*, no?"

"I suppose." Riley hated it when people switched languages on him. Even when they used phrases he understood.

"No recent troubles, though?" Dave asked.

"None," Baxter said.

"No," the manager said.

"Well, then." Riley sighed. "I guess you'd better be on the lookout for something. We'll assume it was a warning."

"We will check the day's accounts," the manager said, "and let you know."

"Better still," said Baxter, "we'll double-check everything from the security tapes to the safe deposit boxes. If anything is amiss, we'll contact you."

"Thanks," Riley said, and led Dave out of that stuffy office.

As they left the bank and headed to the car, Dave said, "That manager couldn't survive without that Baxter guy."

"Sometimes it happens that way in a partnership," Riley said and wondered if he'd said too much.

———

No bank robbery, no missing funds, nothing out of the ordinary in National Bank, and none of the other area banks with similar names had any problems either. That sexy voice on the phone had sent Riley on a wild goose chase that had left him more than a little annoyed.

So, to say that he was surly when she called again, was probably an understatement.

Three days later, same kind of coffee—only without the oil slick— same bleary-eyed morning, after he'd closed two murders and given up on a suicide which would always remain a mystery, the desk phone rang again.

Same sexy voice. Same throaty laugh. Same request—

"Detective Riley Scott?"

"Don't start," he said. "I should get you for lying to a police officer."

That chuckle. He had forgotten the chuckle. It sent little shivers down his back, which was certainly something he didn't want to acknowledge to anyone.

"I didn't lie," she said. "I would like to turn myself in."

"What for this time?" he asked.

"Bank robbery," she said as if he were slightly thick-headed. "Eastern United Bank. The one on Third Street."

"I thought you said you robbed National Bank and Trust."

Dave looked up from his new stack of files. His eyes were blood-shot, and his nose too red. He was also wearing yesterday's shirt. If that kept up, Riley wouldn't be able to cover for him much longer.

"Did I?" She laughed. "I must be confessing to all the wrong things."

"It's beginning to seem that way," he said.

Dave picked up his phone, punched a few numbers, and spoke softly into it. At least he remembered to trace her call, even without Riley making the reminder move.

"So...." Her voice got even huskier. "How's your schedule?"

"Full," he snapped. "But you could come down here, wait a while, talk to somebody—so long as you don't lie again."

"I didn't lie," she said. "And I do want to turn myself in."

He heard the sound of paper turning. She gave a thoughtful little moan, as if she were considering making a date, and then said,

"You know, this week really isn't good for me. How's next week?"

"How's right now?" he said. "I just got in, have a few things to work on but nothing new. Come on over."

"You want to work on me?" And the innuendo was unmistakable.

"Right now," he said, tired of the game. She'd played with him enough. He'd lost half a day, asked embarrassing questions, and made work for a bunch of people who didn't need more aggravation.

"Oh, honey," she said softly. "Most things are better if you wait."

And then she hung up.

Riley clung to the receiver for a moment, listening to the silence, knowing she wasn't going to come back on. That voice had his number—not the words, but that throaty just-back-from-bed sound, the slight accent (what was it? A little Grace Kelly, a lotta Katharine Hepburn), and that sly tone, the kind a woman would use when she was making a private promise in a public place.

Shiver was probably the wrong word for what was going on under his skin. He thanked whatever god would still listen to him that he wasn't in his twenties any more.

"Same thing," Dave said. "Disposable cell phone."

"Same tower?" Riley asked.

Dave shook his head.

"Did we ever get someone to track the phone the last time?" Riley asked.

"Yeah," Dave said. "It hasn't been turned back on since she called. This's a different one or so the guys in tech assure me."

"Lovely," Riley said.

"She tell you what imaginary robbery she committed today?" Dave asked.

"Eastern United Bank," Riley said, "on Third."

Dave picked up the phone and shook the receiver at Riley. "Can we just call or do we have to go through the whole thing again?"

He almost gave in, almost said, "Call, go ahead," and then changed his mind.

"Have the uniforms drive by," he said. "We're going back to chasing geese."

───────

The thing was, back when he was a kid, he used to play Dictionary with a group of friends. Not the stupid board game, which didn't even exist back then, but a made-up game using an actual dictionary. One guy would pick a word, everyone else would write down the definitions, and the person who got it right or came close would get a point. If no one got it, the person who chose the word got all the points.

Nerdy yes, but valuable, and probably the only reason he got "A"s in English Comp in college. Couldn't beat a vocabulary like his.

One particular game stuck in his brain. His best friend Cal was the third to pick a word. On the first word, he listed the definition as "a form of currency in medieval Poland." He was wrong. When he used that same definition for the second word, the gang laughed.

When he chose his word, nobody got the right definition. Because he'd set them up: the word—some crapoid thing that sounded made-up— actually was a form of currency used in medieval Poland.

Riley didn't have that kind of brain, not then, not now. But he'd learned his lesson. If the first one and the second one were false, then the third one—or the one after that—might actually be true.

But by then, the average detective wouldn't be vigilant any more. The average detective wouldn't take her up on her offer of turning herself in.

Brilliant, in its own way, but wouldn't it be just as easy to rob and not confess?

He had no idea, and because he had no idea, he wasn't going to tell Dave his suspicions.

At Eastern United Bank, the two detectives went through the same old rigmarole—oblivious customers, hard-working tellers, calm security guards. The manager was on the floor of this bank—it was a 1950s building with low ceilings and mustard-colored carpet—and he knew his own bank history, reciting it proudly:

Not a single theft since he started his watch in 1997. He upgraded the security system the moment he came in because before that, Eastern United had had the highest incidents of theft in the state.

Not embezzlement—the bank had systems for that—but actual gun-in-the-hand, note-on-the-counter theft. You wanted money for free in this town, word used to be go to Eastern United.

The manager told them all that as if he expected them personally to award him some kind of medal of honor. Dave actually seemed a little impressed, but Riley wasn't fond of smug bastards with middle-management jobs. So he insisted on some heightened security, a review of the accounts that went back a few months instead of a few days, and every single tape the bank had stored.

But there was nothing, just like Riley expected.

He had the chief send notice to every bank in the area, warning them that there'd been threats of theft, and to heighten security. The notices also included warnings of embezzlement, theft of a single (non-currency) item, and other non-traditional ways to take something out of a financial institution.

For his part, Riley warned the chief that this could all be a hoax, and the chief didn't care.

"I always figure heightened security is better than that lackadaisical crap most of these places employ these days," the chief said, and left it at that.

So Riley was ready, the banks were ready, the entire force was ready.

And she didn't call.

———

One month, five smash-and-grabs, two gang-shootouts, three murders, and yet another suicide later, the phone rang on Riley's desk. He wasn't contemplating his mug of coffee—he'd graduated to a styrofoam cup of designer joe at the suggestion of Dave, whose divorce became final the week before.

Riley still wasn't a morning person, still hadn't learned how to shut off the tube late at night or how to shut off his brain once he went horizontal, so he still stared at his desk with bleary eyes, only now he would try to figure out what each and every stain was, and whether it came from yesterday's lunch or last week Thursday's.

When the phone rang, he picked it up, only to discover the receiver was sticky from the mocha he'd spilled the night before.

"What?" he barked.

"Why, Detective Scott," said that sexy, sexy voice. "Did you miss me that much?"

He hadn't missed her at all. He hadn't even thought of her (except maybe a little—that voice in the middle of the night, when he had nothing better to do than stare at naked women on HBO2. Lately he'd kept the sound turned off, so the women—every single one of them—had a throaty, sexy voice that sent shivers down his back).

"You haven't called," he said, sounding more like a jilted lover than he wanted to.

He snapped his fingers at Dave, whose eyebrows went up. Dave knew the routine for finding that cell phone, if indeed, that's what she was calling on, but he also had other duties this time. He had to make sure that the banks were notified, particularly the one she mentioned.

"I've been meaning to call," she said, "but I told you. I've had a busy week."

"It's been more than a week since you called." Yep. Jilted lover. Not that he had much of a choice. He wanted to keep her on the line, figure out what she was doing, what she was really up to.

"It's been two. Don't you have busy weeks?" Her voice had a plaintive edge.

"Sometimes," he said. "Rob another bank?"

"A couple," she said. "First Federal Savings and Loan, although I don't know if that qualifies as a bank. And McAdams Family Bank, on Eighteenth. I've been very busy."

"Sounds like it." He wrote down the two banks, although he didn't have to. People were listening in. "You still planning to come in?"

"I never said I'd come in." Her voice had a pretty pout to it. "I said I'd turn myself in."

Interesting distinction. "Have you changed your mind?"

"Should I?"

"You're the one that's been calling me, Miss—"

"Oh, detective," she said. "That's cheating. I've told you what I've been doing. I know what you've been doing. You've been increasing security at area banks."

"Does that create a problem for you?"

"I wouldn't use the word problem," she said. "I rarely have problems with security."

"Why is that?" he asked.

"Because no one's caught me yet," she said.

"Is that why you're offering to turn yourself in?" he asked.

"Detective." There was just a hint of sarcasm in her tone. "I have other reasons for calling you."

"What are they?" he asked.

She chuckled. He wasn't sure he could survive many more of those chuckles.

"How about I call you on Wednesday, and we'll discuss the terms of my capture?"

"Why not now?" he asked, but he was talking to a dead line.

Dave came in from the other room, sighing. "New phone, again. Different tower. She likes to tease you, Riley."

"She's doing a good job of it." He hated that she knew he'd raised the security levels at the banks. "You checking out those banks?"

"They've all been notified," Dave said.

"Then let's go."

———

Riley wondered if she was watching him as he went to the two banks she'd mentioned. Despite its name, First Federal Savings and Loan was a bank, and had more security systems than Fort Knox. And despite its name, McAdams Family Bank had no McAdams working for it, no family in charge, and was barely a bank by federal regulations.

Riley would have loved to get the financial geek squad on McAdams Family, but that wasn't his job. At the moment, preventing a robbery at the so-called bank was all he was supposed to do.

And while he went through the same questions over and over—Robbery? (no) Embezzlement? (no) Missing items? (no)—he mulled this case over and over in his head.

All he had was her word that she had done something, and if she had, her word wasn't worth much. She had once told him she had never lied. And all of these banks had been robbed before.

So he sent Dave on a new part of the wild goose chase: he had to go through the archives to find out if the previous bank robbers had ever been caught.

Riley continued going through the motions, asking, receiving the answers he already knew, and going over and over those conversations with her in his head.

Finally, he hit on something she shouldn't have known.

Increased security. It had never been a problem for her in the past. Why would it be a problem now?

Why indeed?

So he finally got to ask a new question, and he asked it of the president of McAdams Family Bank. "Did you update your security like we asked a few weeks ago?"

"Oh, yeah," said the president, a man so young he could have been Riley's son. "We hired a new firm and everything."

"When did they test the systems?" Riley asked.

"A few days ago," the president said.

"Did they run a mock robbery?" Riley asked.

The president smiled. "How did you know?"

———

The firm, Blue Chip Security Ltd., had offices on the far edge of town. Riley called Dave off the deep background, and picked him up on the way to Blue Chip's offices.

They looked secure enough. Various cameras, bugging devices, and computers stood on shelves around the reception area. As Riley and Dave walked in, Riley saw himself reflected on a hundred surfaces. He couldn't locate all the cameras in such a short period of time.

The owner of Blue Chip, Bob O'Dell, was slender, young, and balding, the kind of guy who would seem more at home behind a computer than running a security firm.

Of course, security had changed since Riley was young. Now it was about cameras and lasers and motion detectors instead of muscle and proficiency with a gun.

O'Dell's office which was in the back didn't seem like an office at all. He didn't even have a conventional desk. Instead, two laptops sat on tables, and other computers ran in the next room.

He readily admitted to doing security for all the banks mentioned, and like a good security guru, wouldn't mention any problems with the systems at all, except to say that they were now properly updated.

"And tested?" Riley asked.

"We'd be remiss if we didn't test," O'Dell said.

"How do you test?" Riley asked. "Run diagnostics?"

O'Dell grinned. "You know how we do it. We have outsiders try to break in."

"They have any success?" Dave asked.

"Can't tell you if they do or not," O'Dell said. "Confidentiality. You'd have to get a warrant, which might be hard, since there was no crime."

"Only the admission of one," Riley said. "We'd like to be able to check."

O'Dell nodded. He grabbed a file from a desk drawer, shoved it forward, and grinned. "Y'know," he said. "I need a bathroom break. I'll be back in about five minutes."

He headed for the door. When he reached it, he stopped.

"You do realize that we have pretty tight security here, too."

Dave nodded, looking a bit clueless, but Riley wasn't. He glanced at the file, and flipped open the manila edge.

"He said there's security," Dave said.

"Plain sight," Riley said. "That's clear, even on the tapes."

"Digital," Dave said.

"What?" Riley asked.

"No one uses tape any more," Dave said.

Riley didn't care. What he did care about was the names of all the banks and credit unions that O'Dell provided security for. Only five of them refused to upgrade their systems after break-ins.

Five, and Riley knew the name of four of them: National Bank and Trust; Eastern United; First Federal; and McAdams Family. All of them had been tested a few days before the phone calls. All of them had failed, and all of them, when contacted, said they couldn't afford the additional outlay of security.

Four of the five—the same four—accused O'Dell of creating the flaws in the system so that he could charge extra money.

Riley closed the file and sat back in his chair. A minute later, O'Dell came back into the room.

"One more question," Riley said. "Do you have a favorite company for security testing?"

O'Dell smiled. "We have several. If I were you, I'd start with Kat and Mouse Incorporated. They specialize in systems first. I'll give you a list of the others."

Kat and Mouse. Somehow Riley'd expected something with Goose in the title. But that would have been much too obvious.

———

She wasn't at all what he had expected, sitting behind her desk in that tiny office, with thousands of dollars of computer equipment behind her. She was a few pounds heavier, a few years younger, and a few degrees plainer.

But that voice made up for everything.

"And you call yourself a detective," she said, leaning back in the leather chair that was the center of the small room. "Three phone calls. *Three*, before you could clear your schedule enough to come and see me."

Riley smiled at her. Her name was on the door: Katharine Mauser, Detective. Only of the private kind, specializing in security systems, computer fraud, and white-collar crime.

Kat, of Kat and Mouse.

"You didn't rob any banks," he said, leaning against the doorjamb, effectively blocking Dave's entry into the space. For some reason, Riley wanted this interview all to himself.

"Oh, but I did," she said, giving him a half smile that made up for even more. Those eyebrows added a bit too—made a few promises that no naked woman on HBO2 could ever fulfill.

"You didn't take anything," he said. "Did you?"

"Only their security," she said. "And silly them, they really didn't want it back."

"So you called me. How come you didn't call anyone else?" he asked.

She smiled. "Have you looked in the mirror, Detective Riley?"

He had. He'd only seen a craggy face that got more and more lined as time went on.

"Have we met?" he asked, thinking he'd remember her.

"I've only watched," she said. "But since I got to choose a detective, I figured I'd choose one worth talking to."

"What made you come to the police?" he asked. "No crime had been committed."

She shrugged. "I'm supposed to protect people from fraud and crime. Call me cynical, but banks that don't update their security get robbed. Banks that get robbed get federal insurance money. I've noticed, in my line of work, that a number of those banks then close. And sometimes, no one notices that the banks ignored procedures—at least, they don't notice in time to prevent the managers and presidents from disappearing to some warm place that lacks extradition treaties with the United States."

"You don't like that, huh?" Riley said.

"I've seen it too often," she said.

"You think anyone on your list is a potential?" he asked.

"They all have potential," she said. "But until I called you, I would have banked on the family bank. There was always something a little shady about them."

"So," Riley said, "you were doing this out of the goodness of your heart."

Kat stood. She was short—not even five feet—but well proportioned. When she stood, the weight redistributed into all the right places.

"Actually," she said, those eyebrows dancing and that voice lowering even more, "I was getting tired of playing with myself."

Which was when Dave excused himself and went back to the car.

"Need someone else to play with, do you?" Riley asked, his eyes twinkling.

She waved a ringless left hand at him. "It gets lonely, sneaking around in the middle of the night, robbing things."

"You just want to get caught?" he asked.

She chuckled, that throaty, throaty chuckle. And he got another shiver —and enjoyed it.

"I'd rather do this properly," she said. "Y'know, dinner first? And then, maybe, we could turn in—together."

His breath caught. "All right. How's your schedule look?"

"Free, detective," she said with a smile. "Quite free."

THE PERFECT MAN

KRISTINE KATHRYN RUSCH

THE PERFECT MAN

Paige Racette stared at herself in the full-length mirror, hands on hips. Golden cap of blond hair expertly curled, narrow chin, high cheekbones, china blue eyes, and a little too much of a figure—thanks to the fact she spent most of her day on her butt and sometimes (usually!) forgetting to exercise. The black cocktail dress with its swirling party skirt hid most of the excess, and the glittering beads around the collar brought attention to her face, always and forever her best asset.

Even with the extra pounds, she was not blind date material. Never had been. Until she quit her day job at the television station, she'd had to turn men away. Ironic that once she became a best-selling romance writer, she couldn't get a date to save her life. Part of the problem was that after she quit, she moved to San Francisco where she'd always wanted to live. She bought a Queen Anne in an old, exclusive neighborhood, set up her office in the bay windows of the second floor, and decided she was in heaven.

Little did she realize that working at home would isolate her, and being in a new city would isolate her more. It had taken her a year to make friends—mostly women, whom she met at the gym not too far from her home.

She saw interesting men, but didn't speak to them. She was still a small town girl at heart, one who was afraid of the kind of men who lurked in the big city, who believed that the only way to meet the right man was after getting to know him through mutual interests—or mutual friends.

In fact, she wouldn't have agreed to this blind date if a friend hadn't convinced her. Sally Myer was her racquetball partner and general confidant who seemed to know everyone in this city. She'd finally tired of Paige's complaining and set her up.

Paige slid on her high heels. Who'd ever thought she'd get this desperate? And then she sighed. She wasn't desperate. She was lonely.

And surely, there was no shame in that.

———

Sally had picked the time and location, and had told Paige to dress up. Sally wasn't going to introduce them. She felt that would be tacky and make the first meeting uncomfortable. She asked Paige for a photograph to give to the blind date—one Josiah Wells—and then told Paige that he would find her.

The location was an upscale restaurant near the Opera House. It was The Place To Go at the moment—famous chef, famous food, and one of those bars that looked like it had come out of a movie set—large and open where Anyone Who Was Someone could see and be seen.

Paige arrived five minutes early, habitually prompt even when she didn't want to be. She adjusted the white pashmina shawl she'd wrapped around her bare shoulders and scanned the bar before she went in.

It was all black and chrome, with black tinted mirrors and huge black vases filled with calla lilies separating the booths. The bar itself was black marble and behind it, bottles of liquor pressed against an untinted mirror, making the place look even bigger than it was.

She had only been here once before, with her Hollywood agent and a movie producer who was interested in her second novel. He didn't buy it—the rights went to another studio for high six figures—but he had bought her some of her most memorable meals in the City by the Bay.

She sat at the bar and ordered a Chardonnay which she didn't plan on touching—she wanted to keep her wits about her this night. Even with

Sally's recommendation, Paige didn't trust a man she had never met before. She'd heard too many bad stories.

Of course, all the ones she'd written were about people who saw each other across a crowded room and knew at once that they were soul mates. She had never experienced love at first sight (and sometimes she joked to her editor that it was lust at first sight) but she was still hopeful enough to believe in it.

She took the cool glass of Chardonnay that the bartender handed her and swiveled slightly in her chair so that she would be in profile, not looking anxious, but visible enough to be recognizable. And as she did, she saw a man enter the bar.

He was tall and broad-shouldered, wearing a perfectly tailored black suit that shimmered like silk. He wore a white scarf around his neck—which on him looked like the perfect fashion accent—and a red rose in his lapel. His dark hair was expertly styled away from his chiseled features, and she felt her breath catch.

Lust at first sight. It was all she could do to keep from grinning at herself.

He appeared to be looking for someone. Finally, his gaze settled on her, and he smiled.

Something about that smile didn't quite fit on his face. It was too personal. And then she shook the feeling away. She didn't want to be on a blind date—that was all. She had been fantasizing, the way she did when she was thinking of her books, and she was simply caught off guard. No man was as perfect as her heroes. No man could be, not and still be human.

Although this man looked perfect. His rugged features were exactly like ones she had described in her novels.

He crossed the room, the smile remaining, hand extended. "Paige Racette? I'm Josiah Wells."

His voice was high and a bit nasal. She took his hand, and found the palm warm and moist.

"Nice to meet you," she said, removing her hand as quickly as possible.

He wore tinted blue contacts, and the swirling lenses made his eyes seem shiny, a little too intense. In fact, everything about him was a little too intense. He leaned too close, and he seemed too eager. Perhaps he was just as nervous as she was.

"I have reservations here if you don't mind," he said.

"No, that's fine."

He extended his arm—the perfect gentleman—and she took the elbow in her hand, trying to remember the last time a man had done that for her. Her father maybe, when they went to the father-daughter dinner at her church back when she was in high school. And not one man since.

Although all the men in her books did it. When she wrote about it, the gesture seemed to have an old-fashioned elegance. In real life, it made her feel awkward.

He led her through the bar, placing one hand possessively over hers. This exact scene had happened in her first novel, *Beneath a Lover's Moon*. Fabian Garret and Skye Michaels had met, exchanged a few words, and were suddenly walking together like lovers. And Skye had thrilled to Fabian's touch.

Paige wished Josiah Wells's fingers weren't so clammy.

He led them to the maitre d', gave his name, and let the maitre d' lead them to a table near the back. See and Be Seen. Apparently they weren't important enough.

"I asked for a little privacy," he said, as if reading her thoughts. "I hope you don't mind."

She didn't. She had never liked the display aspect of this restaurant anyway.

The table was in a secluded corner. Two candles burned on silver candlesticks and the table was strewn with miniature carnations. A magnum of champagne cooled in a silver bucket, and she didn't have to look at the label to know that it was Dom Perignon.

The hair on the back of her neck rose. This was just like another scene in *Beneath a Lover's Moon*.

Josiah smiled down at her and she made herself smile at him. Maybe he thought her books were a blueprint to romancing her. She would have said so not five minutes before.

He pulled out her chair, and she sat, letting her shawl drape around her. As Josiah sat across from her, the maitre d' handed her the leather bound menu and she was startled to realize it had no prices on it. A lady's menu. She hadn't seen one of those in years. The last time she had eaten here had been lunch, not dinner, and she had remembered the prices on the menu from that meal. They had nearly made her choke on her water.

A waiter poured the champagne and left discretely, just like the maitre d' did. Josiah was watching her, his gaze intense.

She knew she had to say something. She was going to say how nice this was but she couldn't get the lie through her lips. Instead she said as warmly as she could, "You've read my books."

If anything, his gaze brightened. "I adore your books."

She made herself smile. She had been hoping he would say no, that Sally had been helping him all along. Instead, the look in his eyes made her want to push her chair even farther from the table. She had seen that look a hundred times at book signings: the too-eager fan who would easily monopolize all of her time at the expense of everyone else in line; the person who believed that his connection with the author—someone he hadn't met—was so personal that she felt the connection too.

"I didn't realize that Sally told you I wrote."

"She didn't have to. When I found out that she knew you, I asked her for an introduction."

An introduction at a party would have done nicely, where Paige could smile at him, listen for a polite moment, and then ease away. But Sally hadn't known Paige that long, and didn't understand the difficulties a writer sometimes faced. Writers rarely got recognized in person—it wasn't their faces that were famous after all but their names—but when it happened, it could become as unpleasant as it was for athletes or movie stars.

"She didn't tell me you were familiar with my work," Paige said, ducking her head behind the menu.

"I asked her not to. I wanted this to be a surprise." He was leaning forward, his manicured hand outstretched.

She looked at his fingers, curled against the linen tablecloth, carefully avoiding the miniature carnations, and wondered if his skin was still clammy.

"Since you know what I do," she continued in that too-polite voice she couldn't seem to shake, "why don't you tell me about yourself?"

"Oh," he said, "there isn't much to tell."

And then he proceeded to describe his work with a software company. She only half listened, staring at the menu, wondering if there was an easy —and polite—way to leave this meal, knowing there was not. She would make the best of it, and call Sally the next morning, warning her not to do this ever again.

"Your books," he was saying, "made me realize that women looked at men the way that men looked at women. I started to exercise and dress appropriately and I..."

She looked over the menu at him, noting the suit again. It must have been silk, and he wore it the way her heroes wore theirs. Right down to the scarf, and the rose in the lapel. The red rose, a symbol of true love from her third novel, *Without Your Love*.

That shiver ran through her again.

This time he noticed. "Are you all right?"

"Fine," she lied. "I'm just fine."

———

Somehow she made it through the meal, feeling her skin crawl as he used phrases from her books, imitated the gestures of her heroes, and presumed an intimacy with her that he didn't have. She tried to keep the conversation light and impersonal, but it was a battle that she really didn't win.

Just before the dessert course, she excused herself and went to the ladies room. After she came out, she asked the maitre d' to call her a cab, and then to signal her when it arrived. He smiled knowingly. Apparently he had seen dates end like this all too often.

She took her leave from Josiah just after they finished their coffees, thanking him profusely for a memorable evening. And then she escaped into the night, thankful that she had been careful when making plans. He didn't have her phone number and address. As she slipped into the cracked backseat of the cab, she promised herself that on the next blind date—if there was another blind date—she would make it drinks only. Not dinner. Never again.

———

The next day, she and Sally met for lattes at an overpriced touristy café on the Wharf. It was their usual spot—a place where they could watch crowds and not be overheard when they decided to gossip.

"How did you meet him?" Paige asked as she adjusted her wrought iron café chair.

"Fundraisers, mostly," Sally said. She was a petite redhead with freckles that she didn't try to hide. From a distance, they made her look as if she were still in her twenties. "He was pretty active in local politics for a while."

"Was?"

She shrugged. "I guess he got too busy. I ran into him in Tower Records a few weeks ago, and we got to talking. That's what made me think of you."

"What did?"

Sally smiled. "He was holding one of your books, and I thought, he's wealthy. You're wealthy. He was complaining about how isolating his work was and so were you."

"Isolating? He works for a software company."

"Worked," Sally said. "He's a consultant now, and only when he needs to be. I think he just manages his investments, mostly."

Paige frowned. Had she heard him wrong then? She wasn't paying much attention, not after she had seen the carnations and champagne.

Sally was watching her closely. "I take it things didn't go well."

"He's just not my type."

"Rich? Good-looking? Good God, girl, what is your type?"

Paige smiled. "He's a fan."

"So? Wouldn't that be more appealing?"

Maybe it should have been. Maybe she had over-reacted. She had psyched herself out a number of time about the strange men in the big city. Maybe her overactive imagination—the one that created all the stories that had made her wealthy—had finally betrayed her.

"No," Paige said. "Actually, it's less appealing. I sort of feel like he has photos of me naked and has studied them up close."

"I didn't think books were that personal. I mean, you write romance. That's fantasy, right? Make-believe?"

Paige's smile was thin. It was make-believe. But make-believe on any level had a bit of truth to it, even when little children were creating scenarios with Barbie dolls.

"I just don't think we were compatible," Paige said. "I'm sorry."

Sally shrugged again. "No skin off my nose. You're the one who doesn't get out much. Have you ever thought of going to those singles dinners? They're supposed to be a pretty good place to meet people..."

Paige let the advice slip off her, knowing that she probably wouldn't discuss her love life—or lack of it—with Sally again. Paige had been right in the first place: she simply didn't have the right attitude to be a good blind date. There was probably nothing wrong with Josiah Wells. He had certainly gone to a lot of trouble to make sure she had a good time, and she had snuck off as soon as she could.

And if she couldn't be satisfied with a good-looking wealthy man who was trying to please her, then she wouldn't be satisfied with any other blind date either. She had to go back to that which she knew worked. She had to go about her life normally, and hope that someday, an interesting guy would cross her path.

"...even go to AA to find dates. I mean, that's a little crass, don't you think?"

Paige looked at Sally, and realized she hadn't heard most of Sally's monologue. "You know what? Let's forget about men. It's a brand-new century and I have a great life. Why do we both seem to think that a man will somehow improve that?"

Sally studied her for a moment. "You know what I think? I think you've spent so much time making up the perfect man that no flesh-and-blood guy will measure up."

And then she changed the subject, just like Paige had asked.

———

As Paige drove home, she found herself wondering if Sally was right. After all, Paige hadn't dated anyone since she quit her job. And that was when she really spent most of her time immersed in imaginary romance. Her conscious brain knew that the men she made up were too perfect to be real. But did her subconscious? Was that what was preventing her from talking to men she'd seen at the opera or the theater? Was all this big city fear she'd been thinking about simply a way of preventing herself from remembering that men were as human—and as imperfect—as she was?

She almost had herself convinced as she parked her new VW Bug on the hill in front of her house. She set the emergency brake and then got out, grabbing her purse as she did.

She had a lot of work to do, and she had wasted most of the day obsessing about her unsatisfying blind date. It was time to return to work —a romantic suspense novel set on a cruise ship. She had done a mountain of research for the book—including two cruises—one to Hawaii in the winter, and another to Alaska in the summer. The Alaska trip was the one she had decided to use, and she had spent part of the spring in Juneau.

By the time she had reached the front porch, she was already thinking of the next scene she had to write. It was a description of Juneau, a city that was perfect for her purposes because there was only two ways out of it: by air or by sea. The roads ended just outside of town. The mountains hemmed everything in, trapping people, good and bad, hero and villain, within their steep walls.

She was so lost in her imagination that she nearly tripped over the basket sitting on her porch.

She bent down to look at it. Wrapped in colored cellophane, it was nearly as large as she was, and was filled with flowers, chocolates, wine and two crystal wine goblets. In the very center was a photo in a heart-shaped gold frame. She peered at it through the wrapping and then recoiled.

It was a picture of her and Josiah at dinner the night before, looking, from the outside, like a very happy couple.

Obviously he had hired someone to take the picture. Someone who had watched them the entire evening, and waited for the right moment to snap the shot. That was unsettling. And so was the fact that Josiah had found her house. She was unlisted in the phonebook, and on public records, she used her first name—Giacinta—with no middle initial. And although her last name was unusual, there were at least five other Racettes listed. Had Josiah sent a basket to every one of them, hoping that he'd find the right one and she'd call him?

Or had he had her followed?

The thought made her look over her shoulder. Maybe there was someone on the street now, watching her, wondering how she would react to this gift.

She didn't want to bring it inside, but she felt like she had no choice. She suddenly felt quite exposed on the porch.

She picked up the basket by its beribboned handle and unlocked her door. Then she stepped inside, closed the door as her security firm had instructed her, and punched in her code. Her hands were shaking.

On impulse, she reset the perimeter alarm. She hadn't done that since she moved in, had thought it a silly precaution.

It didn't seem that silly any more.

She set the basket on the deacons bench she had near the front door. Then she fumbled through the ribbon to find the card which she knew had to be there.

Her name was on the envelope in calligraphed script, but the message inside was typed on the delivery service's card.

> Two hearts, perfectly meshed.
> Two lives, perfectly twined.
> Is it luck that we have found each other?
> Or does Fate divine a way for perfect matches to meet?

Those were her words. The stilted words of Quinn Ralston, the hero of her sixth novel, a man who finally learned to free the poetry locked in his soul.

"God," she whispered, so creeped out that her hands felt dirty just from touching the card. She picked up the basket and carried it to the back of the house, setting it in the entryway where she kept her bundled newspapers.

She supposed most women would keep the chocolates, flowers, and wine even if they didn't like the man who sent them. But she wasn't most women. And the photograph bothered her more than she could say.

She locked the interior door, then went to the kitchen and scrubbed her hands until they were raw.

————

Somehow she managed to escape to the Juneau of her imagination, working furiously in her upstairs office, getting nearly fifteen pages done before dinner. Uncharacteristically, she closed the drapes, hiding the city view she had paid so much for. She didn't want anyone looking in.

She was cooking herself a taco salad out of Bite-sized Tostitos and bagged shredded lettuce when the phone rang, startling her. She went to answer it, and then some instinct convinced her not to. Instead, she went to her answering machine and turned up the sound.

"Paige? If you're there, please pick up. It's Josiah." He paused and she held her breath. She hadn't given him this number. And Sally had said that morning that she hadn't given Paige's unlisted number to anyone. "Well, um, you're probably working and can't hear this."

A shiver ran through her. He knew she was home, then? Or was he guessing.

"I just wanted to find out of you got my present. I have tickets to tomorrow night's presentation of *La Boheme*. I know how much you love opera and this one in particular. They're box seats. Hard to get. And perfect, just like you. Call me back." He rattled off his phone number and then hung up.

She stared at the machine, with its blinking red light. She hadn't discussed the opera with him. She hadn't discussed the opera with Sally either, after she found out that Sally hated "all that screeching." Sally wouldn't know *La Boheme* from *Don Giovanni*, and she certainly wouldn't remember either well enough to mention to someone else.

Well, maybe Paige's problem was that she had been polite to him the night before. Maybe she should have left. She'd had this problem in the past—mostly in college. She'd always tried to be polite to men who were interested in her, even if she wasn't interested in return. But sometimes, politeness merely encouraged them. Sometimes she had to be harsh just to send them away.

Harsh or polite, she really didn't want to talk to Josiah ever again. She would ignore the call, and hope that he would forget her. Most men understood a lack of response. They knew it for the brush-off it was.

If he managed to run into her, she would just apologize and give him the You're Very Nice I'm Sure You'll Meet Someone Special Someday speech. That one worked every time.

Somehow, having a plan calmed her. She finished cooking the beef for her taco salad and took it to the butcher block table in the center of her kitchen. There she opened the latest copy of *Publisher's Weekly* and read it while she ate.

———

During the next week, she got fifteen bouquets of flowers, each one an arrangement described in her books. Her plan wasn't working. She hadn't run into Josiah, but she didn't answer his phone calls. He didn't seem to understand the brush off. He would call two or three times a day to leave messages on her machine, and once an hour, he would call and hang up. Sometimes she found herself standing over the Caller ID box, fists clenched.

All of this made work impossible. When the phone rang, she listened for his voice. When it wasn't him, she scrambled to pick up, her concentration broken.

In addition to the bouquets, he had taken to sending her cards and writing her long e-mails, sometimes mimicking the language of the men in her novels.

Finally, she called Sally and explained what was going on.

"I'm sorry," Sally said. "I had no idea he was like this."

Paige sighed heavily. She was beginning to feel trapped in the house. "You started this. What do you recommend?"

"I don't know," Sally said. "I'd offer to call him, but I don't think he'll listen to me. This sounds sick."

"Yeah," Paige said. "That's what I'm thinking."

"Maybe you should go to the police."

Paige felt cold. The police. If she went to them, it would be an acknowledgement that this had become serious.

"Maybe," she said, but she hoped she wouldn't have to.

———

Looking back on it, she realized she might have continued enduring if it weren't for the incident at the grocery store. She had been leaving the house, always wondering if someone was watching her, and then deciding that she was being just a bit too paranoid. But the fact that Josiah showed up in the grocery store a few moments after she arrived, pushing no grocery cart and dressed exactly like Maximilian D. Lake from *Love at 37,000 Feet* was no coincidence.

He wore a new brown leather bomber jacket, aviation sunglasses, khakis and a white scarf. When he saw her in the produce aisle, he whipped the sunglasses off with an affected air.

"Paige, darling! I've been worried about you." His eyes were even more intense that she remembered, and this time they were green, just like Maximilian Lake's.

"Josiah," she said, amazed at how calm she sounded. Her heart was pounding and her stomach was churning. He had her trapped—her cart was between the tomato and asparagus aisles. Behind her, the water jets, set to mist the produce every five minutes, kicked on.

"You have no idea how concerned I've been," he said, taking a step closer. She backed toward the onions. "When a person lives alone, works alone, and doesn't answer her phone, well, anything could be wrong."

Was that a threat? She couldn't tell. She made herself smile at him. "There's no need to worry about me. There are people checking on me all the time."

"Really?" He raised a single eyebrow, something she'd often described in her novels, but never actually seen in person. He probably knew that no one came to her house without an invitation. He seemed to know everything else.

She gripped the handle on her shopping cart firmly. "I'm glad I ran into you. I've been wanting to tell you something."

His face lit up, a look that would have been attractive if it weren't so needy. "You have?"

She nodded. Now was the time, her best and only chance. She pushed the cart forward just a little, so that he had to move aside. He seemed to think she was doing it to get closer to him. She was doing it so that she'd be able to get away.

"I really appreciate all the trouble you went to for dinner," she said. "It was one of the most memorable—"

"Our entire life could be like that," he said quickly. "An adventure every day, just like your books."

She had to concentrate to keep that smile on her face. "Writers write about adventure, Josiah, because we really don't want to go out and experience it ourselves."

He laughed. It sounded forced. "I'm sure Papa Hemingway is spinning in his grave. You are such a kidder, Paige."

"I'm not kidding," she said. "You're a very nice man, Josiah, but—"

"A nice man?" He took a step toward her, his face suddenly red. "A nice man? The only men who get described that way in your books are the losers, the ones the heroine wants to let down easy."

She let the words hang between them for a moment. And then she said, "I'm sorry."

He stared at her as if she had hit him. She pushed the cart passed him, resisting the impulse to run. She was rounding the corner into the meat aisle when she heard him say, "You *bitch*!"

Her hands started trembling then, and she couldn't read her list. But she had to. He wouldn't run her out of here. Then he'd realize just how scared she was.

He was coming up behind her. "You can't do this, Paige. You know how good we are together. You know."

She turned around, leaned against her cart and prayed silently for strength. "Josiah, we had one date, and it wasn't very good. Now please, leave me alone."

A store employee was watching from the corner of the aisle. The butcher had looked up through the window in the back.

Josiah grabbed her wrist so hard that she could feel his fingers digging into her skin. "I'll make you remember. I'll make you—"

"Are you all right, miss?" The store employee had stepped to her side.

"No," she said. "He's hurting me."

"This is none of your business," Josiah said. "She's my girlfriend."

"I don't know him," Paige said.

The employee had taken Josiah's arm. Other employees were coming from various parts of the store. He must have given them a signal. Some of the customers were gathering too.

"Sir, we're going to have to ask you to leave," the employee said.

"You have no right."

"We have every right, sir," the employee said. "Now let the lady go."

Josiah stared at him for a moment, then at the other customers. Store security had joined them.

"Paige," Josiah said, "tell them how much you love me. Tell them that we were meant to be together."

"I don't know you," she said, and this time her words seemed to get through. He let go of her arm and allowed the employee to pull him away.

She collapsed against her cart in relief, and the store manager, a middle-aged man with a nice face, asked her if she needed to sit down. She nodded. He led her to the back of the store, past the cans that were being recycled and the gray refrigeration units to a tiny office filled with red signs about customer service.

"I'm sorry," she said. "I'm so sorry."

"Why?" The manager pulled over a metal folding chair and helped her into it. Then he sat behind the desk. "It seemed like he was harassing you. Who is he?"

"I don't really know." She was still shaking. "A friend set us up on a blind date, and he hasn't left me alone since."

"Some friend," the manager said. His phone beeped, and he answered it. He spoke for a moment, his words soft. She didn't listen. She was staring at her wrist. Josiah's fingers had left marks.

Then the manager hung up. "He's gone. Our man took his license number and he's been forbidden to come into the store again. That's all we can do."

"Thank you," she said.

The manager frowned. He was looking at her bruised wrist as well. "You know guys like him don't back down."

"I'm beginning to realize that," she said.

———

And that was how she found herself parking her grocery-stuffed car in front of the local precinct. It was a gray cinderblock building built in the late 1960s with reinforced windows and a steel door. Somehow it did not inspire confidence.

She went inside anyway. The front hallway was narrow, and obviously redesigned. A steel door stood to her right and to her left was a window made of bullet-proof glass. Behind it sat a man in a police uniform.

She stepped up to the window. He finished typing something into a computer before speaking to her. "What?"

"I'd like to file a complaint."

"I'll buzz you in. Take the second door to your right. Someone there'll help you."

"Thanks," she said, but her voice was lost in the electronic buzz that filled the narrow hallway. She opened the door and found herself in the original corridor, filled with blond wood and doors with windows. Very sixties, very unsafe. She shook her head slightly, opened the second door, and stepped inside.

She entered a large room filled with desks. It smelled of burned coffee and mold. Most of the desks were empty, although on most of them, the desk lamps were on, revealing piles of papers and files. Black phones as old as the building sat on each desk, and she was startled to see that typewriters outnumbered computers.

There were only a handful of people in the room, most of them bent over their files, looking frustrated. A man with salt and pepper hair was carrying a cup of coffee back to his desk. He didn't look like any sort of police detective she'd imagined. He was squarely built and seemed rather ordinary.

When he saw her, he said, "Help you?"

"I want to file a complaint."

"Come with me." His deep voice was cracked and hoarse, as if he had been shouting all day.

He led her to a small desk in the center of the room. Most of the desks were pushed together facing each other, but this one stood alone. And it had a computer, screen showing the SFPD logo.

"I'm Detective Conover. How can I help you, Miss...?"

"Paige Racette." Her voice sounded small in the large room.

He kicked a scarred wooden chair toward her. "What's your complaint?"

She sat down slowly, her heart pounding. "I'm being harassed."

"Harassed?"

"Stalked."

He looked at her straight on, then, and she thought she saw a world-weariness in his brown eyes. His entire face was rumpled, like a coat that had been balled up and left in the bottom of a closet. It wasn't a handsome face by any definition, but it had a comfortable quality, a trustworthy quality, that was built into the lines.

"Tell me about it," he said.

So she did. She started with the blind date, talked about how strange Josiah was, and how he wouldn't leave her alone.

"And he was taking things out of my novels like I would appreciate it. It really upset me."

"Novels?" It was the first time Conover had interrupted her.

She nodded. "I write romances."

"And are you published?"

The question startled her. Usually when she mentioned her name people recognized it. They always recognized it after she said she wrote romances.

"Yes," she said.

"So you were hoisted on your own petard, aren't you?"

"Excuse me?"

"You write about your sexual fantasies for a living, and then complain when someone is trying to take you up on it." He said that so deadpan, so seriously, that for a moment, she couldn't breathe.

"It's not like that," she said.

"Oh? It's advertising, lady."

She was shaking again. She had known this was a bad idea. Why would she expect sympathy from the police? "So since Donald Westlake writes about thieves, he shouldn't complain if he gets robbed? Or Stephen King shouldn't be upset if someone breaks his ankle with a sledgehammer?"

"Touchy," the detective said, but she noticed a twinkle in his eye that hadn't been there before.

She actually counted to ten, silently, before responding. She hadn't done that since she was a little girl. Then she said, as calmly as she could, "You baited me on purpose."

He grinned—and it smoothed out the care lines in his face, enhancing the twinkle in his eye and, for a moment, making him breathlessly attractive.

"There are a lot of celebrities in this town, Ms. Racette. It's hard for the lesser ones to get noticed. Sometimes they'll stage some sort of crime for publicity's sake. And really, what would be better than a romance writer being romanced by a fan who was using the structure of her books to do it?"

She wasn't sure what she objected to the most, being called a minor celebrity, being branded as a publicity hound, or finding this outrageous man attractive, even for a moment.

"I don't like attention," she said slowly. "If I liked attention, I would have chosen a different career. I hate book signings and television interviews, and I certainly don't want a word of this mess breathed to the press."

"So far so good," he said. She couldn't tell if he believed her, still. But she was amusing him. And that really pissed her off.

She held up her wrist. "He did this."

The smile left Conover's face. He took her hand gently in his own and extended it, examining the bruises as if they were clues. "When?"

"About an hour ago. At San Francisco Produce." She flushed saying the name of the grocery store. It was upscale and trendy, precisely the place a "celebrity" would shop.

But Conover didn't seem to notice. "You didn't tell me about the attack."

"I was getting to it when you interrupted me," she said. "I've been getting calls from him—a dozen or more a day. Flowers, presents, letters and e-mails. I'm unlisted and I never gave him my phone number or my address. I have a private e-mail address, not the one my publisher hands out, and that's the one he's using. And then he followed me to the grocery store and got angry when the store security asked him to leave."

Conover eased her hand onto his desk, then leaned back in his chair. His touch had been gentle, and she missed it.

"You had a date with him—"

"A blind date. We met at the restaurant, and a friend handled the details. And no, she didn't give him the information either."

"—so," Conover said, as if she hadn't spoken, "I assume you know his name."

"Josiah Wells."

Conover wrote it down. Then he sighed. It looked like he was gathering himself. "You have a stalker, Ms. Racette."

"I know."

"And while stalking is illegal under California law, the law is damned inadequate. I'll get the video camera tape from the store, and if it backs you up, I'll arrest Wells. You'll be willing to press charges?"

"Yes," she said.

"That's a start." Conover's world-weary eyes met hers. "but I have to be honest. Usually these guys get out on bail. You'll need a lawyer to get an injunction against him, and your guy will probably ignore it. Even if he gets sent up for a few years, he'll come back and haunt you. They always do."

Her shaking started again. "So what can I do?"

"Your job isn't tied to the community. You can move."

Move? She felt cold. "I have a house." A life. This was her dream city. "I don't want to move."

"No one does, but it's usually the only thing that works."

"I don't want to run away," she said. "If I do that, then he'll be controlling my life. I'd be giving in. I'd be a victim."

Conover stared at her for a long moment. "Tell you what. I'll build the strongest case I can. That might give you a few years. By then, you might be willing to go somewhere new."

She nodded, stood. "I'll bring everything in tomorrow."

"I'd like to pick it up, if you don't mind. See where he left it, whether he's got a hidey hole near the house. How about I come to you in a couple of hours?"

"Okay," she said.

"You got a peephole?"

"Yeah."

"Use it. I'll knock."

She nodded. Then felt her shoulders relax slightly, more than they had for two weeks. Finally, she had an ally. It meant more to her than she had realized it would. "Thanks."

"Don't thank me yet," he said. "Let's wait until this is all over."

All over. She tried to concentrate on the words and not the tone. Because Detective Conover really didn't sound all that optimistic.

———

The biggest bouquet waited for her on the front porch. She could see it from the street, and any hope that the meeting with Conover aroused disappeared. She knew without getting out of the car what the bouquet would be: calla lilies, tiger lilies and Easter lilies, mixed with greens and lilies of the valley. It was a bouquet Marybeth Campbell was designing the day she met Robert Newman in *All My Kisses*, a bouquet he said was both romantic and sad. (Not to mention expensive: the flowers weren't in season at the same time.)

She left the bouquet on the porch without reading the card. Conover would be there soon and he could take the whole mess away. She certainly didn't want to look at it.

After all this, she wasn't sure she ever wanted to see flowers again.

When she got inside, she found twenty-three messages on her machine, all from Josiah, all apologies, although they got angrier and angrier as she didn't answer. He must have thought she had come straight home. What a surprise he would have when he realized that she had gone to the police.

She rubbed her wrist, noting the soreness and cursing him under her breath. In addition to the bruises, her wrist was slightly swollen and she wondered if he hadn't managed to sprain it. Just her luck. He would damage her arm, which she needed to write. She got an ice pack out of the freezer and applied it, sitting at the kitchen table and staring at nothing.

Move. Give up, give in, all because she was feeling lonely and wanted to go on a date. All because she wanted a little flattery, a nice evening, to meet someone safe who could be—if nothing else—a friend.

How big a mistake had that been?

Big enough, she was beginning to realize, to cost her everything she held dear.

———

That night, after dinner, she baked herself a chocolate cake and covered it with marshmallow frosting. It was her grandmother's recipe—comfort food that Paige normally never allowed herself. This time, though, she would eat the whole thing and not worry about calories or how bad it looked. Who would know?

She made some coffee and was sitting down to a large piece, when someone knocked on her door.

She got up and walked to the door, feeling oddly vulnerable. If it was Josiah, he would only be a piece of wood away from her. That was too close. It was all too close now.

She peered through the peephole, just like she promised Conover she would, and she let out a small sigh of relief. He was shifting from foot to foot, looking down at the bouquet she had forgotten she had left there.

She deactivated the security system, then unlocked the three deadbolts and the chain lock she had installed since this nightmare began. Conover shoved the bouquet forward with his foot.

"Looks like your friend left another calling card."

"He's not my friend," she said softly, peering over Conover's shoulder. "And he left more than that."

Conover's glance was worried. What did he imagine?

"Phone calls," she said. "Almost two dozen. I haven't checked my e-mail."

"This guy's farther along than I thought." Conover pushed the bouquet all the way inside with his foot, then closed the door, and locked it. As he did, she reset the perimeter alarm.

Conover slipped on a pair of gloves and picked up the bouquet.

"You could have done that outside," she said.

"Didn't want to give him the satisfaction," Conover said. "He has to know we don't respect what he's doing. Where can I look at this?"

"Kitchen," she said, pointing the way.

He started toward it, then stopped, sniffing. "What smells so good?"

"Chocolate cake. You want some?"

"I thought you wrote."

"Doesn't stop me from baking on occasion."

He glanced at her, his dark eyes quizzical. "This hardly seems the time to be baking."

She shrugged. "I could drink instead."

To her surprise, he laughed. "Yes, I guess you could."

He carried the bouquet into the kitchen and set it on a chair. Then he dug through the flowers to find the card.

It was a different picture of their date. The photograph looked professional, almost artistic, done in black and white, using the light from the candles to illuminate her face. At first glance, she seemed entranced with Josiah. But when she looked closely, she could see the discomfort on her face.

"You didn't like him much," Conover said.

"He was creepy from the start, but in subtle hard-to-explain ways."

"Why didn't you leave?"

"I was raised to be polite. I had no idea he was crazy."

Conover grunted at that. He opened the card. The handwriting inside was the same as all the others.

My future and your future are the same. You are my heart and soul.
Without you, I am nothing.
    —Josiah

She closed her eyes, felt that fluttery fear rise in her again. "There'll be a ring somewhere in that bouquet."

"How do you know?" Conover asked.

She opened her eyes. "Go look at the last page of *All My Kisses.* Robert sends a forgive-me bouquet and in it, he puts a diamond engagement ring."

"This bouquet?"

"No. Josiah already used that one. I guess he thought this one is more spectacular."

Conover dug, and then whistled. There, among the stems, was a black velvet ring box. He opened it. A large diamond glittered against a circle of sapphires in a white gold setting.

"Jesus," he said. "I could retire on this thing."

"I always thought that was a gaudy ring," Paige said, her voice shaking. "But it fit the characters."

"Not to your taste?"

"No." She sighed and sank back into her chair. "Just because I write about it doesn't mean I want it to happen to me."

"I think you made that clear in the precinct today." He put the ring box back where he found it, returned the card to its envelope and set the flowers on the floor. "Mind if I have some of that cake?"

"Oh, I'm sorry." She got up and cut him a piece of cake, then poured some coffee.

When she turned around, he was grinning.

"What did I do?" she asked.

"You weren't kidding about polite," he said. "I didn't come here for a tea party, and you could have said no."

She froze in place. "Was this another of your tests? To see if I was really that polite?"

"I wish I were that smart." He took the plate from her hand. "I was getting knocked out by the smell. My mother used to make this cake. It always was my favorite."

"With marshmallow frosting?"

"And that spritz of melted chocolate on top, just like you have here." He set the plate down and took the coffee from her hand. "Although in those days, I would have preferred a large glass of milk."

"I have some—"

"Sit." If anything, his grin had gotten bigger. "Forgive me for being so blunt, but what the hell did you need with a blind date?"

There was admiration in his eyes—real admiration, not the sick kind she'd seen from Josiah. She used her fork to cut a bite of cake. "I was lonely. I don't get out much, and I thought, what could it hurt?"

He shook his head. That weary look had returned to his face. She liked its rumpled quality, the way that he seemed to be able to take the weight of the world onto himself and still stand up. "What a way to get disillusioned."

"Because I'm a romance writer?"

"Because you're a person."

They ate the cake in silence after that, then he gripped his coffee mug and leaned back in the chair.

"Thanks," he said. "I'd forgotten that little taste of childhood."

"There's more."

"Maybe later." And there was no smile on his face any more, no enjoyment. "I have to tell you a few things."

She pushed her own plate away.

"I looked up Josiah Wells. He's got a sheet."

She grabbed her own coffee cup. It was warm and comforting. "Let me guess. The political conferences he stopped going to."

Conover frowned at her. "What conferences?"

"Here in San Francisco. He was active in local politics. That's how my friend Sally met him."

"And he stopped?"

"Rather suddenly. I thought, after all this started, that maybe—"

"I'll check into it," Conover said with a determination she hadn't heard from him before. "His sheet's from San Diego."

"I thought he was from here."

Conover shook his head. "He's not a dot-com millionaire. He made his money on a software system back in the early nineties, before everyone was into this business. Sold his interest for 30 million dollars and some stock, which has since risen in value. About ten times what it was."

Her mouth had gone dry. Josiah Wells had lied to both her and Sally. "Somehow I suspect this is important."

"Yeah." Conover took a sip of coffee. "He stalked a woman in San Diego."

"Oh, God." The news gave her a little too much relief. She had been feeling alone. But she didn't want anyone else to be experiencing the same thing she was.

"He killed her."

"What?" Paige froze.

"When she resisted him, he shot her and killed her." Conover's soft gaze was on her now, measuring. All her relief had vanished. She was suddenly more terrified than she had ever been.

"You know it was him?"

"I read the file. They faxed it to me this afternoon. All of it. They had him one hundred percent. DNA matches, semen matches—"

She winced, knowing what that meant.

"—the fibers from his home on her clothing, and a list of stalking complaints and injunctions that went on for pages."

The cake sat like a lump in her stomach. "Then why isn't he in prison?"

"Money," Conover said. "His attorneys so out-classed the DA's office that by the end of the trial, they could have convinced the jury that the judge had done it."

"Oh, my god," Paige said.

"The same things that happened to you happened to her," Conover said. "Only with her those things took about two years. With you it's taking two weeks."

"Because he feels like he knows me from my books?"

Conover shook his head. "She was a TV business reporter who had done an interview with him. He would have felt like he knew her too."

"What then?" Somehow having the answer to all of that would make her feel better—or maybe she was just lying to herself.

"These guys are like alcoholics. If you take a guy through AA, and keep him sober for a year, then give him a drink, he won't rebuild his drinking career from scratch. He'll start at precisely the point he left off."

She had to swallow hard to keep the cake down. "You think she wasn't the only one."

"Yeah. I suspect if we look hard enough, we'll find a trail of women, each representing a point in the escalation of his sickness."

"You can arrest him, right?"

"Yes." Conover spoke softly. "But only on what he's done. Not on what he might do. And I don't think we'll be any more successful at holding him than the San Diego DA."

Paige ran her hand over the butcher block table. "I have to leave, don't I?"

"Yeah." Conover's voice got even softer. He put a hand on hers. She looked at him. It wasn't world-weariness in his eyes. It was sadness. Sadness from all the things he'd seen, all the things he couldn't change.

"I'm from a small town," she said. "I don't want to bring him there."

"Is there anywhere else you can go? Somewhere he wouldn't think of?"

"New York," she said. "I have friends I can stay with for a few weeks."

"This'll take longer than a few weeks. You might not be able to come back."

"I know. But that'll give me time to find a place to live." Her voice broke on that last. This had been her dream city, her dream home. How quickly that vanished.

"I'm sorry," he said.

"Yeah," she said quietly. "Me, too."

———

He decided to stay without her asking him. He said he wanted to sift through the evidence, listen to the phone messages, and read the e-mail. She printed off all of it while she bought plane tickets on-line. Then she e-mailed her agent and told her that she was coming to the City.

Already she was talking like the New Yorker she was going to be.

Her flight left at 8 a.m. She spent half the night packing and unpacking, uncertain about what she would need, what she should leave behind. The only thing she was certain about was that she would need her laptop, and she spent an hour loading her files onto it. She was writing down the names of some moving and packing services when Conover stopped her.

"We leave everything as is," he said. "We don't want him to get too suspicious too soon."

"Why don't you arrest him now?" she asked. "Don't you have enough?"

Something flashed across his face, so quickly she almost didn't catch it.

"What?" she asked. "What is it?"

He closed his eyes. If anything, that made his face look even more rumpled. "I issued a warrant for his arrest before I came here. We haven't found him yet."

"Oh, God." Paige slipped into her favorite chair. One of many things she would have to leave behind, one of many things she might never see again because of Josiah Wells.

"We have people watching his house, watching yours, and a few other places he's known to hang out," Conover said. "We'll get him soon enough."

She nodded, trying to look reassured, even though she wasn't.

———

About 3 a.m., Conover looked at her suitcases sitting in the middle of the dining room floor. "I'll have to ship those to you. No sense tipping him off if he's watching this place."

"I thought you said—"

"I did. But we need to be careful. One duffel. The rest can wait."

"My laptop," she said. "I need that too."

He sighed. "All right. The laptop and the biggest purse you have. Nothing more."

A few hours earlier, she might have argued with him. But a few hours earlier, she hadn't yet gone numb.

"I need some sleep," she said.

"I'll wake you," he said, "when it's time to go."

———

He drove her to the airport in his car. It was an old bathtub Porsche—with the early seventies bucket seats that were nearly impossible to get into.

"She's not pretty any more," he said as he tucked Paige's laptop behind the seat, "but she can move."

They left at 5, not so much as to miss traffic, but hoping that Wells wouldn't be paying attention at that hour. Conover also kept checking his rearview mirror, and a few times he executed some odd maneuvers.

"We being followed?" she asked finally.

"I don't think so," he said. "But I'm being cautious."

His words hung between them. She watched the scenery go by, houses after houses after houses filled with people who went about their ordinary lives, not worrying about stalkers or death or losing everything.

"This isn't normal for you, is it?" she asked after a moment.

"Being cautious?" he said. "Of course it is."

"No." Paige spoke softly. "Taking care of someone like this."

He seemed even more intent on the road than he had been. "All cases are different."

"Really?"

He turned to her, opened his mouth, and then closed it again, sighing. "Josiah Wells is a predator."

"I know," she said.

"We have to do what we can to catch him." His tone was odd. She frowned. Was that an apology for something she didn't understand? Or an explanation for his attentiveness?

Maybe it was both.

He turned onto the road leading to San Francisco International Airport. The traffic seemed even thicker here, through all the construction and the dust. It seemed like they were constantly remodeling the place. Somehow he made it through the confusing signs to Short Term Parking. He found a space, parked, and then grabbed her laptop from the back.

"You're coming in?" she asked.

"I want to see you get on that plane." He seemed oddly determined.

"Don't you trust me?"

"Of course I do," he said and got out of the car.

San Francisco International Airport was an old airport, built right on the bay. The airport had been trying to modernize for years. The new parts were grafted on like artificial limbs.

Paige took a deep breath, grabbed her stuffed oversized purse, and let Conover lead her inside. She supposed they looked like any couple as they went through the automatic doors, stopping to examine the signs above them pointing to the proper airline. Conover was watching the other passengers. Paige was checking out the lines.

She had bought herself a first class ticket—spending more money than she had spent for her very first car. But she was leaving everything behind. The last thing she wanted was to be crammed into couch next to a howling baby and an underpaid, stressed businessman.

She hurried to the first class line, relieved that it was short. Conover stayed beside her, frowning as he watched the people flow past. He seemed both disappointed and alert. He was expecting something. But what?

Paige stepped to the ticket counter, gave her name, showed her identification, answered the silly security questions, and got her E-ticket with the gate number written on the front.

"You've got an hour and a half," Conover said as she left the ticket counter. "Let's get breakfast."

His hand rested possessively on her elbow, and he pulled her close as he spoke. She glanced at him, but he still wasn't watching her.

"I have to make a stop first," she said.

He nodded.

They walked past the arrival and departure monitors, past the newspaper vending machines and toward the nearest restrooms. This part of the San Francisco airport still had a seventies security design. Instead of a bank of x-ray machines and metal detectors blocking entry into the main part of the terminal, there was nothing. The security measures were in front of each gate: you couldn't enter without going past a security checkpoint. So different from New York, where you couldn't even walk into some areas without a ticket. Conover would have no trouble remaining beside her until it was time for her to take off.

She went into the ladies room, leaving Conover near the departure monitors outside. The line was long—several flights had just arrived—but Paige didn't mind. This was the first time she had a moment to herself since Conover had arrived the night before.

It seemed like weeks ago.

She was going to be sorry to say good-bye to him at the gate. In that short period of time, she had come to rely on him more than she wanted to admit. He made her feel safe for the first time since she had met Josiah Wells.

As she exited the ladies room, a hand grabbed her arm and pulled her sideways. She felt something poke against her back.

"Think you could leave me?"

Wells. She shook her arm, trying to get away, but he clamped harder.

"Scream," he said, "and I will hurt you."

"You can't hurt me," she said. "You can't have weapons in an airport."

"You can bring a gun into an airport," he said softly, right in her ear. "You just can't take it through security."

She felt cold then. He was as crazy as Conover said, then. And as dangerous.

"Josiah." She spoke loudly, hoping that Conover could hear her. She didn't see him anywhere. "I'm going to New York on business. When I come back, we can start planning the wedding."

Wells was silent for a moment. He didn't move at all. She couldn't see his face, but she could feel his body go rigid. "You're playing with me."

"No," she said, letting her voice work for her, hoping it sounded convincing. She kept scanning the crowd, but Conover was gone. "I got your ring last night. I decided I needed to settle a few things in New York before I told you I'd say yes."

Wells put his chin on her shoulder. His breath blew against her hair. "You're not wearing the ring."

"It didn't fit." she said. "But I have it with me. I was going to have it sized in New York."

"Let me see it," he said.

"You'll have to let me dig into my purse."

She wasn't sure he'd believe her. Then, after a moment, he let her go. She brought up her purse, pretended to rummage through it, and took a step toward the ladies room door, praying her plan would work.

He was frowning. He looked like any other businessman in the airport, his suit neat and well tailoredwell-tailored, his trench coat long and expensive, marred only by the way he held his hand in the pocket.

She waited just a split second, until there were a lot of people around from another arriving plane, and then she screamed, "He's got a gun!" and ran toward the ladies room.

Only she didn't make it. She was tackled from behind, and went sprawling across the faded carpet. A gunshot echoed around her, and people started screaming, running. The body on top of hers prevented her from moving, and for a moment, she thought whoever had hit her had been shot.

Then she felt arms around her, dragging her toward the departure monitors.

"You little fool," Conover said in her ear. "I had this under control."

He pushed her against the base of the monitor, then turned around. Half the people around Wells had remained, and two of them had him in their grasp, while another was handcuffing him. Plainclothes airport police officers. More airport police were hurrying to the spot from the front door.

Passengers were still screaming and running out of the airport. Airline personnel were crouched behind their desks. Paige looked to see whether anyone was shot, but she didn't see anyone lying injured anywhere.

Her breathing was shallow, and she suddenly realized how terrified she had been. "What do you mean, under control? This doesn't look under control to me."

Security had Wells against the wall and were searching him for more weapons. One of the uniformed airport police had pulled Wells' head back and was yelling at him. Some of the passengers, realizing the threat was over, were drifting back toward the action.

Conover kept one hand on her, holding her in place. With the other, he pulled out his cell phone. He hit the speed-dial and put the small phone against his ear.

"Wait a minute!" Paige said.

He turned away slightly, as if he didn't want to speak to her. Then he said into the phone, "Frank, do me a favor. Call the news media—everyone you can think of. Tell them something just happened at the airport.... No. I'm not going through official channels. That's why I called you. Keep my name out of it and get them here."

He hung up and glanced at Paige. She had never felt so many emotions in her life. Anger, adrenaline, confusion. Then she saw security lead Wells away.

Conover took her arm and helped her up. "What's going on?" she asked again.

"Outside," he said, and pushed her through the crowd. After a moment, she remembered to check for her laptop. He had it, and somehow she had retained her purse. They reached the front sidewalk only to find it a confusion of milling people—some still terrified from the shots, others just arriving and trying to drop off their luggage. Cabs honked and nearly missed each other. Buses were backing up as the crowd spilled into the street.

"Oh, this is so much better," she said.

He moved her down the sidewalk toward another terminal. The crowd thinned here.

"What the hell was that?" she asked. "Where were you? How did he get past you?"

"He didn't get past me," Conover said softly.

She felt the blood leave her face. "You set me up? I was bait?"

"It wasn't supposed to happen like this."

"Oh, really? He was supposed to drag me onto the nearest flight? Or shoot me?"

"I didn't know he had a gun," Conover said. "He was ballsier than I expected. And he wouldn't have taken you from San Francisco."

"You know this how? Because you're psychic?"

"No, he wanted to control you. He couldn't control you on a plane. I had security waiting outside. A few plainclothes had been around us since we arrived. He was supposed to grab you, but you weren't supposed to try to get away."

"Nice if you would have told me that."

He shook his head slightly. "Most people wouldn't have fought him. Most people would have cooperated."

"Most people would have appreciated an explanation!" Her voice rose and a few stray passengers looked her direction. She made herself take a deep breath before she went on. "You knew he was going to be here. You knew it and didn't tell me."

"I guessed," he said.

"What did you do, tip him off?"

"No," Conover said softly. "You did."

"I did? I didn't talk to him."

"You booked your e-ticket on-line." His face was close to hers, his voice as soft as possible in all the noise. "He'd hacked into your system weeks ago. That's how he found your address and your phone number. Your public e-mail comes into the same computer as all your other e-mail. He's been following your every move ever since."

"Software genius," she muttered, shaking her head. She should have seen that.

Conover nodded. Across the way, reporters started converging on the building, cameras hefted on shoulders, running toward the doors. Conover shielded her, but she knew they would want to talk to her.

"Why didn't you warn me?" she asked again.

"I thought you'd be too obvious then, and he wouldn't try for you. I didn't expect you to be so cool under pressure. Telling him about the ring, pretending you were interested, was smart."

One of the reporters was working the crowd. People were turning toward the camera.

"Where were you?" she asked. "I looked for you."

"I was behind you all the time."

"So if he took me outside...?"

"I would have followed."

"I don't understand. Why didn't you tell me not to get the ticket on line?"

"The ticket was a gift," Conover said. "I didn't realize you were going to do it that way. You told me when you finished. His file from the previous case mentioned how he had used the internet to spy on his first victim. He was obviously doing that with you."

"But the airport, how did they know?"

"I called ahead, said that I was coming in, expecting a difficult passenger. I faxed his photo from your place while you were asleep. I asked them to wait until I got him outside, unless he did something threatening."

She frowned. More reporters were approaching. These looked like print media. No cameras, but lots of determination. "You could have waited and caught him at home."

"I could have," Conover said. "But this is better."

She turned to him, remembering the feel of the gun against her back, the screaming passengers, the explosive sound when the gun went off. "Someone could have been killed."

"I didn't expect a gun," Conover said. "And I didn't think he'd be rash enough to use it in an airport."

"But he did," she said.

"And it's going to help us." Conover watched another set of reporters run into the building. "First, his assault on you in an airport makes it a federal case. The gun adds to the case, and all the witnesses make it even better. Then there is the fact that airports are filled with security cameras. There's bound to be tape on this."

She frowned, trying to take herself out of this, trying to listen like a writer instead of a potential victim.

"And then," Conover said, "he attacked you. You're nationally known. It'll be big news. Our DA might have lost a stalking case against Wells, but the feds aren't going to let a guy who went nuts in an airport walk, no matter how much money he has."

"You set him up," she said. "If this had failed—"

"At the very least, I would have been fired," Conover said. "But it wouldn't have failed. I wouldn't have let anything happen to you. I didn't let anything happen to you."

"But you took such a risk." She raised her head toward his. "Why?"

He put a finger under her chin, and for a moment, she thought he was going to kiss her.

"Because you didn't want to leave San Francisco," he said softly.

"I get to stay home?" she asked.

He smiled, and let his finger drop. "Yeah."

He stared at her uncertainly, as if he were afraid she was going to yell at him again. But she felt a relief so powerful that it completely overwhelmed her.

She threw her arms around him. For a moment, he didn't move. Then, slowly, his arms wrapped around her and pulled her close.

"I don't even know your first name," she whispered.

"Pete," he said, burying his face in her hair.

"Pete." She tested it. "It suits you."

"I'd ask if I could call you," he said, "but I'm not real good on dates."

That pulled a reluctant laugh from her. "Obviously I'm not either. But I make a mean chocolate cake."

"That's right," he said. "Let's go finish it."

"Don't we have to talk to the press?"

"For a moment." He pulled back just enough to smile at her. "And then I get to take you home."

"Where I get to stay." She couldn't convey how much this meant to her. "Thank you."

He nodded. "My pleasure."

She leaned her head against his shoulder, feeling his strength, feeling the comfort. It didn't matter how he looked or whether he knew *La Boheme* from *Don Giovanni*. All that mattered was how he made her feel.

Safe. Appreciated. And maybe even loved.

Ten Stories by
Dean Wesley Smith

SPRINKLE ON A MEMORY

DEAN WESLEY SMITH

ONE

Red sugar sparkles on white cookie icing.

Blood drops on a snowdrift.

Who would have thought that decorating Christmas cookies with my kid would remind me of a murder. A murder I had no real memory of doing, yet I had no doubt I had done.

I could bring back a few details. The feel the cold of the night air, the white of the snow under the light from my car's headlights, and the smell of hot blood from the woman's throat. I have a memory of her blood spraying, just like all my victim's blood did. Her blood had left red dots all over the snow bank. Why hadn't I remembered her, or that night, or the blood on the snow before now?

Had I killed too many? Or maybe she was one I had yet to kill.

"You all right, Dad?" my daughter, Jennifer, asked.

My mind snapped out of the vision, or the memory, and came back to the kitchen table. The bright-lit room smelled of baking cookies and felt too warm by a few degrees.

I was sitting at our tablecloth-covered oak table, across from my daughter, Jennifer. My wife, Lisa, was taking another batch out of the oven. Decorating cookies had been a tradition in our family since before

Jennifer was born. I always enjoyed it. It made it feel like the Christmas season.

I had my hand poised over a cookie, the few bits of red sprinkles still in my hand, the rest on the white icing.

Like blood drops on snow.

"Changed my mind," I said, smiling at Jennifer. "I think this one needs green."

"You're strange, Dad," Jennifer said, laughing and shaking her head before going back to work on getting the exact right color on an angel cookie.

My wife Lisa laughed also, but it was a fond laugh. For some reason she loved me and all my quirks. Why such a beautiful, brown-haired, brown-eyed smart woman would love me, I had no idea. But I was very glad she did.

Neither she nor Jennifer had any idea about my little hobby, as I thought of my killing. Everyone in the city, I was sure, had heard of me. I was what the newspapers and police called "The Foothills Killer." I got the nickname because of I always dumped my victims up in the foothills above the city of Boise.

I picked up the bottle of green sugar sparkles and started to put them on the half-decorated cookie. But again the red specks on the white frosting distracted me, brought back a memory I clearly had been holding back for a long time.

Blood splatters on the snow.

I remembered the woman now. It was my first kill, my first wife, actually, long before Lisa.

Her name was Stephanie, and we had met in college. She had been tall, blonde, with green eyes. Everything about her shouted sex, and I remember liking that the most about her.

For some reason Stephanie and I had been arguing the night I killed her. The police had never found her body, and never would. I had buried her up in the Boise National Forest, deep, very deep, and then killed our dog Harvey and buried him two feet above her, so anyone digging would find the dog bones and stop.

Since she had no parents or close family, I told friends she had taken Harvey and left me for New York City. She had always talked about going to New York to try to break into acting in the theater, and every friend we had knew that we fought all the time. So her leaving me was no surprise to anyone.

I acted upset, angry, then upset again.

Everyone bought my little hurt-husband play-acting.

And after some time had passed, I got a divorce and people stopped asking about her.

That was over twenty years and thirty-five other kills ago. And not once during that time had anyone even questioned me about any of the deaths. I was that good, and that careful. The Foothills Killer had the police stumped.

Now I was happily married, had a wonderful daughter, and taught school in a local high school. I even was an assistant couch on the football team. I only killed once or twice a year, always in my private storage building near the river that I had bought to store sports equipment.

Only Stephanie had been killed out in the open, where I couldn't control every detail. In the storage building, I controlled the details, controlled the mess, even had a shower to wash up in, along with a washer and dryer to clean my clothes. With gloves and hot water I washed down every woman I killed, then stood them up to dry. I always left them nude, never left any trace of myself on them, and dumped them by keeping my van on the pavement of a well-traveled road in the foothills.

I also changed vans every year.

So why now, sitting in my kitchen, did seeing red specks on a cookie take me back to the memory of that first murder? I hadn't thought of Stephanie for a decade.

Suddenly around the cookie I could feel the wonderful kitchen, the image of Lisa, slipping away. I tried to hold onto it, but I couldn't.

Two

The fresh smell of baking cookies was still around me, but now instead of a covered oak dining table, I was sitting at a Formica kitchen table. The room around me was smaller, clearly less expensive.

"Jason!" my wife demanded, glaring at me from across the room. "Are you all right?"

I glanced up into Stephanie's face, the face of the woman I had thought about killing for twenty-five years.

"Fine," I said. "Just day-dreaming."

Stephanie snorted and shook her head, clearly disgusted. "Wow, that's a surprise."

She always complained that I never seemed to be there, never talked to her, never wanted to touch her anymore. The truth was that she was right. I was always off daydreaming, imaging a life where I had killed her.

I glanced around, wondering what had happened to me? How I had become this weak person?

I had the memories of Lisa and Jennifer, yet I knew that in reality Stephanie and I had gotten married right out of college, had two children, one named Craig and one named Leslie. Both kids were now off at college and would be coming home in the next day or so.

Stephanie had wanted us to decorate cookies like we always did, so the kids would have some.

"Make it feel like Christmas," she had said.

I had agreed because it was just easier to agree with Stephanie than fight her. I had learned that long ago.

The cookie in front of me had white frosting with red sparkles, just like I imagined the snow would have after I cut Stephanie's neck. For twenty years I had imagined killing Stephanie, imagined doing my dream job of teaching high school.

I also imagined killing dozens of other women I had met in my corporate job, women like Stephanie who deserved to be killed and hung naked to dry.

But instead of acting, I simply did nothing.

That was the story of my life it seemed. I only dreamed of acting while doing nothing. And by doing nothing, I got nowhere. I agreed with my wife, worked my boring job, and came home to the same old bitching. Somehow I had lost the person I might have become.

All I had left was my daydreams.

I stared at the white icing on the cookie, letting the red specks become something besides sugar as I imagined killing Stephanie, slicing her throat, letting her blood spurt out over the snow.

THREE

"Jason," Lisa said, putting her hand on my shoulder as I stared at the cookie. "Can I get you something?"

"Yeah, Dad, take a break," Jennifer said. "You're acting even stranger than normal."

The memory of cutting Stephanie's neck, of killing all those other women was there again.

"I'm fine," I said. I glanced up at my beautiful Lisa. "Honest. I was just thinking how lucky I am to be here with you two."

"Oh, weird," Jennifer said.

Lisa laughed and kissed me. "I'm glad you're here too." She gave me a wonderful hug and went to get another batch out of the oven.

I looked around the kitchen, at my perfect family, at the wonderful, rich-textured room filled with the smell of fresh-baked sugar cookies. I had made a life for myself with Lisa. Not Stephanie. And it was in this life where I wanted to live.

I stared at the cookie with the red sprinkles, remembering how wonderful it had felt to cut Stephanie's neck and watch the blood spray.

Then I took another cookie, put white frosting on it, and again put the red sprinkles on it, just to remind myself how lucky I had it.

Miss Smallwood's Goodies

A Pilgrim Hugh Incident

Dean Wesley Smith

ONE

Pilgrim Hugh stared at the lifelike statue of the naked and blue woman.

Actually, she wasn't completely naked. She wore a large cowboy hat and carried a large revolver in her right hand pointed upward. Her finger was on the trigger like she was about to blow a hole in the rim of her hat.

The last days of summer were just starting to fade, but the temperature for the Portland, Oregon area still seemed too high at eighty-five. The statue stood in a park in a suburban town of Portland called Hillsboro. The Chief of Police of Hillsboro had called Pilgrim to figure out where the statue had come from. The statue seemed to have just appeared late last night and a couple mothers of small children had complained this morning.

Hillboro, it seemed, wasn't used to getting statues donated to their parks in the middle of the night.

Over the last few years as a freelance private detective and lawyer, Pilgrim had gotten some strange calls, and this was another of the strange ones, of that there was no doubt.

After he'd gotten out of law school, he had tried to work in corporate law. He had managed two years, the exact same amount of time his first marriage lasted. Basically he had become bored with both.

Then his grandmother on his long-dead mother's side, a woman he barely knew, died and left him more money than even he could imagine or try to spend.

Two months after being divorced and out of work he had become free to do what he wanted.

His choice, as any young person might do, was a year of drinking and traveling around the world. Somewhere in the alcoholic haze, there was another even shorter marriage.

Eventually he went back to school to become a private detective, figuring that wouldn't be as boring as the law practice was.

Most of the training was not like the books about private detectives he loved to read. In fact most of what he had done was learn how to track someone by computer and look up financial records.

Finally, out of desperation to do something interesting, he set up his own combination law and private detective firm, hired a couple of talented associate lawyers to handle the really boring cases, and offered his services for free to the different city police departments around the Portland metropolitan area.

Hugh and Associates now occupied three floors in a downtown Portland high-rise. He had started out rich from his grandmother and managed to get even richer by hiring the right people and taking the right cases over the last few years.

Carrie, Pilgrim's assistant, limo driver, and best friend, stood beside him, staring at the blue statue. Today Carrie had on a green University of Oregon sweatshirt (that didn't hide her figure much at all) and a pair of white shorts that also hid little. Even in her late thirties, she could still have been modeling.

Pilgrim was over six feet tall and Carrie usually seemed to tower over him because of tall heels. But today they were the same height since she had on a rare pair of tennis shoes that matched her outfit perfectly.

Carrie was about to finish her last year of law school at the University of Oregon and join the legal side of Pilgrim's firm. But until that day, she paid for her apartment and food and school by being his assistant and driver when she wasn't in class.

He was going to miss her when her last year of law school started back up later in the month. They were such a good team.

The statue was anchored to what looked like a concrete slab and on the face of the slab was a name. "Miss Smallwood."

"Very lifelike," Carrie said, moving around the statue.

The blue statue did look very, very lifelike. No question there. Except the skin was perfectly smooth, the naked breasts had no nipples and were perfectly smooth, and the crotch of the statue looked like it came from a doll, also perfectly smooth with no attempt to make it lifelike in any way.

The eyes were open, yet showed no detail.

The entire thing felt creepy. Even in the bright sunlight and hot day.

Two

The park that now held the Miss Smallwood stature was only one block wide and a block long, surrounded by a sidewalk. A few other sidewalks wound into the trees and to a new playground in the far corner. A very nice neighborhood park, very well maintained.

The statue had been placed near the sidewalk facing an apartment complex across the street. In fact, it seemed to really be staring at that apartment building.

Pilgrim looked over at it, following the direction of the statue's look. The apartment looked to be a renovated old hotel of some sort. Stone and brick exterior, large windows. A nice place from the looks of it.

Pilgrim moved over and stared at the large revolver in the statue's hand. It looked real and from what he could tell the artist had depicted it with one shell missing.

"Know anything about guns?" Pilgrim asked Carrie.

"It's a revolver," Carrie said. "That's about it."

Pilgrim laughed. "I knew that much."

"Frank from the estate planning part of your office is a gun nut," Carrie said. "You want me to send him a picture?"

"Might as well," Pilgrim said. He doubted it would make any difference but it never hurt to get the details together.

Carrie started back toward the limo that served as an office for them. Pilgrim had every possible modern device he could think of in that car, from high-speed computer connections to sophisticated camera and listening equipment.

He moved closer and tapped the hard surface of the statue. It felt like a plastic resin of some sort.

He moved around the statue, studying every tiny detail. Clearly the statue had been made by a mold. And then polished and finished with a clear, thick blue resin compound. The resin looked to be almost a quarter inch thick in some places.

Fantastic work. Not a mark or seam anywhere.

The statue was clearly made from the mold of a real woman. Her legs were slightly too long for her final height, her hips just a touch too wide, and the right breast was slightly larger than the other.

A perfect statue, no marks at all, yet not a perfect woman as the subject.

Pilgrim stepped back and realized he was shivering slightly even with the heat of the day.

This statue just flat gave him the creeps.

He walked in a large circle around the statue, just trying to let his mind take in the details. It had been placed near the entrance to the park, between where a sidewalk split. But it hadn't been placed looking directly at the walkway, but instead at a slight angle staring off at the nearby apartment across the street.

With as perfect as this statue was done, why mess up the placement? Pilgrim would bet it wasn't messed up. It was intentional.

Carrie came back with the camera, snapped a couple of close-ups of the revolver in the statue's hand and then sent the images from the camera back to the office.

Then she placed the camera down and picked up what looked like an iPad and aimed it at the statue.

"Shit!" she said, staring at the device in her hands.

"What?" Pilgrim asked, moving over toward her.

She had turned her back on the statue and was clearly trying to catch her breath.

"You all right?" he asked.

She shook her head yes, then showed him the image on the device.

"I wanted to see what the inside of the statue looked like," she said.

All Pilgrim could do was stare at the image on the device. No wonder the statue wasn't perfect. It was an actual woman inside that resin.

He could see every detail of her skeleton. Her insides had been cleaned out like they did with embalming. Metal bars ran up both legs. Another was up her spine and through her neck to hold her head.

Pilgrim turned to look at the woman frozen like a statue. "Whoever did this cut off the woman's nipples and smoothed over any sign."

"And covered or removed her crotch as well," Carrie said. "And covered or removed her eyes."

"Took and kept all the goodies," Carrie said.

"Better call Chief Benson," Pilgrim said, "tell him he has a crime scene here. The statue isn't a statue, it's a body."

"He's going to love this," Carrie said. "To find the killer he has to look for a woman's nipples and crotch."

"Might not want to tell him that on the phone," Pilgrim said.

"Not a chance," Carrie said, heading for the limo again, picking up the camera along the way.

THREE

Pilgrim did another slow walk about the woman's body, looking at it with a new perspective. He was convinced that the placement in this park, in that exact position had something to do with all this.

He needed to find out what she was looking at with those blank eyes.

He headed back for the coolness of the limo and crawled into the back just as Carrie hung up. "Detectives and crime scene crew on the way. Benson said he would be here in fifteen minutes and we're not to move."

"Yeah, I bet," Pilgrim said.

"So," Carrie said, "any idea on The Case of Miss Smallwood's Goodies?"

Carrie loved to give each of the investigations they did with a strange case name that almost always stuck.

"Some," Pilgrim said. "Search the area data bases for a woman of that height and size and age being reported missing in the last month. Might want to go all the way down to San Francisco and up to Seattle as well in the search."

"Got it," Carrie said.

She was sitting with her back to the front compartment and a large computer complex of keyboards and screens opened out of the seat beside her, sliding out to almost surround where she was sitting with a keyboard on her lap and a large screen in front of her.

Pilgrim was on the seat near the wet bar. He turned and punched a hidden button on the bar, letting it turn into another computer center with a large screen and two small screens where the drinks had been.

He loved this limo. He felt like a super hero at times. The car was the most sophisticated computer center on wheels that he knew of. He loved it and never once questioned the costs to build it and keep it completely outfitted with any new device that would help him with a case.

In this car he could almost see through walls, hear something whispered two hundred yards away, and tap into any phone line he wanted to. This was a dream car for any private detective.

He immediately typed in the address of the apartment complex the woman statue was looking at.

Then on one screen he pulled up a floor plan of the building and on the other a list of tenants.

The landlord, a man by the name of Steven Frome lived in a large apartment on the main floor with his wife, Sue. It was the only apartment on the first floor, the rest of the space was filled with a large lobby and entrance area. He had been right, the building had been an old hotel at one time in the past called The Wellington Inn. It had been converted to apartments in 1962 and Frome had bought it in 2001.

There was nothing in the full basement that showed on the floor plan and four apartments per floor from the second floor through the fifth, all fairly large.

Pilgrim couldn't see anything at all odd about any of the tenants or the building or the landlord.

"No missing person meets her look size or shape," Carrie said, "anywhere in the Pacific Northwest in the last six months."

"Yeah, that would have been too easy," Pilgrim said, shaking his head.

"So why would someone do this to a person and put them in this park?" Carrie asked as outside the first police car arrived on the scene.

"Figure that out and I bet we find Miss Smallwood's goodies," Pilgrim said. "I'll go talk to the police. Bring up pictures and background checks of anyone in that building there. I'll bet anything there is a reason she's looking in that direction."

Carrie nodded and went to work as Pilgrim crawled back out in to the heat.

"Where's the body?" the dark, heavy-set policeman asked. His name on his uniform was Wells.

Pilgrim pointed at the shiny, blue statue that seemed to be glistening in the sunlight as if she was sweating, even with the big cowboy hat and revolver.

"You're kidding?" Officer Wells asked. "That statue?"

"I wish I was," Pilgrim said.

Pilgrim went back to staring at the statue for a moment as Officer Wells started to tape off the area. More than likely the hat and gun the woman had were clues as well, but damn if Pilgrim could even figure out how to start on them.

At that moment Chief of Police Benson pulled up and got out into the heat.

"You're telling me that's a body?" he asked, as Pilgrim met him halfway across the lawn toward the statue.

"Sealed in resin and disguised, yes," Pilgrim said.

"You mean like that traveling science exhibit where bodies were frozen in movement in some sort of resin. The one that showed all the body's muscles and other parts most of us didn't want to see or even know about?"

"Might be like that," Pilgrim said, shaking his head. "I didn't know you were into science, Chief?"

"The kid loves the Omsi Center. That exhibit just grossed me out and I've seen a lot of bodies in my day." Chief Benson stopped a few feet from the statue. "What happened to her nipples and crotch?"

"The killer must have wanted to keep them. Or thought them too private to show," Pilgrim said.

Suddenly he realized what he had just said. The missing parts were the answer after all.

FOUR

"Hang on, Chief. I'm not so sure this is a crime after all. At least not a murder."

Pilgrim turned and headed back for the limo with Chief Benson right behind him.

Inside the cool interior, the Chief sighed as he closed the door. "I sure wish the city would spring for one of these for me."

"More than the city budget for a year," Carrie said, not looking up from the computer screen in front of her.

"Carrie," Pilgrim said, "can you do a search of death notices in the last year. Pictures of woman the age of the statue out there."

"Sure," Carrie said, frowning.

While she was doing that, Pilgrim looked up the occupations of all the tenants in the building, including the landlord.

He found exactly as he figured he would find. Steven Frome, the owner of the building, owned three of the area funeral homes.

"Look for a death notice for Sue Frome," Pilgrim said to Carrie.

"Already found her," Carrie said, swinging around he computer screen showing a picture of Sue Frome. "Maiden name Smallwood."

There was no doubt it was the woman in the statue.

"She died three months ago of terminal brain cancer," Carrie said.

"She went very quickly. In fact, this park is named after her since her husband donated a ton of money in her memory to upgrade it and put in new kid's swings and such."

"He made her into a statue and stuck her here?" Benson asked. "Creepy."

"Death makes people do strange things at times," Pilgrim said.

"She liked to spend time in the park her last weeks," Carrie said. "And she was a top shot and loved to ride horses. All in the obituary."

"That explains the gun and the hat," Pilgrim said, nodding.

'Oh, shit, now what am I supposed to do?" Benson asked. "I'm fairly certain there's a rule against this somewhere."

"I'd go talk to Steve Frome, get him to remove her to a more appropriate place and then put a real statue in her place."

"Yeah, makes sense," Benson said. "Better than the press getting wind of this. Can you imagine the news?"

"Ask him what he did with her goodies," Carrie said as the Chief started to climb out.

"Her what?"

Pilgrim shook his head. "Never mind. Just Carrie's name for this case is all."

"You two are weird," Benson said, smiling. "But thanks."

After Benson got out and the computers were back into their hiding places, Carrie said, "Don't you want to know what happened to the woman's goodies?"

"Not even in the slightest," Pilgrim said, shaking his head. "Curiosity about another man's wife's private parts can only lead to problems."

"And you know this how?" Carrie asked, smiling.

Pilgrim dug out a Diet Coke for himself and handed Carrie a regular Coke. "How about we just let your imagination and memory work on that one while you drive us back to the office."

"You are no fun at all, boss," Carrie said, smiling as she took the offered can and started to climb out of the limo to move up to the front seat.

"That's not what she said," Pilgrim said, smiling.

All Carrie did was groan and then slam the door.

The Remarkable Way
She Died

A Cold Poker Gang Story

Dean Wesley Smith

THE REMARKABLE WAY
SHE DIED

Retired Las Vegas Detective Debra Pickett had seen a lot of death over her decades-long career. And now that she was a member of the Cold Poker Gang task force with the mission to solve cold cases, she saw even more.

But how Connie Dipkin had died was maybe the strangest of them all.

She had died standing up, alone, in the middle of a sidewalk. She had no marks on her body, no wounds, nothing medical or poison that anyone could find.

And she had remained standing in the middle of that sidewalk, completely dead, for almost three hours before someone actually noticed something was wrong with her.

That alone shouldn't have been possible, but yet it had happened. There was even surveillance film of her from the moment she died, completely alone, until the police arrived three hours later.

One moment Connie was walking along seemingly just fine. Then she slowed and just stopped.

The day had been a nice, calm spring day in 2010, no winds, not too hot either.

The medical examiner had labeled Connie's death as unexplained, thus it was investigated. Since nothing was ever found to push it toward natural causes or murder, the case went cold.

And now Pickett was holding the thin summary file in her hand while sipping her morning coffee and waiting for Retired Detective Ben "Sarge" Carson to get out of the shower and get dressed.

Around her the morning Las Vegas sun filled their large condo with bright light. It was late October and the weather was about as perfect as it got here in the valley.

Their three cats, Pete, Ree, and Nose, had finished their morning routine of chasing each other through the place, followed by bathing, which was now followed by naps in the sun.

This morning Ree, a large orange tabby, had taken over one of the brown armchairs, while Nose, a black-and-white tuxedo occupied one end of the tan cloth couch and Pete, another large orange tabby, the other end.

Pickett loved those three cats and couldn't imagine this large place without them. They gave it life and energy.

At the moment it was nap energy, but still energy.

And massive cuteness.

Their condo had been decorated in shades of wood and tan and browns, sort of like the desert, only richer. And the kitchen she stood in was state-of-the-art modern, with white granite counters and a fridge that was larger than anything Pickett had seen before. Sarge had once said that a small family could live in the stupid thing. Pickett had not disagreed.

But what she loved more than anything else about their penthouse condo was the natural light that flooded the entire main room and kitchen. Even though they were on the top of one of downtown Las Vegas's largest buildings, it felt like the outside was being invited in, but without all the heat and wind.

Behind her Sarge came from the master bedroom area, his thick silver and gray hair still damp. He had on a light green dress shirt with rolled up sleeves and jeans. He had his badge on his belt and his gun in his holster under his arm.

She wore her normal as well, this time a tan silk blouse and jeans. She carried her gun and badge the same way Sarge did.

Every morning she was struck by how handsome he was with his deep hazel eyes and square jaw. She couldn't believe he had fallen in love with her and how lucky she was to find him this late in life.

They had only been together for a year now, but it felt like she had always known him.

And even though she was a lot shorter than he was at five-four, people said they made a great couple. More than likely it was because they were both always smiling and laughing and joking.

She handed him a cup of coffee and he took a sip, then glanced at the Connie Dipkin file.

"Any idea on that one?" he asked.

Pickett just shook her head. "Never seen a dead person remain standing before."

Sarge laughed. "That's a new one on me as well. Seen a couple vics propped up, one against a jukebox like in the song, but never standing on a sidewalk right out in the open."

"I was at one funeral," Pickett said, "where they stood the deceased near a pool table with a pool cue in his hand."

"Now that's weird," Sarge said.

"It actually felt sort of right for the guy who had died. Creepy, but right."

"To each his own," Sarge said, shaking his head.

"I'm not sure this was murder," Pickett said, pointing to the file on the counter.

Sarge took another sip of his coffee and nodded to that. "Let's hope Robin and her magic computers can come up with something, because I got nothin'."

"I'm still stuck on the woman dying standing up," Pickett said.

Retired Detective Robin Sprague was Pickett's best friend and when they had been active detectives, they had been partners. Now the three of them worked together on cold cases for the task force. Pickett and Sarge did the legwork while Robin did all the computer work.

Together they had solved a lot of cases in just a year working together. Sometimes Pickett and Sarge found the leads, other times Robin did with her computer. They had balanced well.

Sarge finished his coffee and they both put on light jackets to cover their badges and guns, then headed out for the five-block walk to breakfast at the Golden Nugget Buffet.

Pickett loved the morning walk and the routine of it. They ate at the Golden Nugget Buffet every morning and Pickett never got tired of the food because when she wanted, she just changed it up and ate something different. And she never had to do dishes. Or cook. Good food, someone to wait on her, no dishes to wash. To her, that was retirement heaven.

Robin was already there and eating, completely absorbed in reading something on her computer.

While Pickett was thin and short, Robin was solid and square, like a swimmer. She wasn't overweight in the slightest, just solid. She had always been that way.

Sarge and Pickett got their breakfast from the buffet and went back to sit with Robin. The three of them had the same table every morning, away from the tourists on the other side of the room near a massive wall of windows looking out over the hotel pool.

The room was decorated in oak tones, lots of plants, and brass everywhere. It actually worked as a décor and felt comfortable. And the staff knew the three of them and saved their table every morning and also made sure to not sit anyone close to them. Sarge had asked for that favor and made sure he tipped generously to keep the favor alive.

They talked about cats through most of breakfast until Robin smiled and said, "I know what killed Connie Dipkin."

Sarge laughed and Pickett just shook her head. That was so like Robin to do something like that.

"Connie was injected with a very rare drug out of Australia that causes slow paralysis of the muscles. The drug shut off her breathing and stopped her heart."

Robin got out a picture of Connie standing on the sidewalk, dead.

"Three reasons she stayed standing," Robin said. "One, there was no wind to knock her down and other people on the sidewalk never touched her. Two, the drug froze her muscles just long enough for rigor to start to set in as the drug cleared. Three, her large shopping bags served as balances."

Pickett stared at the picture. Connie was holding a shopping bag in each hand. And the two bags were wide and low, close to the sidewalk.

"I'll be go to hell," Sarge said. "Strangest thing I have ever seen."

"So how come no one spotted the poison in her system?" Pickett asked.

"Because by the time they found her it was gone," Robin said. "If she had fallen over and died, the tests would have spotted the poison. But since she died standing and remained standing until rigor started to take over, the poison was no longer detectable with surface tests."

"So we have no toxicology proof of this?" Sarge said.

"Oh, we do I'm sure," Robin said. "If a test is done looking only for the specific poison, residual amounts will still be there. They just didn't do that test."

"And it can still be done?"

"Without a problem," Robin said.

"Well, that's darned fast progress," Sarge said. "Great work there. I thought this would be a no-movement case."

"So did I," Pickett said.

Robin smiled. "I got more. Once I came up with the poison, I learned how long it takes to kill a person and freeze them up. Exactly ten minutes."

"So you backtracked Connie's movements?" Pickett asked, smiling.

Robin always had a way of being ahead of puzzles like this one, one of the many things Pickett loved about her.

Robin nodded. "Take a look at this. The detectives on the case originally had pulled all surveillance footage since from what she was carrying they knew exactly what stores she had been in.

Robin started an image of Connie just leaving a women's clothing store, her two bags balanced, one in each hand.

A man in his thirties, dark brown hair, glasses, bumped into her, excused himself, and went on into the store.

"Exactly ten minutes from the moment she stopped on the sidewalk," Robin said.

"And tell me you know who that man is?" Sarge asked a half second before Pickett could ask the same thing.

"His name is Preston Barker. It seems Connie's husband Jake had a secret. He was gay and meeting Preston on the side."

"And Connie had all the money, right?" Pickett asked.

"All of it," Robin said, nodding. "And Preston was working as a pharmacist, so he would know rare poisons like this one."

"Did the detectives at the time interview him?" Pickett asked.

"They didn't know he existed," Robin said. "Jake was deep, deep, deep in the closet. But Preston and Jake are now married and living happily on Connie's money."

"Not for much longer," Sarge said.

Pickett could only agree to that with a smile.

"We have enough evidence to actually get an arrest on this?" Pickett asked.

"The tests will find the traces of the drug that killed her and its time to take effect. I am sure there is evidence of him ordering the poison somewhere, and that film will cinch the deal," Robin said.

"Got a hunch good old Jake will roll on Preston, no pun intended, when faced with first-degree murder charges."

Pickett was certain he was right.

She looked at Robin, then at Sarge. "I think Robin should make the call on this one since she did all the work."

"Hey, I sat here and ate breakfast," Sarge said, smiling. "I should get credit for that at least."

Robin laughed. "Pickett, give him credit, would you?"

"Later tonight he'll get what's coming to him."

"Do I get extra credit?" Sarge asked, smiling.

"Only if you are a very, very good detective," Pickett said, laughing at the man she loved.

Robin waved her hand in the air. "More information than I needed."

Robin grabbed her phone to set up an appointment with one of the active detectives who could take this case and make sure all the details were in place for an arrest.

"In celebration of Robin solving this one," Pickett said to Sarge, "I'm going for dessert."

"Let me guess... bread pudding?" Sarge asked, smiling.

"Damn you are a good detective," Pickett said. "That might be even more extra credit tonight."

Pickett leaned over and kissed Sarge and he kissed her back.

"Would you two get a room," Robin said, shaking her head.

"No," Pickett said, standing and pulling Sarge to his feet. "But we will get some bread pudding."

"I'm going to need the energy," Sarge said.

All Robin did was groan and that made Pickett laugh all the way across the dining room.

A Life in Whoopees

Dean Wesley Smith

My name is Bill Wallace, I'm seventy-two years old, and I feel like one of the lucky people in life. I had a good marriage, great children and grandchildren, a good career. And I had five whoopee moments.

I hear some people never even have one.

MY FIRST WHOOP

I was ten. It was the last day of school before Christmas, and it was snowing lightly outside our family house in Madison, Wisconsin. As I came through the door, the warmth of the house hit me in the face, combined with the fantastic smell of Mom baking Christmas cookies.

"Yes!" I shouted. I dropped my backpack on the hall table and headed toward the kitchen.

"Billy!" my mom shouted from the kitchen. "Take off your boots at the door."

I stopped, yanked off my boots and went sliding in my stocking feet on the hardwood floors to get a cookie.

That Christmas turned out to be the best Christmas ever, since Grandma and Grandpa were there, Dad was still living at home, and Mom seemed happy. None of that would ever happen again, so I still look back at that Christmas as the best ever.

MY SECOND WHOOP

Debbie pushed me away and slid back across the front seat of the car. She was clearly breathing hard and as excited as I was.

We had parked on a canal road a good four miles outside of town. The only thing close was a farmer's house a half mile away. I still had the car radio on, and the light from it and the moon through the steamed-up windows was enough for me to see Debbie's face.

Her short brown hair was messed up slightly, and her cheeks were red.

Debbie and I were both sophomores in high school and had been sort of hanging out for a month or so together. It was common knowledge that we were together, and we went out on sort-of dates a lot, but that was about as far as it had gotten.

Twice after I had gotten my drivers license, we had parked out here on the canal bank, and both times all we had done was kissed. I was hoping tonight might be a little different, but so far it was turning out to be the same.

The seat between us was one of those bench seats that only Dodges and pick-up trucks had during the seventies. Luckily my mom had bought a Dodge.

"Billy, you promise you won't tell anyone we're parking?"

"Who am I going to tell?" I asked. "Of course I promise. What happens here, what we talk about here, is just between you and me."

She looked at me for a long time, but of course, in that situation, any amount of time seemed long. Then, in a quick motion, she slipped her sweater over her head and tossed it into the back seat.

Her white bra was like a beacon in the night. All I could say was "Wow!"

Five years later, during our second years in college, we were married. I have to admit that even after we were married the sight of her in a bra still took my breath away.

My Third Whoop

The letter came from the State Bar association. Four years of college and three years of law school and it all came down to one stupid envelope in my hand.

I just stood there in the doorway our apartment, staring at the envelope. I couldn't stop my hand from shaking.

Debbie, who had spent seven years putting me through college, looked at what I was holding, then gently took it out of my hand.

I was already an associate at *David, David, and Jennings*, one of the best law firms in town. But I still had to pass the bar, and the results of that bar exam were inside the envelope. Three weeks ago I had walked out of the exam convinced I had passed, but with every day since I became less and less sure, to the point where I could hardly sleep I was worrying about it so much.

I couldn't watch as Debbie quickly opened the letter.

Then, in the loudest release of breath I had ever heard, she handed me the letter and then hugged me, smiling and crying at the same time.

I glanced at the letter. I had passed.

"Oh, thank God!" I said.

"You did it," Debbie said.

I looked her right in the eye and shook my head. "We did it."
All both of us could do after that was just smile.

My Fourth Whoop

My secretary knew what I liked. We'd been having an affair for almost a year, and she said that she had something very special for me for Christmas this year.

Debbie and I had had two kids, a boy named Ben and a daughter named Karen. With Debbie focusing on the kids and me focusing on building my law practice, we sort of drifted apart. At some point a few years back we just sort of stopped making love, one or the other of us seeming to always be too busy. We talked about it once in a while, but never really acted on the talk.

We also fought a lot, especially right after the kids were born. It seemed I never knew when I went home if Debbie was going to be angry or not.

I don't think Debbie knew I was having an affair with my secretary, Heather, and I never wanted her to find out. She had developed a real temper over the years, and I sure didn't want her letting that temper lose on me for something as major as an affair. It was bad enough on the small stuff with the kids and the house and money.

Heather knew I was never going to leave Debbie, and she didn't much care. She was open sexually and had no thoughts at all of wanting me as a husband.

"So what's this surprise you've been talking about?" I asked Heather as I came back into my office after my last meeting. It was a little after six in the evening three days before Christmas, and Debbie didn't expect me home for at least another few hours.

Heather beamed at me, her twenty-something smile lighting up the room. She had long blonde hair, even longer legs, and a body that looked far too good in a lace bra and underwear.

"This way," she said, motioning me with a finger.

She had that sexy look on her face and I knew I was in for something fun.

She led me into my darkened office, and then before I could turn on the light, she put her hand on mine and said, "Not yet. I'll tell you when."

She closed the door and turned the lock, sending the room into almost complete blackness, since the blinds were down on the window and it was a dark night outside.

I could hear a faint rustling in the dark. Then Heather said, "Go ahead."

I snapped on the light. The sight that greeted me was something I could have only dreamed about. Heather and another young woman were both sitting on the edge of my desk. Both were wearing only lace under-wear. The sight took my breath away, so it was a moment before I finally said, "Wow!"

Heather smiled at me. "This is Heidi, a friend of mine. She's going to help me give you a very special Christmas present."

Two and a half hours later I finally managed to stagger to my car. Never, in all my life, had a Christmas been like this one.

My Fifth and Final
Whoop

I was just over an hour late getting home after my special present from Heidi and her friend. I expected to find Debbie sitting in her favorite chair, watching television, wrapped in her blue bathrobe, more than likely angry at me. But instead, when I opened the door, I was greeted with the wonderful smell of baking cookies.

I took off my coat and dropped my briefcase on the hall table, then headed for the kitchen. I had skipped dinner because of Heather's little surprise, so the smell of the cookies was almost more than my rumbling stomach could handle.

When I went through the kitchen door, I got a sight that not in a million years would I have expected to see. Debbie was leaning over the stove in her white lace bra and underwear, taking out a fresh batch of cookies.

Until that moment I hadn't realized just how attractive she still was. Even after having two children, she had kept herself fit.

"Wow!" I said, for the second time in the same night.

She looked up at me and smiled. "Welcome home. I thought I'd give you a little surprise."

I glanced around, then back at her. "Where are the kids?"

"At my mothers for the night," Debbie said, smiling her old sexy smile. "So we're all alone."

She put the hot batch of cookies on the stovetop, closed the oven, and moved over to a plate of cookies already frosted. "I bet you're hungry," she said, offering the plate to me.

"I am," I said, taking two cookies. "And these smell wonderful. And you look wonderful."

I almost swallowed the first cookie whole, it tasted so good.

"I do, don't I?" she asked, turning around so that I could see her from all sides.

"You do," I agreed between bites of the second cookie. "Really good."

"As good as Heather and her friend Heidi?"

I froze in mid-bite, staring at her smile.

She laughed, twirling around to give me another look. "I'm surprised you would even be interested after what those two young things put you through in your office."

I had no idea what was happening, how she knew about Heather and what had happened in my office, or how she was even going to react. So being a good attorney and a fearful husband, I ventured nothing, and said nothing.

She leaned against the counter across the kitchen from me, that damned white lace bra of hers making her look very sexy. "Surprised, huh?"

I nodded slightly and she laughed.

It was getting damned hot in that kitchen at that moment. Too hot.

"Didn't you know I would find out what you were doing? Hell, I went to take you dinner to talk about things and even got a little show tonight."

Damn, she had a key to my office. I had made her one years ago.

"So I thought I'd just come home and give you a little show of my own."

I could feel my heart racing, my blood pounding through my head. I couldn't seem to think straight.

I tried to say something, but the words didn't want to come out.

"Oh, good," Debbie said, laughing and coming toward me, "the poison is working."

I wanted to say, "Cookies?" but again nothing came out.

The next instant, instead of staring at Debbie's white bra, I was watching the tile Debbie and I had picked out specially for the kitchen come rushing up at my face.

I woke up six hours later in the hospital. A woman who looked like a doctor was standing over me, frowning.

"Poison," I managed to croak out.

"We know," she said, nodding and staring at some instrument beside me. Then she patted my arm. "Just rest."

I must have rested, because the next thing I remembered was waking up to the blinding light from the window, my head pounding so hard I thought it might explode.

Debbie was already in jail. She served a total of six years in prison for trying to kill me.

I lost my position in the firm and had to hang out my own shingle because it came out in court what Heather and I were doing that caused Debbie to snap.

The kids lived with me, with my parents helping out, and visited their mother every other Sunday while she was in jail, and every other week after she got out and got a job. I never did make as much money as I had been making at the firm, but I did all right for myself over the years. And never once hired a secretary.

I never remarried either. Couldn't see much point in it.

I was thirty-two when Debbie poisoned me with that cookie. Now I'm seventy-two, no longer practice law, and have three wonderful grand-kids. But in all those years, I never had another whoopee moment.

I guess I should be happy to have a five-whoopee life.

From what I understand, some people never even have one.

I feel sad for them.

A Bad Day
for the Dream
A Cold Poker Gang Story

Dean Wesley Smith

PROLOGUE

March 3rd, 1990
Las Vegas, Nevada

Becky Penn tied her long brown hair back away from her face and laughed as her mom stood in their bathroom door, arms crossed over her chest, the worried look that Becky saw so much from her.

Her mom had raised her since their father had left when Becky was three. The two of them were more like sisters at times and Becky loved that.

Becky was dressed in a light skirt, a new blouse she had just bought, and had on sandals, since the weather was already starting to warm up.

Becky's mom had already changed from her nursing scrubs into a light sweatshirt and jeans. She seldom wore shoes around the house and tonight was no exception.

"It's all right, mom," Becky said, smiling as she finished up and turned from the mirror. "Paul and I are just headed to a party just off the strip. I'm going to meet him there."

"I wish you wouldn't," her mom said, shaking her head.

"I know, I know," Becky said. "You don't like him."

"I'm not sure why you do," her mom said.

Becky laughed. Paul was a good guy who worked hard. And he was a very gentle soul. Becky liked that about him.

Becky kissed her mother lightly on the cheek as she went past and out into the hallway toward the front door. "You worry too much."

"Sometimes I wish you worried more," her mom said.

Then both of them laughed. That exchange had happened for every date Becky had ever gone on from a freshman in high school and all the way through four years at UNLV. It made them both feel better.

"Don't wait up," Becky said.

A minute later she was in her red two-door Toyota and headed out toward the Strip.

It was the last time anyone saw her. She just simply vanished.

And just like so many other missing persons, after no leads came up, her case went cold.

Thirty years cold.

ONE

April 10th, 2020
Las Vegas, Nevada

Retired detective Bayard Lott ran a hand through his short white hair and sighed. They weren't supposed to find a body. Lott hated every time they did that. It was never the way they wanted to close missing person's cases. But more often than not, it was exactly how they closed them.

"Looks like we found Becky," Retired Detective Julia Rogers said.

Julia stood beside Lott staring down at the skeleton that was slowly emerging from the desert sand and dirt where it had been buried for almost thirty years, as far as they could tell.

Julia had on a light white blouse and a sports bra under it. She wore jeans and tennis shoes and a wide-brimmed white golf hat to keep the sun off her face.

Lott had on a short-sleeved dress shirt, jeans, tennis shoes and a wide-brimmed Panama hat. They had expected to spend time in the sun in the desert to the north of Las Vegas, so they were both also smeared with sunscreen that smelled like they belonged on a beach instead of out in the desert.

They might have looked silly and smelled funny, but he was in his mid-sixties and Julia in her late fifties and they were smart enough to take no chances. At their age, too much sun did not do well on either of them.

The open grave in front of them was being carefully worked by a couple of Las Vegas police's best forensic lab people. They were in white suits that had to be hot in the morning April sun in the desert. And they were being very careful to brush away sand and then shovel it into containers to be sifted.

Lott could visualize the wonderful college graduation picture of Becky Penn. She had been a beautiful woman with a promising future. She vanished on March 3rd, 1990, on her way to a party to meet her boyfriend.

It was her boyfriend, Paul Vaughan, that had reported to Becky's mother three hours after they were supposed to meet that Becky had not shown up. He had called concerned that Becky had been sick or something.

Her mother filed a missing person's report.

Nothing had ever come of it. The detective assigned to the case did some fine interviews, found nothing.

Two months ago, Retired Detective Andor Williams brought the thin file on Becky Penn's case to the weekly meeting of the Cold Poker Gang.

Lott loved the weekly sessions in his card room in his house. Retired detectives got together, played poker, and talked about cold cases. Then during the week between games, they worked the cold cases.

The Las Vegas Chief of Police had given the Cold Poker Gang special status to carry badges and guns because they had solved so many cold cases and wanted no credit for any of it.

For the retired detectives, it was just the sense of feeling valued that mattered and continuing at their own pace, without paperwork, the job they had loved for decades.

When Julia joined the group, she had retired from Reno because of a shattered bone in her leg where she had been shot. For almost two years, she was the only woman in the gang until six months ago two of Las Vegas's best women detectives had retired. Both had taken a month vacation and then joined the group.

Now the Cold Poker Gang often had seven or eight people at the table on a Tuesday night. There were eleven official members and every detective on the force liked helping them.

At any given moment, the gang might have eight or nine cold cases they were working in some fashion or another.

"Let's sit in the car for awhile," Julia said, turning from the grave.

Lott agreed to that idea. The sun was getting warmer by the minute and there was absolutely nothing they could do to help in that shallow hole. Getting Becky Penn's remains out of that hole would take time and painstaking work. Lott was just glad he wasn't doing the work, especially in one of those white suits they wore these days.

Lott got his white Cadillac SUV started and the air-conditioning running as Julia dug them both out a cold bottle of water from the ice chest sitting on the back seat.

Then they just sat in silence for a moment, cooling down and watching the two men in the shallow hole work.

Lott was always surprised at how wonderful cold water tasted after being out in the Nevada sun for a while.

"I can't believe we found her," Julia said after a moment.

"We're still not one hundred percent it is her," Lott said.

And they weren't, but that was just a technical issue now. They had figured out where she was buried exactly from notes in a journal left by her boyfriend, Paul Vaughan, when he killed himself twenty years ago.

From what they could tell when they got the journal, still stored with Paul's things by his sister, he and Becky had gotten into a fight and he had killed her.

The journal went on to give exact directions to where he had buried her and then what he had done to cover his crime.

Lott had found the writing creepy. Impassionate while being angry. Paul blamed Becky's death on her, taking no responsibility at all.

Lott had been upset that the guy was dead. But if he hadn't been dead, there was no telling if they ever would have solved Becky's cold case. They were lucky in a couple of ways. That he was dead and that his sister had just stored what few things he owned in boxes in her basement.

But something felt off to both Julia and Lott. And Lott couldn't put his finger on it at all. First, they had no idea why a killer like Paul would write down what he had done, then give exact directions to the grave.

And his sister had told them that Paul hated to write anything, let alone in a journal.

But it seemed, at least on the surface, that Paul had started the journal when he and Becky started dating and they had confirmed with Becky's mother some of the dates and times in the journal as best as she could remember.

So it all seemed real enough.

The second thing that seemed off was no one knew what had happened to Becky's red Toyota. The car had simply vanished and Paul made no mention of it in his strange journal. And he should have. Getting rid of that car had to be a lot harder than burying her in the desert.

Something was off on all of this, but darned if Lott could figure out what was bothering him about it all.

Then, in front of them, one of the two men in white suits working in the shallow grave stood up, turned and waved for Lott and Julia to come over.

Then both men climbed out of the shallow grave and one headed for their vehicle, pulling off his white suit as he went.

"Something went wrong," Julia said as both she and Lott climbed out of the car.

The other man who had waved them over had pulled off the top of his white suit as well and was working on a bottle of water. His face was covered in sweat.

"What did you find?" Lott asked.

The guy just pointed for them to look into the grave and kept drinking.

It took a moment for Lott to see it, but then he did.

Nowhere in any report did it say that Becky had three arms.

"There's another body with her," Julia said softly.

"Shit," Lott said. "Just shit."

TWO

April 12th, 2020
Las Vegas, Nevada

Lott set the bucket of Kentucky Fried Chicken on his kitchen table while Julia pulled out three bottles of water from the fridge. Andor had just parked outside in the driveway and was going to join them for lunch.

The smell of the chicken filled Lott's remodeled kitchen. In the remodel two years ago, he had put in the best counters, all new cabinets and flooring, and new appliances. But the floor plan of the kitchen was exactly as it had been when he and his wife had lived here.

His wife of thirty years had died of cancer almost five years before and it wasn't until Julia walked into his life that he could ever imagine enjoying the company of another woman. But now he did.

So now he and Julia and Andor, Lott's former partner back on the force before they both had retired to take care of sick wives, formed a team.

And outside of the nights with the Cold Poker Gang playing cards, the three of them often met over KFC in Lott's kitchen to talk over cases.

But Lott had a hunch today wasn't going to be much of a good lunch, no matter how wonderful the bucket of KFC smelled. The topic was Becky Penn's case.

Lott spread around three paper plates and Julia got some forks for pulling the hot chicken apart and some spoons for the sides that came with the bucket. They didn't often eat much of the sides. All three of them just loved the fresh chicken.

Lott came in the back door, his solid frame and balding head moving like a bull. He had a cold towel around his neck and was sweating.

Julia handed him a fresh towel to wipe off his face and head and neck, then she sat next to Lott at the table.

Andor dropped some files at the back of the table and all three of them dug into the chicken.

Finally, after pretty much demolishing his first piece and starting on a second, Lott couldn't take it any longer.

He looked at Andor. "Well, was one of them Becky Penn?"

When the other body was found in Becky's grave, the case had reverted back to the regular younger detectives. By the end of the day, the techs doing the digging had found a total of four bodies in that grave, all stacked on one another with a very thin layer of dirt between them.

From what Lott had heard, they were now doing ground radar sweeps around the grave to see if others were buried close by.

Paul Vaughan's journal had led them to the location, but he had said nothing about killing and burying other women.

Andor nodded, wiping chicken grease off his mouth with a paper towel. "It was Becky on top," Andor said. "Confirmed by remnants of what she was wearing, hair color, and the remains of her ID buried with her. They will run some DNA tests, but no one is doubting it is her."

"And the other three?" Julia asked.

"They don't have a clue," Andor said. "But they are treating all three as live murder cases at the moment."

"Three?" Lott asked.

Again Andor nodded. "They are closing Becky's case. Seems we solved another cold case."

Lott glanced at Julia who was shaking her head. He felt the same way. Becky's case was far, far from closed.

Andor just looked at them. "We're out of this one for now. You both know that, don't you?"

Lott knew they were. As long as the younger detectives considered the three other bodies open and live murder cases, there was nothing anyone retired in the Cold Poker Gang could do.

And actually, by doing anything, they might jeopardize the entire existence of the Cold Poker Gang.

They worked cold cases. Period.

That was the firm rule the Chief of Police had put on them.

Becky's case was officially closed and the other three were live murder cases.

The Cold Poker Gang was done with them.

Julia was nodding, and not looking happy.

Lott just sat there, not even interested in another piece of cold chicken.

"This day just sucks," Lott said.

"Yeah, it does," Andor said. "But we have to give the hotshot young detectives a crack at this first. Remember, we were young once as well."

"Speak for yourself," Julia said. "I'm still young, thank you very much."

Lott and Andor both laughed.

Julia smiled. "Not sure how I should take that laughing."

"Oh, oh," Andor said, winking at Lott.

"So what are the files?" Julia asked, indicating the folding files that Andor had at the top of the table.

"I brought them for storage here," he said, starting into another piece of chicken.

Lott laughed at that. He knew what they were without even asking. After the decades of the two of them working together, Lott knew how his partner thought.

Lott had Julia hand them to him and then without looking at their contents, he stood and put them in an empty cabinet above the fridge.

Storage.

"All four files for the bodies in the grave?" Julia asked, starting to catch on.

Andor nodded. "I'll get more from downtown and update them as the young hotshots find information."

Lott laughed and sat down and took another piece of chicken.

"And if they solve the cases?" Julia asked.

Lott laughed. "If they solve them like they think we solved Becky's murder, then we go to work on all four of the cases."

"And if they don't solve them, then we go to work on the cases," Andor said, smiling. "But that's going to be years down the road I'm afraid."

Lott nodded. "So the day officially sucks. We are officially fired from these cases."

"We move on," Julia said, nodding and taking another piece of chicken.

"We move on," Andor said, wiping chicken juice from his face again.

"There are no shortages of cold cases for us to solve," Julia said.

"Amen to that," Andor said.

Lott knew that was the truth. But he just hated failing, hated having a case taken from him, hated everything about this.

The Cold Poker Gang hadn't really solved a cold case. They had just found more murders that, more than likely, would turn into cold cases in a year or two.

Lott knew that all three of them hated failing. They didn't volunteer their time in their retirement to fail.

But sometimes it happened. Sometimes even the Cold Poker Gang failed.

Or, as they say in poker, you can't win every hand, even on good nights.

But down the road, way down the road, they just might get to play this hand again.

Mated From The Morgue

A Fun Romance of Near Death

Dean Wesley Smith as
Dee W. Schofield

ONE

I'm on one damn cold metal table, bright lights shining on my naked body, my brand new, enhanced breasts aiming at the ceiling tile of this stupid hospital morgue like they were supposed to. And what do I feel? Annoyed. Just annoyed. Not cold, not embarrassed, just annoyed.

And just a little scared.

Panic?

Sure. That was in the mix as well.

I'm about to be very, very dead if someone doesn't catch a clue real quick that I am still inside this stupid body of mine and very much alive, even though it doesn't look like I am.

Some pimply-faced kid set up a tray of sharp knives and bone spreaders beside my table, looked at my breasts, then my crotch, and left.

This felt like sitting in a dentist's chair getting ready for the dentist to use all his nasty-looking instruments. Only, that tray of stuff was sitting there just waiting for some lowlife mortician to come in and cut me open like a stupid trout.

While I'm still alive and can feel it! Okay, maybe panic was a little closer to the surface than I thought.

Can't any of the idiots out there see that I'm still alive, that some blood was pumping? Otherwise, how could I be lying here on this damn cold metal table thinking that if I ever did get out of this, I was going to kill someone.

Anyone.

From across the embalming room I heard a door open. I sure as hell wanted to turn my head and smile at the person just to give them a shock. I tried.

Nothing.

Not even a muscle twitch.

Suddenly, a hunk of a good-looking guy in a rubber apron and a hairnet appeared over me like an angel. He had flashing dark eyes, longish, dark brown hair under the net, and a smile that just wouldn't stop.

And he was looking right in to my eyes.

"You are far too good-looking to be here on this table," he said.

I tried to shout, *No Shit, Sherlock!*

My mouth wouldn't move. Not even a grunt came out.

He walked slowly down along the table, clearly taking in all my naked assets.

Now I was starting to feel embarrassed. This was not really the way I wanted a hunk of a guy to see me. He looked at the toe tag on my foot, then came back up and checked off something on a clipboard.

"Debbie," he said, smiling at me again. "My name is Mathew. I'm here to try to find out why you just keeled over dead in your tuna salad."

I'm not dead! I tried to scream.

Nothing.

I was facing a young hunk of a doctor who talked to the bodies. Even with that bad habit, I still wanted to jump his bones.

I wanted to jump anything, actually. Getting cut open on a morgue table was not my idea of a good way to leave the planet.

How the hell did I end up here?

And what the hell was a guy like him doing here? He could be modeling for a men's magazine in sweaters with golf clubs in his hands. Instead he was cutting open dead people.

And more than likely a not-so-dead one in just a moment.

I had two degrees in business and ran my own company. He clearly had a medical license of some sort to call himself a doctor. He couldn't be dumb. Maybe, just maybe, he might figure this all out. The idiots in the ambulance and the bitch doctor in the emergency room sure hadn't.

Having yourself declared dead while you are listening is just not a good time. If I got out of here, I was going to need counseling for years.

The door to the room opened again, and Doctor Mathew turned those wonderful, dark eyes away from me.

"I won't need you anymore today, Jim," he said.

His voice sort of echoed, so the room had to be fairly large. More than likely he was talking to the kid with the face-full of pimples, but I couldn't see the kid.

Doctor Mathew disappeared from my limited sight, and I heard the kid mumble something, then the door closed.

And then there was the sound of a lock turning.

Oh, shit!

This might turn even more ugly than it was. I just went from a horror sit-com to a full-out horror movie.

Two

Now the panic was starting to swell up. I had seen far too many movies where the good-looking doctor was some sort of perv.

My brain told me I wanted to swallow and then scream for help, but none of that was happening.

In horror movies, they always made the poor victim unable to move as well.

The hunk of a man appeared above me again, smiling. At least he was a good-looking monster.

"We're all alone now, Debbie. Just you and me. Maybe we could call this a date. You would be the first date I've had in a year. Since my wife died."

Oh, shit! Oh, shit! I was doomed. I just hoped I didn't remind the guy of his dead wife.

"You remind me a little of Marcie," he said, smiling and checking out my scalp with very tender fingers and a light touch.

Oh, shit! Oh, Shit! Oh, Shit!

"But she was shorter and had green eyes," he said, "instead of pretty blue ones like yours. She also wanted to have breast enhancements like yours, but was killed in a car crash before she got the chance. Life is so short. Clearly it was for you as well."

He kept working over my scalp, very carefully, like a lost hairdresser trying to pad her bill and find her way to the door by Braille.

"I'm afraid I won't be a very good date," he said, smiling at me and looking right into my eyes. "I just don't think it's been long enough for me since my Marcie left."

He laughed in a strained way and shook his head.

Wasn't it bad enough that I was on a morgue table, thought to be dead, and now some guy was going to get his jollies on my naked body?

"But don't worry," he said as he smiled down at me. "I have always been a complete gentleman on a first date."

I'd believe that if I wasn't as naked as the day I came into this stupid world. Except for the toe tag.

He started to check out my neck with those wonderful hands of his, then he stepped back, a frown on his face. "Your skin is still warm to the touch."

Could he be figuring this out?

He stepped away and I could no longer see him. From what I could tell he was flipping through some sort of paperwork.

"It's been three hours since you collapsed," he said, clearly still talking to me. "Two hours since you were declared dead. And you've been down here on this table for over an hour now. That's just weird."

I should be as cold as a rock. Right? Come on, Doc! Figure it out.

Next I could hear him rummaging through a drawer, and a moment later he was back, a stethoscope around his neck and a small device in one hand.

He held the device in my ear for a moment, then looked at it.

"Weird," he said. "Just weird." He looked into my eyes again. "You are as strange as you are beautiful."

If I could have even blushed I would have right at that moment. Maybe I did, just a little. I couldn't tell.

He put one hand on my chest, right on my brand new, specially-enhanced left breast, and leaned forward, not noticing at all what he was touching. I was still just dead meat to him, like I had been to my first husband for two years of that disaster laughingly called a marriage.

With his other hand he held the cold stethoscope to my chest.

For a moment he listened, then he moved the stethoscope to a location just under my enhancement and held it there. His eyes were distant, intense, as he tried to listen.

I'm in here, Doc! I wanted to shout.

After a moment he pushed down fairly hard on my chest with one hand while listening.

And then he pushed again, right on my breast.

Gentleman, hell!

But I knew he had no real idea what part of my body he was touching and pushing on. And that was damn fine with me. I wanted out of this nightmare – then he could push on my new breasts as much as he wanted. In a nice soft bed at his place or mine.

Suddenly he jumped back as if I had shocked him.

My new breasts were good, but not that good.

THREE

"Not possible!" he said.

Then he was back at my chest, leaning over, breathing gently into my chin as he leaned way down and almost put his ear against my chest with the stethoscope pressed in hard.

He listened and listened and then suddenly jumped back again, knocking over the tray of instruments.

"Oh, hell, Debbie, are you still in there?"

If I could have moved I would have jumped up and kissed him.

Suddenly, he vanished out of my vision and I could hear him grab a phone. He called in some sort of code and unlocked the door. Then he was back at my side, staring into my eyes.

"Hang on, Debbie. Help is on the way."

He took my hand and squeezed it gently.

I just stared into those wonderful dark eyes of his and said nothing. Not like me, but I had no choice.

It was still a very, very nice moment.

What seemed like only a few seconds later the door exploded open and help arrived.

Six of them, including Doctor Mathew, moved me onto a stretcher, put an oxygen mask over my nose and mouth, covered me with a sheet, and banged me out of the room so fast I thought I was on a ride in an amusement park.

Doctor Mathew never left my side as he and two other doctors talked all the way down the hall and up an elevator, clearly headed into more tests than I wanted to think about. I had no idea what they were talking about, but to be honest, it all sounded wonderful. A ton better than having someone declare you dead when you were really just fine.

For the moment my nightmare in the morgue was over. Now if I died, it wouldn't be because I was sliced and diced. It would be with real doctors trying to save me.

They arrived in a place with dozens of people swarming around all seeming to talk at the same time. They hooked me up to a dozen monitors and confirmed I still had a very, very slowly beating heart.

And that my brain was still working.

I knew that, but it sure felt better to have some doctor say that.

"Oh, wow," I heard Doctor Mathew say as someone else announced the test results. "I could have killed her on that table."

Some other male doctor said, "But you didn't. Nice work, doctor."

So after what seemed like only a moment since they shoved me out of the morgue, Doctor Mathew leaned in over me again and smiled.

His smile got more wonderful every time I saw it. And those dark eyes of his could melt an iceberg.

I was almost dead and still in lust. How sad was that? It had clearly been too long since I had been laid.

"Hang in there, Debbie. We're going to put you under while we do more tests and figure out just what is happening to you. But don't worry, I'll be right here when you wake up."

Then he gently reached forward and closed my eyelids.

"Sleep well."

He could do that to me for years if he wanted to.

And that was the last thing I remembered as that little cloud of blackness sort of came in from all sides.

FOUR

And then the blackness pushed back.

Weird. It seemed I didn't want to be knocked out.

Or all of that had been some horrible nightmare.

Around me, I could hear the beeping of machines; and in the background, the sounds of a people talking.

And a television was on, softly going over some sort of news.

I blinked and opened my eyes to the lights of the room.

I was in a very different room than the one the tests had been in. And CNN was on the television. I had a light oxygen mask on my nose.

And holy crap, I had moved my eyelids!

I tried a finger and could feel it move as well.

And then an arm.

And then a leg.

Everything moved!

And I could feel I had a tube stuck in my arm.

And my chest hurt something awful.

And I was beyond thirsty.

"Water?" I tried to say, and I actually think what I managed to croak out sounded like a word.

Instantly Doctor Mathew was standing over me, smiling. He had been sitting beside my bed watching television.

"Glad to have you back, Debbie," he said, again giving me that wonderful smile of his.

He eased a tiny ice cube toward my lips and managed to help me get it in my mouth.

"Just let that melt for a moment."

In all my life, an ice cube had never tasted or felt as good.

Doctor Mathew smiled as I worked the tiny ice chip over like it was a seven-course meal.

"My name is Doctor Mathew Stevens," he said. "I have no idea how much you remember, but you were declared dead."

I nodded slightly, and indicated he should come closer. He leaned in and I somehow managed to whisper. "A weird first date, Mathew. Thank you for saving me."

He leaned back, smiling and blushing, realizing I had heard every word he had said in the morgue. Somehow, with that handsome face of his bright red, he managed to recover a little and go on.

"We had to remove your breast implants," he said. "You had an allergy to them that just shut you down. It would have killed you completely in another few hours. Don't worry, you can get the implants replaced with a different type later."

At that moment I didn't care. Who knew having large breasts could kill a woman? My original, factory-issued breasts weren't that bad in the first place. Dumb idea by me to think they might help me with men.

I just nodded to Mathew, so he went on.

"You've been out for about five days," he said, "in a drug-induced coma so the toxins could clear your system completely. You should be up and around in a few days and feeling back to normal in a week."

He leaned in and gave me another piece of ice, which again felt wonderful.

I sure liked having him close.

"Thank you for saving me," I said again, my voice gaining strength.

"That's what we try to do," he said, nodding and blushing a little again. "You are welcome."

A bashful doctor. Who knew there was such a thing?

I smiled at him.

"You have a beautiful smile," he said. "Glad I could see it."

"So am I," I said.

Then I smiled again. "I understand about your wife, at least what little you told me. But if you are willing to give it a try and are ready, I would be up for a second date. The first one turned out so well."

He stood there just staring at me, then, after a long few seconds, he finally laughed.

"Honestly," I said, "I don't expect you to save my life every date."

"That's good," he said, shaking his head and laughing. "I would love to try a second date. Especially since that was a first date I could never imagine happening. I normally don't date patients."

"Why?" I asked, smiling so hard I was going to knock the small oxygen mask off my nose.

"Because I'm a forensic pathologist," he said. "I only deal with the dead."

"Thanks to you," I said, "I am far from dead."

"Good. Because I only really date the living."

I just sat there smiling, trying not to laugh because my chest hurt too much. It seemed that those larger breasts really had helped me get a man.

I Killed the
Clockwork Key

A Bryant Street Story

Dean Wesley Smith

I Killed the
Clockwork Key

The early morning on Bryant Street seemed like any other early spring-morning day in a subdivision that looked like most other middle-class subdivisions in America. Young trees, well-kept green lawns watered by automatic sprinkler systems, clean sidewalks, and a dozen for-sale signs every two blocks.

Half the houses along Bryant Street were bank-owned, and most of the other half had huge mortgages that would never be paid off and would soon also become bank owned.

Barb's and my place was no exception. The Bryant Street subdivision was a small, but beautiful subdivision that might as well be a ghost town.

And I was one of the only remaining ghosts. A ghost of past times on Bryant Street just as any ghost was from a past where life had once existed, but had been killed in a brutal and ugly fashion.

Tuesday had arrived. Monday was finished. The week stretched ahead of me like a dull highway across a flat desert. Or at least I thought it did, until I killed the Clockwork Key, the thing inside of me that wound me up and kept me moving along the same path, in the same circle day after day after day.

We all have Clockwork Keys, but most of us never notice we have them or seem to care.

When I killed my Clockwork Key, I was halfway to my sixty-three-payments-left black Lexus. All normal, until Barb came out of the front door.

"Ram!" she shouted.

She called me Ram because of my days playing football in college where we met. It had been my nickname and she still called me that, even though my real name and the one I liked was Raymond. To her calling me Ram reminded her of better times, better nights of sex and lots of drinking and laughing and throwing parties where kids threw up in garbage cans and behind hedges and called it the "good old days."

I turned, not really caring what she had to say. We had gone through the morning routine. I had kissed her at the door, she had said she thought she was going to have better luck today finding a job. I had told her I thought she would as well.

All simple morning lies to keep us walking along in our circles and not thinking about anything in our life or how we would eventually have to leave Bryant Street and her dream house that we had paid far, far too much to build back when "times were better" as people said.

I'm not sure I remember those times, but people do tell me they existed.

"You forgot your briefcase!" Barb shouted, as if I couldn't hear her in the complete silence of the early morning in a mostly empty subdivision. I was usually the first out of the subdivision these days of the few people that actually left, since I was one of the few on the street who actually pretended to still have a job.

She held up the black briefcase and instead of coming down the side-walk to bring it to me, she just stood there, waiting for me to come back to her to get it.

And I just stood there waiting for her to bring it to me.

We had a marriage standoff.

Barb and I had had many such standoffs over the years.

But back in the "good old days" or when "times were better," I usually was the one to break the marriage standoff. Now I couldn't care.

I had walked down the sidewalk, I had done my bit to keep the morning moving, to stay in my routine, to continue to pay for the house and the cars and the food for as long as I could, even though we were within six months of being out of money.

She had done her bit to cook the breakfast and to make small talk and to pretend she was preparing to go looking for a job even though we both knew there were no jobs to be had and she would never leave the house or get out of her bathrobe.

We had both played our parts perfectly, just as we did every morning.

Now, standing there on that wide sidewalk with the carefully manicured edges so that the grass wouldn't touch the pavement, neither Barb nor I knew what to do.

We did not know, in our perfectly ordered world, who had the responsibility for the briefcase.

A marriage standoff.

Sure, the black briefcase was supposed to have my job paperwork in it, paperwork I brought home to work on every night, but never did, because I hadn't had a job for over a year.

And in a year of looking, I had found nothing.

And had never told Barb I had lost my job. It just hadn't been worth the problems telling her would have caused me every day. We had long before stopped acting as partners.

And the last thing I had wanted to do was stay in the house with her all day long. I felt bad enough about losing my job and not finding a new one. I didn't need that kind of punishment as well.

My former job was nothing more than crunching numbers to determine who would be laid off next. I assigned numbers, calculations, statistics to people, real people, and then gave those special living numbers to my boss who pretended to check them and then give them to his boss and so on up the corporate ladder until someone decided to act.

Because of my numbers, a certain person or numbers of people each week had been laid off to keep the company profitable (on paper) for the shareholders who continued to send the stock higher and higher making everyone happy who owned the stock.

At first I had felt remorse for the people that my calculations had caused to lose their job. But then, after a few years of doing the same thing every day, every week, I no longer cared about the faces and the lives destroyed behind those simple numbers.

And then one day I had become a number as well. Someone above me had figured the numbers for me and I had been laid off.

Now in our marriage standoff, Barb, once a good-looking woman with brown hair and good teeth, stood there in her blue bathrobe and blue matching slippers on the brown welcome mat in front of our brown and tan home, smiling and holding the worthless lie of a briefcase that contained nothing of value in it.

My life had become nothing of value, either.

It seemed logical I should carry a briefcase that carried nothing.

I stared at her and she smiled at me, holding the briefcase.

And I smiled back and made no movement toward her.

The morning sun felt warm against my back, and I realized that in all the years of mornings I had walked from the house to the car I had never noticed any feeling about anything.

Now I felt warmth.

And the smell of the freshly mowed grass suddenly caught my attention.

And the sounds of birds chirping in the young trees almost distracted me from staring at Barb.

Slowly, her smile faded.

"Ram, don't you need your briefcase?"

I turned my back to her and looked around at the neighborhood.

It was a perfect neighborhood, a perfect, Hollywood-version of a neighborhood, as if some screenwriter had written in a few words at the beginning of a script, "Standard Subdivision: Well-kept and manicured."

I had not really, really stopped and looked at Bryant Street and the homes along the street for a long time. And now that I had stopped, thanks to the marriage standoff, I could actually see what I had missed.

The paint on a few of the empty homes was starting to show weathering. The shrubs on a few homes hadn't been trimmed in years and had grown too large for the yards.

Windows on two of the closest bank-owned homes were dirty, and the drapes in one window were torn and looked faded.

And as I watched, a woman's face appeared beside the torn curtain, staring at me with sunken eyes and hair that looked like it hadn't been combed in weeks.

A ghost of a former resident, maybe.

I recognized her after a moment. DeAnna Sterling. Or what was left of DeAnna Sterling. She used to be a large, almost obese woman. Now she looked more like a model for a bad fashion designer.

Her husband, Dan had been laid off two years ago and the bank had foreclosed on their home over a year ago.

That home had been DeAnna's dream home, and she and Barb used to be best friends.

I had a vague memory of Barb telling me DeAnna had had a breakdown and had refused to leave her home.

Now I understood why our grocery bill had grown higher. Barb did the shopping, telling me about the inflation. The inflation was that we were feeding DeAnna.

I looked down the street. I wondered how many other ghosts were in these empty buildings and what they did when I was working.

DeAnna ducked back into the darkness of her home.

I turned back to face Barb who had that "worried look" I knew so well on her face. She had not expected a marriage stand-off either this fine morning. More than likely she was missing her morning program and her second cup of coffee, and that was not right.

Or more likely she was worried that I had seen DeAnna.

I stared at my home. I had somehow managed to continue making payments on this "perfect" home. I had started to do the yard work myself when I could no longer afford a gardener, and I drained most of the remains of my estate from my parents to keep walking this routine.

To keep pretending that I was living a life I wanted to live.

I was nothing more than calculations and statistics and numbers as well. My entire life consisted of walking the same routine, doing the same thing, trying to find a job that didn't exist to pay bills I didn't want to pay so that I could keep doing the same thing again and again and again.

And now, because of a briefcase and a marriage standoff, I could see clearly for the first time what I had been doing.

I had broken the cycle.

I had broken my Clockwork Key.

I reached up and undid my tie because I was getting warm standing there on the sidewalk in my black suit.

Barb's "worry look" switched to her "puzzlement look" mixed with her "slight-panic look." I knew all her expressions. I knew how she thought at every moment of every day.

I dropped my tie on the grass I had mowed yesterday after I had gotten home from my pretend job.

"You keep the briefcase," I said to Barb.

"Ram!" she shouted, her voice rising to the level I hated, the level that made her sound like a record had spun up just a little too fast while she spoke. "What are you doing?"

"You keep it all," I said, waving at the home I had come to hate and the neighborhood I had never really looked at in years.

"Ram? What's wrong?"

She had still not moved off the porch, and was now clutching my briefcase against her chest as a symbol of the life she didn't want to lose. An empty briefcase that meant far more to her than I ever did.

"Nothing's wrong," I said, smiling at her. "I've got to go. You keep it. You keep it all. You win."

With that I turned and walked the short distance to my car and got in.

She still stood there in front of the worthless home, in her blue bathrobe with perfectly matching blue slippers, my empty briefcase clutched against her chest.

I still had enough savings left to get a divorce, give her the house in the settlement, pay off my car, get a nice, cheap apartment in some other town where there were still a few jobs to be had, and maybe eat for a year or more.

After all, I was a numbers man and I knew the numbers. I had lived those numbers for years now, walking in clock-like service to a life I did not want with a woman I had grown to hate.

I pulled out of the driveway and stopped in the middle of Bryant Street, giving it one more look.

Barb clutched my briefcase, staring at me.

I smiled at her, a real smile for the first time in years. Not a pretend smile, but a smile I actually felt.

I waved at her. Then, with my hand solidly planted on the horn, I drove down Bryant Street for one last time, letting the loud sound of my leaving echo off the ghost-like remains of my former life.

HALF A CLUE

A COLD POKER GANG SHORT STORY

DEAN WESLEY SMITH

PROLOGUE

October 21st, 2005

Vicki Dix spent the twenty-minute drive from her office near the university to her new home north of Las Vegas listening to a talk show about the new Supreme Court term. She had been a lawyer now for five years and loved everything about the law, including listening to political discussions about the high court.

And she didn't mind the perks that came with loving the law, like her new red Lexus she had just bought a week before. It had a fantastic climate-controlled interior and amazing sound system. In the morning, on the way to the office, she listened to a jazz station just to remind herself how good she had it.

In three days, she had a date with a guy she had met at a reception for a client a few days before. It would be her first date in a while, since her job had pretty much swallowed any free time.

And what little free time she did manage to get she had spent on her new home, getting it just the way she wanted it to be.

She clicked off the talk show as she pulled into the driveway of her three-bedroom ranch-style home and hit the garage door opener.

Her next-door neighbor, Sarah, was working on her yard and looked up and waved with a smile. Sarah had on a wide-brimmed hat that covered her skin. She was in her sixties and living alone, just as Vicki was, because Sarah's husband had died of cancer two years before.

Vicki chose to live alone. She liked it that way at the moment. And she loved her house and felt safe in it.

Sarah had encouraged Vicki to date and Vicki had done the same for Sarah, which had gotten a headshake and a laugh and a comment about being far too old to start over.

"Who said anything about starting over?" Vicki had said. "Just go for the sex."

Sarah had blushed and laughed and said she would think about that.

Vicki really liked Sarah. Vicki didn't really know anyone else in the neighborhood yet, but Sarah had promised to do introductions when there was time.

Vicki waited for the garage door to open and then pulled her Lexus inside as Sarah went back to working on her yard.

As the garage door rolled closed, it was the last time anyone saw Vicki Dix.

She vanished without a trace.

And her case went cold after one of the most massive investigations done by the Las Vegas Police Department.

ONE

"There isn't even half a clue to start with in this file," Retired Detective Debra Pickett said, tossing the thin summery folder on the table in front of the remains of her morning buffet breakfast. "Not a damned thing has changed."

Around her the sounds of the Golden Nugget Buffet in downtown Las Vegas seemed a little louder than normal, more than likely because she was annoyed. Normally she never noticed the sounds of the tourists talking and laughing on the other side of the large dining room, or the clanking of dishes from the buffet area.

This morning the sounds seemed intrusive, like they were aimed only at her.

Retired Detective Ben "Sarge" Carson sat beside her just nodding. Pickett could tell he was just as annoyed. His square-jawed face looked more like a rock. He had a full head of silver-gray hair and even annoyed he was the most handsome man she had ever known.

She was much shorter than he was and four years younger at sixty-one. Her hair was still its golden natural brown and both of them kept thin by exercising and trying to eat healthy.

Pickett forced herself to take a deep breath and look around, working to calm herself some. The Golden Nugget Buffet was on the second floor of the main casino, isolated up an escalator and surrounded by oak planters and brass railings.

The ceiling was coffered with oak and brass and bright lights. On the other side of the buffet from where they sat, one wall was all windows and looked down over the huge hotel pool area and a shark tank. A tunnel slide sent kids through the shark tank and out the other side.

She and Sarge sat on the side of the large room away from the windows every morning.

The tables were oak, with brass chairs covered with brown cloth. Everything about the place felt comfortable. Pickett loved that she and Sarge walked here every morning for breakfast. That walk was one of the favorite parts of her day.

This morning had started out fine, with the air clear and crisp and the sky blue. The walk had been wonderful just like normal. They had eaten breakfast, then had looked at the new cold case file Andor from the Cold Poker Gang had given them.

The case was what had annoyed her.

Andor was a retired detective who was the liaison between the Cold Poker Gang task force of retired detectives working on cold cases and the Chief of Police.

Andor must have thought it funny to give them Vicki Dix's missing person's file. Pickett had been a full detective when this case hit. She and Robin, her partner, hadn't taken lead on the case. The Chief of Police at the time had done that, but the case had everyone working on it. Vicki Dix had been a young, up-and-coming attorney for one of the city's most powerful law firms. One of that firm's members didn't just go missing without it causing a lot of detectives to jump.

Pickett and Robin had been in the jumping detectives' bunch. They had found nothing.

No one had.

And that had made Pickett and Robin both angry at the time, the same anger Pickett was feeling now.

Vicki Dix had just pulled into her garage and vanished without a trace.

And now the brown summary file in front of Pickett almost exactly twelve years later haunted her again.

At that moment, Retired Detective Robin Sprague came off the top of the escalator and turned toward the buffet entrance. She didn't look that happy either. Robin had brown hair and was square, built like a swimmer.

Robin and Pickett had been partners and best friends for over twenty years when they were both active. Pickett knew all of her moods and Robin wasn't in a good one this morning, of that there was no doubt.

The three of them made a great team in solving cold cases. And so far they hadn't failed to solve one. Pickett and Sarge did the legwork, Robin did the computer side of things.

Looks like that record of solving them all was about to end with Vicki Dix.

Robin dropped her file in front of her seat, put her laptop bag on her chair, and without a word headed for the buffet to get food.

"I think this morning calls for dessert," Sarge said, pushing back his chair to follow Robin.

"Bread pudding," Pickett said, also standing. "I deserve bread pudding."

The Golden Nugget Buffet was known for its fantastic bread pudding, served all day long. Pickett normally tried to stay away from it because it was almost addictive. This morning was an exception.

"In my mind you always deserve bread pudding," Sarge said, smiling at her.

She laughed. "Deserve, maybe. Need, no."

"But we're getting some anyway, right?" Sarge asked.

She took his hand as they headed for the buffet. "You are damned right we are."

And now she felt better. The man she loved beside her, great food for breakfast, her best friend here, and bread pudding. It didn't get much better.

Two

October 19th, 2017

Pickett finished up the last of the warm bread pudding and pushed the small bowl to one side.

Robin had asked about their cats, as she always did at breakfast and they had avoided talking about the missing Vicki Dix until Robin was done eating.

Then Robin got out a notebook and opened it up, which was the signal that the three of them needed to get to work on the case.

Sarge pulled his small notebook out of his shirt pocket and Pickett opened her notebook to a clean page.

"So let's start with what we know," Robin said.

"Not a lot," Sarge said.

"Her neighbor was the last to see her as Vicki pulled into her garage, right?" Robin asked.

Pickett nodded.

"There had to have been twenty detectives chasing down every possible lead," Robin said.

Pickett sat back and held up her hand. "Back then we eliminated every single person who worked in that law firm."

Pickett pushed one finger down on her hand.

"We interviewed every neighbor within a mile of the house," Robin said.

Pickett pushed down another finger.

"We looked into every detail of the poor guy who had an upcoming date with her," Pickett said, pushing down another finger.

"Forensic detectives looked over every inch of the yard and windows and doors," Robin said. "Nothing. No trace she left the house at all that night, since her home alarm was set from the inside and still on two days later."

Pickett pushed down a fourth finger.

"We backtracked over every restaurant she had eaten at in the two weeks before her disappearance," Robin said.

Pickett pushed down the final finger on that hand.

"My partner and I actually helped on sorting through any cases the firm had looking for any reason Vicki Dix had been targeted by an unhappy client," Sarge said. "Nothing at all."

Pickett could feel the same frustration she and everyone had felt all those years earlier. Vicki Dix vanished and no one knew how or why.

"So we know for sure she went into the house," Sarge said. "Or at least the garage."

"No, we know she went into the house," Robin said, opening up the summary file for the first time since they started talking, "because she turned on the alarm near the back door inside the kitchen area."

"And the alarm company was checked completely?" Sarge asked.

Both Robin and Pickett nodded.

"Every employee," Pickett said. "Robin and I were on that part of things back then."

"So she went into the house," Sarge said, "set the alarm, and there is no sign of any foul play or that she left at any point between that night and two days later when someone from work went to check on her."

"Two people went to check together," Robin said, looking at the file. "They were sent by one of the senior partners in the firm because Vicki not even calling in sick was unusual. They found nothing and two hours later the senior partner got the police to shut off the alarm and look for her."

"So when all other alternatives are proven impossible," Pickett said, "that means she never left the house."

Pickett then realized what she had said in frustration actually might be part of the answer to this.

"No sign of any blood or trauma in that house," Robin said. "Vicki had eaten dinner, had the television going, and poof she vanished."

"Aliens," Sarge said, shaking his head. "No other explanation."

Pickett punched him lightly on the arm. Anytime they ran into an impossible situation, Sarge jokingly said aliens had done it.

On this case, it seemed more logical than anything.

"Do you have a floor plan of the house?" Pickett asked.

Robin shrugged and pulled out her laptop and a moment later turned it so Sarge and Pickett could see the plan.

"Standard ranch with a two-car garage," Robin said. "Nothing at all special except a fantastic master suite with large bath and walk-in closet."

"Did she have it built?" Pickett asked, not sure where she was going with this, but clearly something had happened in that house to Vicki Dix.

"She did," Robin said a moment later after turning the laptop back around. "A year before she vanished. There are reports of interviews with the builders. They were all also cleared."

Pickett sat back. "Wish we could get into the place."

"We can," Robin said. "The bank took it back fourteen months after Vicki vanished, then the law firm bought it at auction a number of months later and haven't resold it yet. I am sure they will give us permission to go look around."

"Twelve years and they haven't resold it?" Pickett asked, feeling very surprised at that news. "Why not?"

"One of the partners said they owed Vicki that much," Robin said, in an interview four years after her vanishing, "to hold onto her home for a while to see if she would return."

"That firm can afford it out of petty cash," Sarge said, shaking his head. "I bet no one has even noticed it is still sitting on their books."

"Or they are waiting for a ten-year depreciation schedule to finish," Robin said.

Pickett bet that was the case.

"So shall we go take a look?" Pickett asked.

Robin and Sarge both shrugged and Robin took out her phone to call the law office to get keys.

"Why not go take a look? I got nothing," Sarge said, holding up and showing her the blank page on his notebook before stuffing it back in his shirt pocket.

She also hadn't written anything down.

This was impossible.

THREE

October 19th, 2017

Pickett was surprised at how well-kept Vicki Dix's home was as they pulled up. A frail-looking woman was working in one flower bed, a wide-brimmed hat shading her from the fall sun.

She turned and smiled at them as they climbed out of the car.

Pickett reached the older woman first and introduced herself, then Robin and Sarge.

"I'm Sarah," the woman said. "I live there."

She pointed at the house next door, also well-maintained.

"You been keeping up Vicki's home all these years?" Sarge said, smiling at the woman. "It looks wonderful."

"Well thank you, young man," Sarah said to Sarge, who blushed and smiled. "I don't have much else to do and Vicki vanishing like that bothers me every day."

"Bothers a lot of us," Pickett said. "That's why we are going to take another look around inside. See if something was missed."

Sarah laughed lightly. "As many detectives that there were crawling all over that place and the yard and neighborhood, not sure what you might find after all these years. But from what I understand nothing has been touched in there."

"Thank you," Pickett said.

"And thank you for keeping up this yard," Sarge said. "I'm sure wherever Vicki is, she would be grateful."

Sarah beamed as the three of them turned toward the house.

Pickett was always stunned at how Sarge always seemed to know the right thing to say at the right time.

It took a moment for Robin to get the front door open and then turn off the still-functioning alarm system. Another thing the law firm decided they needed to maintain to protect their investment, more than likely.

Pickett wasn't surprised that a woman living alone with Vicki's salary would have such an alarm. But the alarm made the case even more impossible, since it was never once turned off in those two days after she was last seen.

The power was still working fine and Robin turned on the lights in the living area.

"This is creepy," Sarge said.

Pickett couldn't agree more. A solid layer of gray dust covered everything and the house felt frozen in time.

And dead. Very dead.

It had been a very nice place in its time, of that there was no doubt. Comfortable furniture filled the living room area with a large television on one side of the room. The dining room table was close to the kitchen and if the drapes over the sliding door had been open, the view of the back yard and the mountains beyond would have been nice.

The sliding door still had the brace in the door blocking it from opening and every window in the house had the same braces.

Vicki's dinner dishes still sat in the sink, right where she had left them. Pickett remembered seeing a lot of photos of this place at one point. More than likely they were filed somewhere.

The garage was on the dining room side of the house. A hallway led off the living room to two small regular bedrooms and a small bath and then to a master bedroom with a large spa-like bath.

There was also a large walk-in closet still full of Vicki's clothes and shoes.

They tried to move slowly as to not stir up any dust. Their footprints were the only ones in the dust on the hardwood floors.

Pickett stared at all the clothes in the large closet, hanging on three walls. There was some open shelving under the hanging clothes and some drawers. In the center on the far wall from the door was a seating area. But something felt off and Pickett had no idea what.

"Robin, can you pull up the floor plan again for this place?"

Robin pulled out her laptop and put it carefully on top of a dresser, then a moment later had the floor plan.

The plan showed the massive closet. On the plan it was very large, almost the size of another bedroom. That would make sense if a young, professional woman was designing her own house for herself. If she liked clothes, she would design a large walk-in closet.

Pickett turned to Sarge. "Can you tell me how deep that closet is? Approximately."

Sarge shrugged and moved over to the closet and turned on the light. "Hard to tell with all the clothes and built-in shelves and such. I would say maybe twelve feet deep and the same wide."

"Oh, shit," Robin said at the same moment Pickett realized what she was seeing.

"That's what had bothered me," Pickett said as Sarge came back over to look at the plans. "That closet is square. It shouldn't be. The back half of the closet is blocked off."

"A safe room," Sarge said, shaking his head.

Pickett nodded. Vicki must have had it built privately after the regular contractor was finished. Often safe rooms were built by contractors from out of town and done without fanfare, so not even the neighbors would know about it.

Pickett could feel her stomach twisting. She so wanted to be wrong because she had always hoped that Vicki Dix was out there alive somewhere. But if Vicki was in that safe room, something had gone horribly wrong to trap her in there.

All three of them took out gloves and put them on. Then they carefully went hunting for the hidden switch that would open a safe room.

Sarge found it after ten minutes of dusty looking, hidden behind a moveable piece of trim on the closet door. As with any safe room, hiding the switch was the most important thing.

And the second most important thing was to make the walls impossible to break into.

Robin handed all three of them masks to put on, then when they were ready, Sarge hit the switch.

The seating area in the back wall of the closet slid away from them and then to the right with a loud raking sound. It was clear the false wall in the back of the closet was very thick, made out of steel plates, impossible to break into or break out of if something went wrong.

The lights in the room came up.

"Damn it, just damn it," Robin said.

Pickett felt the same way.

Curled up on the floor in the middle of the small room was the mummified remains of Vicki Dix. An open can of paint was off to one side with a paint tray and dried up brushes.

It looked, at first glance, as if she was painting her safe room.

"She passed out from the fumes in the small space," Sarge said, his voice low.

They all three turned and silently left the bedroom, taking off their masks as they headed for the kitchen and the front door beyond.

As they got outside Pickett peeled off her gloves and tucked them inside her mask to be thrown away.

The morning air felt wonderful. Not hot, not cool.

Just refreshing after being in that tomb.

Robin was on the phone to headquarters and Sarge said he would get them some bottles of water out of the car.

The neighbor Sarah came from around the side of the house and saw them all looking glum.

"Don't tell me you found her in there after all these years?" Sarah asked. "Oh, God, no."

"You might want to call it a day on the gardening," Pickett said. "This place will be swarming again with police in very short order. We'll come over and tell you what we found later, I promise."

Sarah started to open her mouth, then nodded and turned and headed home.

Clearly Sarah had hoped as well that Vicki Dix would just come home one day.

Everyone had.

But the problem was that Vicki Dix had never left home.

It had been her home, trying to improve her home, that had killed her.

That bothered Pickett more than she wanted to admit.

And right now Pickett wished they hadn't found Vicki Dix, that Vicki Dix would have just remained a legend among missing persons, with always a chance of coming home.

In a way, Vicki Dix had come home today. Just not in the way everyone, including Pickett, had hoped she would.

THE CASE OF THE MAN WHO SAW

A PILGRIM HUGH INCIDENT

DEAN WESLEY SMITH

THE CASE OF THE MAN
WHO SAW

The five-lane road cutting through the small city of Tigard outside of Portland, Oregon, was as busy as it always was during the day. Stoplights at every long block, constant stop-and-go traffic, and hundreds of businesses on both sides of the street, from pet shops to thrift stores to restaurants and fast-food standards. You could find almost everything along this ten-mile stretch of highway if you were willing to wait in the traffic long enough.

And at all the stoplights.

Pilgrim usually avoided the highway at all costs. Not today.

Pilgrim Hugh wasn't even driving his stretch limo and the traffic lights had annoyed him. He couldn't even imagine what they were doing to Donna Marks, his assistant and driver.

Donna had short brown hair and wide brown eyes and when smiling she could light up a room. She was divorced, thirty, and an expert on computers, high-speed driving, and weapons. And when annoyed, she could swear like a mythological sailor. He hadn't heard any swearing from her on the way out the Tigard highway, so that meant she was in a good mood today. Always a good thing for a woman as smart and good with guns as she was.

She had only been with him for three months now and he could no longer imagine doing this job without her help. She seemed to read his mind at times, something he actually didn't mind in the slightest.

Today she had arrived to work in tight brown shorts, a white blouse, and tennis shoes. He wore his usual jeans, dress shirt with the sleeves rolled up, and tennis shoes. People often said they looked good together, which just made Donna shake her head and walk away in disgust.

Just after one in the afternoon, Pilgrim had been called by the Chief of Police of Tigard to help out on something very weird that had happened on or along this stretch of highway. Pilgrim liked strange and weird. He lived for cases like that and specialized in puzzles that stumped the police. He worked for free for the police forces around Portland and that's why they called him, because he had also solved every case they had called him for so far.

He considered himself to be the best private detective in the Pacific Northwest, maybe in the country. He really was that good.

His road to being a private eye had gone through a bunch of strange events. First, three of years of law school, a three year event he considered so strange he couldn't believe he survived it. Then a failed first marriage and a corporate law-firm job that proved to him, without a doubt, he sucked at being a lawyer.

Or a regular husband, for that matter.

Then his grandmother had died and left him more money than he could imagine. Failed marriage and job in his wake, the arrival of the money sent him on a year of traveling and drinking, mostly drinking, which got really boring.

So back to school he went to become a private detective because he liked mystery novels and it sounded cool. Even before he hung out his PI shingle, it had become very clear that being a private eye wasn't what the novels described. The job was all computer work and long boring hours of nothingness.

He bored easily, no big surprise to anyone who knew him. He needed some excitement and challenges in his life.

Law didn't do it by itself and neither did being a standard PI. And he had done enough drinking to last for a lifetime.

So he had set up Hugh and Associates, a combination law firm and private investigative firm. Then he had hired a couple great associates who took all the boring cases and made the firm lots of money. They hired even more associates that he had no desire to meet who also made him and the firm lots and lots of money.

He also bought land and homes and apartments around Portland that also made him money. His grandmother's fortune had gotten bigger even with his best efforts to drink and spend it all.

He considered that failure his best success so far.

And that's why he could offer his services free to the different police agencies on really, really difficult and interesting cases. The weirder the case, the better.

And there was seldom a day he wasn't out on one thing or another. A lot of weird stuff happened around the Portland area.

Donna parked the stretch limo that served as their remote office off to the side of a street next to a Mongolian restaurant. Two Tigard police cars were parked closer to the intersection in front of them and neither had their lights on. The drivers might have well been inside the restaurant for all Pilgrim could tell.

The street was a slight hill and a wide sidewalk went down both sides. On the west side of the street he could see out over a shallow valley filled with a Home Depot and a couple other large box stores.

He climbed out of the back of the limo as Donna climbed out of the front. She was going to have to be careful getting too close to the five lanes of traffic flashing past. Those tight brown shorts of hers left little to the imagination and would cause wrecks he was sure.

Chief Bennett climbed out of one of the police cars on the passenger side and came back to meet Pilgrim and Donna. The day was warm, but not hot and the traffic noise wasn't loud enough where they stood to be distracting.

Pilgrim shook Bennett's outstretched hand. The man was solid, about five eight, and wore a billed cap to cover his balding head. He wasn't as tall as Pilgrim who somehow managed to keep himself in shape, Bennett clearly hadn't seen a gym in a long time. He now needed a new and bigger blue shirt before the buttons exploded off his stomach.

"Thanks for coming," Bennett said. "Hope I'm not wasting your time. And mine at that."

"Never a waste to put to rest a mystery," Pilgrim said. "Want to tell us what's happening?"

"Damndest thing I have heard in a while," Bennett said. "A guy by the name of Stephen Neilson is in the front patrol car. He ran into the middle of the street there in the crosswalk, shouting for people to call for help. He then went to help a person he saw there on the road."

"No one on the ground," Pilgrim said, taking the reference from Bennett's words. If there had actually been a person in the road, Bennett would not have said, "...a person he saw there on the road."

Bennett nodded. "This Neilson guy sure was convinced there was someone injured there. No one else stopped to help him, so I don't know if others saw the body or not."

"Who called you?" Pilgrim asked.

"A couple of people saying there was a man down in the street," Bennett said, nodding. "So maybe others did see what Neilson saw."

"Go on," Pilgrim said.

"Neilson kept talking to and comforting the person he saw, shouting for people to get help. When my men showed up, Neilson was looking confused and was back on the sidewalk staring at the street. One of my men got him into the patrol car."

"No body in the street?" Pilgrim asked just to confirm that he was hearing this right.

"No body," Bennett said. "No blood or any other sign of a body either."

"Mental breakdown," Donna said. "Military or something like that?"

Bennett shook his head. "That's what we thought as well, but Neilson is an outstanding father, husband, manager at the local Walmart. Never was in the service and has had no mental problems before that we could find. My people aren't as good as you, but they aren't bad."

Bennett said that to Donna and she nodded thanks, but said nothing.

"So let me talk with Neilson for a minute," Pilgrim said.

"Be my guest," Bennett said. "I'll get him."

Bennett turned and went up to the front patrol car.

Pilgrim turned to Donna. "Check out this Neilson guy and also if there were accidents here on this corner in the recent past. It looks like a dangerous intersection."

Pilgrim glanced up as four lanes of traffic sped past seemingly far too fast.

Donna nodded and climbed into the back of the limo. She had a station there with two major computers that came up out of cabinets and surrounded her. She had to be the best at computers Pilgrim had ever seen and had no fear of finding information in any way she could. He had a hunch he knew what she was going to find this time.

Nothing concerning Neilson.

But she had to search for the information for them to be sure.

Bennett came back down the sidewalk with Neilson, who kept glancing back at the street like he had seen a ghost.

Neilson looked like an average guy, wearing tan slacks, a dress shirt, and loafers. His hair was brown and thinning and Pilgrim figured him to be about thirty.

"Is the person you saw still there?" Pilgrim asked, not even giving Bennett a chance to introduce Neilson.

"No," Neilson said, shaking his head. "Vanished just as the police arrived. But the guy had seemed so real."

"What did the victim look like?" Pilgrim asked.

"Senior guy, about eighty or so," Neilson asked. "Bald. It looked as if he had been hit by a car. Blood on the guy's blue shirt and he was twisted up. I was afraid to touch him so I just shouted for help."

Neilson looked down at his slacks as if seeing them for the first time. "I should be covered in the guy's blood because it was everywhere and I was kneeling beside him. I really wanted to help the guy."

Pilgrim had no doubt at all about that. And he had no doubt at all that Neilson wasn't the problem here, just a Samaritan stuck in this.

"Please hold on for a moment," Pilgrim said to Bennett and Neilson.

Pilgrim then went over to the limo and opened the door. "Senior male victim, pedestrian. About eighty or so. Bald."

"Copy that," Donna said as Pilgrim closed the door and turned back to Neilson.

"Am I going insane?" Neilson asked.

"In our own ways," Pilgrim said, "We all are. But in this case, you are perfectly sane and tried to help what you thought was an injured man. Nothing at all insane about that."

Neilson nodded and managed to take a deep breath and exhale. Pilgrim could see the life coming back into the man.

"You think you know what caused this?" Bennett asked.

"I am pretty sure," Pilgrim said. "But we need to wait for Donna to finish her work first."

"How long will that take?" Bennett asked.

Pilgrim smiled and turned and pointed to the limo. "About now."

At that moment Donna opened the back door and climbed out. Her brown shorts and white blouse giving all three of them a wonderful show of fantastic beauty.

Pilgrim noticed and smiled. He was sure that Neilson didn't notice at all he was so rattled, and Bennett just sucked in his breath and turned to face Pilgrim.

"Victim you were trying to help was David Luke," Donna said. "He was hit in the crosswalk by a hit-and-run driver five months ago and died in the street before help could arrive."

"How is that possible?" Neilson said. "The guy didn't look like a ghost."

"Not believing in ghosts either," Bennett said, shaking his head.

"No ghosts," Pilgrim said. He turned to Donna. "Got a few suspects."

"Auto repair shop just up the hill on the other side of the street," Donna said. "Chinese restaurant right beyond that, depending on who has the angle."

Pilgrim glanced at Bennett and Neilson. "How far into the street was the body?"

"In the crosswalk," Neilson said. "Second lane out on the east-bound side, this side."

Pilgrim nodded. "Chief Bennett, Mr. Neilson, would you please wait here while I take a walk to the corner and back."

"I'll get you both a bottle of water," Donna said turning to the limo as Pilgrim started up the sidewalk.

It took him only about thirty seconds to reach the busy street. Donna was correct, the auto repair shop up the street was a logical target, but the roof wasn't high enough for an angle over the cars in the other lanes and in the turning lane.

If he was right, the image of the body of David Luke was projected on the street by a very powerful laser projector, something only the military might have. That would take some pretty large equipment and computer power and money. The Chinese restaurant had a phony front roofline that could easily hide large equipment behind it on the building's flat roof.

And that roof was high enough to have a clear sight-line to the spot where the body appeared.

Pilgrim turned and headed back down the street. Just a little more research was needed to put the why with the how on this puzzle.

As he approached Bennett and Donna and Neilson, Pilgrim said, "Let's all climb into the limo and I'll explain while Donna tries to figure out exactly who is behind this and why."

Donna nodded and moved over to hold the door for the three men, then climbed in last.

Pilgrim took his normal seat in the back. He had a hidden computer station in his seat as well, but he saw no reason to bring it up at the moment. Bennett and Neilson both took the side seat, both marveling at the leather interior, mahogany woods, and the state-of-the-art computer system Donna had surrounding her behind the driver's seat.

Even with four people in the back of the limo, it still didn't feel crowded at all. Pilgrim loved this moving office more than he liked his penthouse office on the top of his firm.

"Chinese restaurant has the angle," Pilgrim said. "Find out why? And you might want to check their power bills. I'm guessing a laser of that size pulls some real power."

Donna nodded.

"Laser projection?" Bennett asked.

"Technology has come a long ways and images can be made to look very, very real from a distance with a direct line. At night you would have been able to see the beam, but during the day, you only saw the projected image on the ground."

"So if I had touched the guy?" Neilson asked.

"Your hand would have gone right through the image," Pilgrim said. "Just like a ghost, which is my guess why someone is doing this. I'm betting David Luke's case has not been solved, so whoever is doing this wants to haunt the intersection with his ghost."

"Got that in one," Donna said. "Hit-and-run driver never found, but we might be able to solve it if you give me a few minutes to do this other thing first."

Bennett looked at Donna, then back at Pilgrim, shaking his head.

"So I'm not going crazy," Neilson said, smiling.

"Got it," Donna said. She turned slightly to the three men. "David Luke's grandson is named David Luke as well. Luke junior has numbers of major degrees in physics and light refraction from more than one major school. His parents own the Chinese restaurant. His grandfather paid for all the years of college."

Donna turned back to the computers, her fingers moving as fast as Pilgrim had seen them move.

Pilgrim turned to Bennett. "I don't think this young David Luke has broken any laws, do you?"

"Certainly could have gotten someone hurt," Bennett said.

"True," Pilgrim said, "But other than having Neilson here question his sanity, nothing was harmed.

Bennett slowly nodded. "What do you have in mind?"

Pilgrim smiled. "I'll get him to shut the machine down and never do it again. And maybe offer him some support and a job."

"He's not going to want to stop until his grandfather's murderer is caught," Bennett said.

"Don't blame him," Neilson said.

Pilgrim smiled and pointed to a printer that had suddenly started spitting out paper from a hidden panel.

Donna took the three sheets, glanced at them, and handed them to Bennett.

"Your detective's investigation found traces of red truck paint on the victim," Donna said. "Eye witnesses also said it was a red Dodge pickup, fairly new."

"I remember that," Bennett said. "We could never find the truck."

Donna smiled. "An auto repair shop in Walla Walla, Washington, fixed damage on the front of a red Dodge pickup one week after Luke senior was killed and repainted the entire truck green. The owner of the truck that was fixed in Walla Walla lives about a half mile from here and already has three DUI convictions and a revoked driver's license."

"Shit, no wonder we couldn't find the truck," Bennett said.

"Even better news," Donna said, "The auto body shop has not yet thrown away the original bumper and front panel of the truck. They held it expecting insurance to come and investigate at some point. So I would imagine you can match evidence on the bumper to the senior Luke."

Bennett just shook his head and looked at the papers one more time, then said, "Thank you."

Then Bennett turned to Pilgrim. "You'll get the kid to turn off the laser show?"

Pilgrim smiled. "I'll do it and tell him you have a lead on his grandfather's killer thanks to his display."

Bennett turned to Neilson. "You all right?"

"My wife's never going to believe any of this," Neilson said, smiling. "But just happy that man I saw in the street will get some justice now."

"That he will," Bennett said, opening the door and climbing out.

Donna shut down her computer and retracted it as Neilson also climbed out.

Pilgrim followed Neilson and Donna got out behind him.

"Thanks again you two," Bennett said.

With that he and Neilson headed back up the street toward the two cars.

"It's a nice day." Donna said, smiling at Pilgrim. "Shall we walk up to the restaurant?"

Pilgrim laughed. "Are you kidding me? That intersection is deadly. Just get me across there and to the restaurant safely and I'll buy lunch."

"And explain to me over lunch what you meant by offering the kid a job?" Donna asked.

"Just thinking I got that big empty building near the Pearl I just bought last week," Pilgrim said. "That might be great for a research center. I will need someone with real innovation and courage of convictions to run it."

"To research what?" Donna asked.

"Damned if I know," Pilgrim said. "I just thought of the idea."

With that, Donna laughed, shook her head, and then turned to climb into the driver's seat of the limo.

Pilgrim climbed into the back and buckled up his seat belt. He loved it when he made Donna shake her head. Sometimes that was more fun than solving a case.

Or in this instance, they had solved two cases. Even better.

UNDER THE SKIN OF DEATH

A COLD POKER GANG SHORT STORY

DEAN WESLEY SMITH

ONE

The three cats were sleeping in the bright morning sun in the large living room of the condo. Retired Detective Debra Pickett just stared at them as she sipped her coffee in the kitchen, amazed that they didn't get too hot in the bright Las Vegas light.

Sarge's two orange cats, Pet and Ree flanked her cat, Nose, on the big brown cloth couch, all spaced evenly apart. She and Sarge had gotten the cats a year before as kittens, but now they were at full size. Nose, a black and white tuxedo cat was the girl and considerably smaller than the two orange male cats. But Nose seemed to run the house and the boys didn't seem to mind at all.

And all three of them were in top shape considering how much running they did through the two combined condos and up into the loft above the big condo. One thing both Pickett and Sarge had learned was don't get in the way of any of the cats when they were running. It was always a losing proposition.

"I see the morning napping in the sun has begun," Sarge said as he came down the hall. He always let her have the bathroom first and for that privilege she fed the cats and made the coffee.

Pickett kissed him and handed him his cup.

Retired Detective Ben "Sarge" Carson was the most handsome man

Pickett had ever seen. He had deep hazel eyes that didn't seem to miss a detail, thick silver-gray hair, and a square jaw that gave him a slight movie-star quality. And he was in top shape for a man in his sixties. In fact, he was in better shape than most men of any age.

She was much shorter than he was and four years younger at sixty-one. Her hair had not turned gray, but was still a rich brown for reasons beyond her imagining. She kept it short and easy to manage. Every other day they both worked out in the complex gym together and they walked as much as they could to stay in shape.

Today both of them were dressed in their normal way. They both wore jeans and tennis shoes. She had on a silk gray blouse with a running bra under it while he had on a blue dress shirt with the sleeves rolled up.

Both of them had their badges on their belt and their guns in a gun holster under their arms. When they went out they would both wear light jackets to cover the guns and badges.

Every day she was amazed they had been so lucky to get on the Cold Poker Gang task force. It was a group of over twenty retired detectives who met once a week to play poker. During the week they all worked on clearing cold cases. The task force had cleared so many cold cases that the Mayor had given them special status to carry their badges and guns.

And the really nice thing was that they could work on the cases at their own pace and never had to do paperwork. When they made headway on something, they brought in an active detective to take point. She loved that part more than anything else. They got to do all the fun work of solving the cases without all the crap of command and paperwork.

And the regular detectives loved the Cold Poker Gang because not a one of the Gang wanted credit for anything. When one of the Gang cleared a cold case, they just stepped into the background and let the active detectives take the credit.

However, at the weekly poker game, clearing a case always got a standing round of applause from the other retired detectives.

She and Sarge worked with Retired Detective Robin Sprague, Pickett's old partner when they were active. The three of them made a perfect team. Pickett and Sarge did the legwork, Robin did the computer work. They had closed a ton of cases over the last year or so they had all been together.

Today Pickett hoped they would get information that would close another. They had gotten the case file from Andor at the poker game a week ago. Andor was the retired detective who was the direct connection between the Gang and the Chief of Detectives. Andor picked the cases for all of them.

This time he had given the three of them the cold case of a body found two years ago after a fire in the remains of the old Moulin Rouge Hotel and Casino. The Moulin Rouge had only been open for six months in 1955, but during those six months it was the first integrated hotel and casino in the city. For six months it had the top entertainment stars of the time there, not only to perform, but as guests.

The casino had blazed a burning trail through the racial problems of Las Vegas in the 1950s. It hadn't solved them by a long ways, but it had at least forced open a few doors that led to progress.

It had to be one of the most famous casinos of all time, even though it had only been open for a very short time.

There had been dozens of attempts to remodel and reopen the place, especially after it was put on the historic register. But no luck for decades and a series of fires had pretty much left very little of the place remaining.

A body was uncovered during the last fire, clearly dead for a very long time and somehow hidden in the walls of the old hotel. The fire hadn't done the mummified corpse any favors, so all forensics pretty much managed to get was that it was a woman.

The woman's DNA was not in the system and there was just no telling how long she had been in that wall.

After two years the case of the body in the wall had gone cold, so Pickett and Sarge and Robin got it.

Last night Robin had called and said she had a lead and she would share it at breakfast. That was great. Anything was better than nothing. Pickett and Sarge had managed in one week to get nothing at all. They had even spent some time in the ruins of the old hotel, which the county owned as of last auction for the fifteen acres.

Both she and Sarge were figuring this case file might end up as unclosed on the small bar in the game room where they held the weekly poker game. There were only five files up there at the moment. That's how good all the teams of the Cold Poker Gang were.

So far, she and Sarge and Robin hadn't put an unclosed file on the bar. She hoped this one wouldn't be their first.

Staring at the three sleeping cats, they finished their coffee. Amazing how simply staring at sleeping cats can be entertaining, especially in the morning.

"Shall we go find out what Robin has for us?" Sarge asked as he rinsed out his mug and tucked it into the dishwasher.

Pickett handed him her mug. She wished she could say she was excited, but there was nothing about this case that excited her. It had just felt wrong from the start.

And she had a hunch Robin's information today wouldn't help that feeling in the slightest.

Two

The walk from their condo in the Ogden Condominiums to the Golden Nugget Casino and Buffet was always wonderful. It was four blocks through the downtown area and then two blocks under the canopy of lights along Fremont Street. They did it every morning because eating in the buffet was a ton simpler and more enjoyable than cooking.

And the food was amazing. They could vary their diet depending on what they felt like since the buffet served just about everything for breakfast. For the last few weeks Pickett had had oatmeal, a slice of ham, a bowl of fruit, and orange juice. And today that still sounded perfect.

The buffet in the Golden Nugget was up an escalator from the casino floor and surrounded by oak planters and gold railings. As they rode the escalator, the sounds of the slots and people shouting at their winnings faded like they were climbing up into a peaceful cloud.

The buffet was huge and on one side had a wall of windows that overlooked the massive pool and shark tank that filled the center of the hotel complex. The ceilings were varied heights throughout the buffet with bright lights and oak trim. The tables were oak and the chairs a brass color with brown cloth.

She and Sarge and Robin liked sitting on the opposite side of the buffet, tucked away from all the tourists and windows. The staff knew them and saved them the same table every morning. And the staff, thanks to Sarge tipping them well, never sat anyone else close.

It was as if every day they had their own private dining area for their breakfast meetings.

Robin was already there and eating when they arrived and she smiled and waved as they came off the top of the escalator. Robin was square and solid, built like a swimmer. She had been Pickett's best friend for thirty years.

Robin's husband, Will, owned the city's top security agency. Robin was an expert on computers, but when she needed help, she could and often did go to Will's top experts. There was nothing they couldn't do or find it seemed.

It was odd that all three of them were rich, even though they were all retired detectives. Detectives seldom retired rich. Sarge had gotten his money when his parents had died and Pickett had gotten her money when her husband decided his secretary's large chest meant more to him than his money. Pickett had been very glad to take the money, actually.

That's how she and Sarge had both ended up with condos on the top floor of the Ogden, even before they met and fell in love. Knocking an archway between the two condos had given the cats a lot more room to run, that was for sure.

It was Sarge's turn to pay today, so Pickett headed straight for the food with a wave at a few of the staff. Ten minutes later she was sitting next to Robin.

"Will says hi," Robin said. "And how are the cats this morning?"

"Sleeping in the sun when we left them. As normal. Not a one of them even looked up when we said goodbye."

"The gods of the condos," Robin said, laughing.

Sarge set his plate down and shook his head. "Talking about the three cats who own us?"

"Who else?" Pickett asked.

They all ate for a short time before finally Sarge said, "So what is this information on this very cold case?"

"Two things," Robin said, finishing up a last bite of waffle. "First, it is pretty clear the body was stuffed in the back of a storage room and a fake block wall was built to hide it. I got that from looking at the old floor plan of the hotel and where the body was found after the fire and then looking at pictures. A small wall in the fire pictures wasn't on the original plans."

Pickett nodded. The Moulin Rouge Hotel had been made of mostly cinder block walls. That's why many of the walls were still standing in parts of the hotel complex even after over sixty years of desert sun and winter storms and numbers of fires.

She knew this not only because of all the times she had been to the site as a detective, but also because she had studied the history of those incredible six months the casino lived.

"Any idea when the body was put in there?" Sarge asked.

Robin nodded. "I think I know exactly. October 1st, 2001."

Pickett just stared at Robin.

Sarge had his mouth open, also staring at Robin.

"How in the hell can you know that?" Pickett asked.

Robin just grinned. "The body belongs to Cynthia Grimstad of Madison, Wisconsin. She went missing that day, reported by her husband, Ben Grimstad."

Now Pickett really was startled. And confused. "So you want to start over and explain how you got from a burnt mummified body to a name and date?"

"Yes, please," Sarge said.

"Computers are wonderful things," Robin said. "I set up a massive search through missing person's files from 1955 when the Moulin Rouge was open until five years ago. It would take at least five years for a body to mummify like this one was before it was burnt in the fire."

Pickett nodded.

"That's a few hundred thousand cases I bet?" Sarge said.

"A lot," Robin said, nodding. "But not impossible with all of it being entered into the police data base. Thankfully that task has been done for missing persons and murder cases now back to 1945."

Pickett could only nod to that. She didn't want to think about how many people went missing in Las Vegas every day. She had been told the amount once, but instantly forgot it. The number was just too high to consciously think about.

Robin went on. "I then cross-referenced any connection to the Moulin Rouge with every missing person's case."

"How many hundreds did that cut it down to?" Sarge asked.

"Only five cases, actually," Robin said. "One good thing about the place only being open for six months in its entire history."

"So how did you narrow it down to this Cynthia woman?" Pickett asked.

"The first four were easy," Robin said. "They were all men. The body found was of a woman. Cynthia was the only woman in the bunch with any connection to the hotel at all."

"And what was her connection to the Moulin Rouge?" Sarge asked.

"She and her husband were supposedly writing a book on the history of the hotel and had come to Las Vegas to visit it and explore and take photos. From what I gathered from reports, Ben's father worked at the Moulin Rouge for the short time it was open."

Pickett nodded. Family history like that, taking part in a major piece of history like that, would influence an entire family.

"So you know when she went missing?" Pickett asked.

Robin nodded. "She went missing just as the sun was setting on October 1st, 2001 when she and her husband supposedly got separated in the old ruins. Most of the big buildings were still standing at that point, so it was a maze in there."

"He reported her missing?" Pickett asked.

"Of course," Sarge said, shaking his head, the sarcasm in his voice not hidden.

"Within an hour after searching for her," Robin said, nodding. "Police did a quick search, but not much they could do since she was an adult and they figured she had just used the chance to get away from him."

"Were they having problems in their marriage?" Pickett asked.

"Detective on the missing person's case wrote that the husband said their marriage was perfect, but the detective contacted some friends back in Wisconsin who had another story about the two of them always fighting, especially about the book they were writing."

"Collaboration," Sarge said, "the quickest way to divorce."

"Or murder," Pickett said. She didn't like that assumption, but it seemed to hold true that the husband or wife were usually the main suspect. And often the murderer.

Sarge just shook his head. "So we solved the missing person's case and now have a sixteen-year-old murder case."

Robin nodded.

"Where is the husband?" Pickett asked.

"Dead," Robin said shaking her head. "He had moved to Vegas to keep looking for his wife and was killed in an automobile accident on the freeway seven months after she vanished."

"Vegas was not good to that couple," Sarge said, shaking his head.

Pickett could only agree to that.

Sadly.

THREE

They had closed a missing person's case from 2001 and figured out who the body was in the ruins after the fire. And Pickett felt as if she had done nothing. It had all been computer work. She and Sarge had flat made no progress at all and that was frustrating.

Sure, it was a modern world and computers helped a lot, but sometimes so did good old police work. Just not this time.

They had to step back from the case for a few weeks since it was now a murder case with a known identity of the victim, but Andor quickly had the Chief of Detectives give the case back to them to work.

So on a warm fall day, she and Sarge had decided that after breakfast they would walk over to the old ruins of the Moulin Rouge. It was just under the freeway and a ten-block walk from the downtown area. They expected to find nothing, but both of them felt restless enough to take the walk.

It had been years since she had even driven past the site. She had felt great sadness every time she had seen an article in the paper about another fire there.

The place was fenced off with signs warning of danger, but it was clear the fence was doing little to keep out anyone who wanted to go in. There were parts of the old two-story block hotel still standing and not much else besides weeds and the smell of old fire.

Where the main casino building had been was now just flat concrete with some cinder blocks stacked around.

All the windows and doors of the still-standing hotel wings had been boarded up, and gang tags covered many of the walls. The place had a heavy, sad feel to it as far as Pickett was concerned. Far too much history had happened here to ever have let this place end up like this.

She had put the old floor plan of the casino building on her phone and the location where the body was found in the back rooms of the old casino building. Both she and Sarge were fairly certain it had been the husband who had killed her, just because that was the most logical conclusion. No one else had motive to kill her and then go to all the work of putting her behind a block wall.

Robin was using her computer skills to check sales of blocks to the husband, but had come up completely empty. His actions had really been of a grieving man who had lost his wife in a strange city. The detective on the case had kept good notes of every visit the husband had made to ask about progress. The guy didn't seem to waver in the slightest as far as the detective on the case was concerned.

If he wasn't the murderer of his wife, Pickett felt really sorry for him.

The walls of the old casino building where the fire had burnt out had been torn down by the city right after the fire because of the risk of collapse, but it was still clear where everything had been if Pickett followed her phone carefully along the concrete slab.

The smell of fire, even though it had been two years, still choked the air and not even a slight fall breeze could clear it.

They found where the extra wall had been put up and some of the blocks, soot-damaged and broken for the most part.

The area where the wall had been built left not more than a two-foot space between the new wall and the old one. Clearly no one going into the old storage room would even notice, if anyone even went into this area of the building when it was still standing.

"I'm going to need a shower to get this smell off of me," Sarge said, standing in the warm sun and staring at where the woman's body had been hidden.

Pickett agreed to that. She was going to need one as well.

She looked around. The bright sunlight made the black of the fire remains even darker, if that was possible.

The place really did have a creepy feel to it, while at the same time a feeling of sadness from all the lost history.

"Let's assume the husband didn't do it," Pickett said. "We have a young couple from Wisconsin climbing around in here when this was still a building. They had expensive cameras and they looked clearly like tourists."

"A target for just about anyone," Sarge said, nodding. "Especially closer to sunset. Got a hunch this old casino was damn dark back then."

"So she's got a flashlight and a flash on her camera," Pickett said, moving away from the storage room outline. From the floor plan on her phone, this area had been for employees. A kitchen had been down a hallway to Pickett's right and a break room to the left.

Sarge came up and looked over her shoulder at the map.

Pickett was trying to put herself in the shoes of Cynthia that evening. Say someone did catch her in this hallway and killed her.

"Where would a person hide a body until a search by the husband and police was finished? It would take time to build that wall back there in the supply room."

"Good question," Sarge said. "There wouldn't have been many places in this old place in 2001 to hide her."

"And it would take someone who really knew the place, who had been studying it, to understand that a wall in that old storage room would never be noticed."

"True as well," Sarge said. "So Ben knew this place because of their research and any vagrant living in here would know it as well."

Picket looked back at where the wall had been built to hide the body. And she had a horrid thought.

She quickly dialed Robin.

When Robin answered, Pickett said, "Is it possible to figure out when Ben Grimstad flew into town and if it was at the same time as his wife?"

"Sure," Robin said. "Hang on. Easy search."

Sarge looked at Pickett with a puzzled frown.

Pickett smiled because that expression made him look even more handsome than he already was, if that was possible.

"Would you do me a favor?" Pickett said to Sarge. "Would you figure out how many blocks it would take to build that wall there where she was hidden?"

Sarge shrugged and said "Sure."

He turned to where the wall had been, stepping it off and measuring one of the broken blocks.

The sun was starting to get warm and standing in the burnt-out remains of an old building filled with history wasn't helping. She now wished she had worn her hat to at least keep the sun from her eyes.

Just as Sarge finished, Robin came back on the phone. "He came in three days ahead of Cynthia," she said.

"I think if you expand your search you will find him buying cinder blocks during those three days."

"Twenty-four of them plus mortar," Sarge said.

Pickett repeated that to Robin.

"I'll let you know what I find," Robin said and hung up.

"You think Ben came in and planned this, don't you?" Sarge asked.

"No place for anyone to actually hide a body in the old ruin here that the police wouldn't find unless that wall was already mostly built. He killed her, stuffed her behind the wall and finished the wall before calling the police."

"Makes sense, but something else tipped you off, didn't it?" Sarge asked.

"Camera," Pickett said. "Ben said he found her camera in the report that he gave to the police. If a transient or robber killed her, they would have taken the camera."

Sarge nodded. "Really good thinking and I am betting you are right. So how about I reward such wonderful thinking by scrubbing your back in a cool shower."

Pickett laughed. "That sounds absolutely wonderful."

She took Sarge by the hand and the two of them carefully picked their way out of the burnt-out ruins of one of the most famous casinos ever built.

Before they made it back to the Ogden and that wonderful promised shower, Robin called.

"You were right on the money," Robin said. "A guy matching Ben's description bought a bunch of cinder blocks and had them loaded into the trunk and back seat of a rental car two days before Cynthia disappeared."

"How in the world did you find that out?" Robin asked.

"The lumber yard out on the Boulder Highway got so tired of being robbed and bounced checks, they started automatically photographing every customer. They still have all the photos saved on the cloud now and when I gave them the day they pulled up his image and what he bought and a note about how strange it was."

"Damn I love computers," Pickett said.

Robin laughed. "That's usually my line. So how in the hell did you think to have me see if he came in ahead of his wife?"

"Good old-fashioned legwork that we will explain later," Pickett said, winking at Sarge as they got near the Ogden tower. "But in the next few minutes I'm going to be rewarded for my idea with having my back washed by a very handsome man."

"Way too much information," Robin said, laughing again. "Have fun."

"Oh, I intend to," Pickett said as she hung up.

All Sarge could do was shake his head and smile as they headed through the air-conditioned lobby of the Ogden for the elevators.

Pickett had no doubt it felt great to close this case. But the coming shower, after standing in those ruins of what had been a wonderful dream in its time, was going to feel a lot better.

At least now the history of the Moulin Rouge wouldn't be saddled with an unsolved murder. The history of that place needed to be focused on what it did for Las Vegas.

And whatever happens to those ruins going forward, Pickett hoped the memory of the six shining months the hotel existed would always be enshrined for many to study. And learn from.

Newsletter sign-up

Be the first to know!

Please sign up for the Kristine Kathryn Rusch and Dean Wesley Smith newsletters, and receive exclusive content, keep up with the latest news, releases and so much more—even the occasional giveaway.

So, what are you waiting for?
To sign up for Kristine Kathryn Rusch's newsletter go to kristinekathrynrusch.com.
To sign up for Dean Wesley Smith's newsletter go to deanwesleysmith.com.

But wait! There's more. Sign up for the WMG Publishing newsletter, too, and get the latest news and releases from all of the WMG authors and lines, including Kristine Grayson, Kris Nelscott, Dean Wesley Smith, *Fiction River, Smith's Monthly, Pulphouse Fiction Magazine* and so much more.

To sign up go to wmgpublishing.com.

ABOUT THE AUTHOR

New York Times bestselling author Kristine Kathryn Rusch writes in almost every genre. Generally, she uses her real name (Rusch) for most of her writing. Under that name, she publishes bestselling science fiction and fantasy, award-winning mysteries, acclaimed mainstream fiction, controversial nonfiction, and the occasional romance. Her novels have made bestseller lists around the world and her short fiction has appeared in eighteen best of the year collections. She has won more than twenty-five awards for her fiction, including the Hugo, *Le Prix Imaginales*, the *Asimov's* Readers Choice award, and the *Ellery Queen Mystery Magazine* Readers Choice Award.

Publications from *The Chicago Tribune* to *Booklist* have included her Kris Nelscott mystery novels in their top-ten-best mystery novels of the year. The Nelscott books have received nominations for almost every award in the mystery field, including the best novel Edgar Award, and the Shamus Award.

She writes goofy romance novels as award-winner Kristine Grayson.

She also edits. Beginning with work at the innovative publishing company, Pulphouse, followed by her award-winning tenure at *The Magazine of Fantasy & Science Fiction*, she took fifteen years off before returning to editing with the original anthology series *Fiction River,* published by WMG Publishing.

To keep up with everything she does, go to kriswrites.com and sign up for her newsletter. To track her many pen names and series, see their individual websites (krisnelscott.com, kristinegrayson.com, retrievalartist.com, divingintothewreck.com, pulphouse.com).

About the Author

Considered one of the most prolific writers working in modern fiction, *USA Today* bestselling writer Dean Wesley Smith published far more than a hundred novels in forty years, and hundreds of short stories across many genres.

At the moment he produces novels in several major series, including the time travel Thunder Mountain novels set in the Old West, the galaxy-spanning Seeders Universe series, the urban fantasy Ghost of a Chance series, a superhero series starring Poker Boy, and a mystery series featuring the retired detectives of the Cold Poker Gang.

His monthly magazine, *Smith's Monthly*, which consists of only his own fiction, premiered in October 2013 and offers readers more than 70,000 words per issue, including a new and original novel every month.

During his career, Dean also wrote a couple dozen *Star Trek* novels, the only two original *Men in Black* novels, Spider-Man and X-Men novels, plus novels set in gaming and television worlds. Writing with his wife Kristine Kathryn Rusch under the name Kathryn Wesley, he wrote the novel for the NBC miniseries The Tenth Kingdom and other books for *Hallmark Hall of Fame* movies.

Dean also worked as a fiction editor off and on, starting at Pulphouse Publishing, then at *VB Tech Journal*, then Pocket Books, and now at WMG Publishing, where he is the editor of *Pulphouse Fiction Magazine*.

For more information about Dean's books and ongoing projects, please visit his website at www.deanwesleysmith.com and sign up for his newsletter.

f 𝕏

Also from WMG Publishing

Fantastic Detectives
Edited by Kristine Kathryn Rusch

Past Crime
Edited by Kristine Kathryn Rusch

Pulse Pounders
Edited by Kevin J. Anderson

Risk Takers
Edited by Dean Wesley Smith

Alchemy & Steam
Edited by Kerrie L. Hughes

Valor
Edited by Lee Allred

Recycled Pulp
Edited by John Helfers

Hidden in Crime
Edited by Kristine Kathryn Rusch

Sparks
Edited by Rebecca Moesta

Visions of the Apocalypse
Edited by John Helfers

Haunted
Edited by Kerrie L. Hughes

Last Stand
Edited by Dean Wesley Smith & Felicia Fredlund

Tavern Tales
Edited by Kerrie L. Hughes

No Humans Allowed
Edited by John Helfers

Editor's Choice
Edited by Mark Leslie

Pulse Pounders: Adrenaline
Edited by Kevin J. Anderson

Feel the Fear
Edited by Mark Leslie

Superpowers
Edited by Rebecca Moesta

Justice
Edited by Kristine Kathryn Rusch

Wishes
Edited by Rebecca Moesta

Pulse Pounders: Countdown
Edited by Kevin J. Anderson

Hard Choices
Edited by Dean Wesley Smith

Feel the Love
Edited by Mark Leslie

Special Edition: Spies
Edited by Kristine Kathryn Rusch

Special Edition: Summer Sizzles
Edited by Kristine Kathryn Rusch

Superstitious
Edited by Mark Leslie

Doorways to Enchantment
Edited by Dayle A. Dermatis

Stolen
Edited by Leah Cutter

Chances
Edited by Denise Little & Kristine Kathryn Rusch

Dark & Deadly Passions
Edited by Kristine Kathryn Rusch

Broken Dreams
Edited by Kristine Kathryn Rusch

Pulphouse Fiction Magazine

Pulphouse Fiction Magazine, edited by Dean Wesley Smith, made its return in 2018, twenty years after its last issue. Each new issue contains about 70,000 words of short fiction. This reincarnation mixes some of the stories from the old *Pulphouse* days with brand-new fiction. The magazine has an attitude, as did the first run. No genre limitations, but high-quality writing and strangeness.

For more information or to subscribe, go to www.pulphousemagazine.com.